Blinding Mirror

Shelley Halima

Copyright © 2009 Shelley Halima

All rights reserved.

ISBN: 0615584667
ISBN-13: 978-0615584669

DEDICATION

I dedicate this novel in loving memory of James Danner Sr., James Danner Jr., James Edward Davis, Edward Quinn Sr., and Mia Moreno.

Shelley Halima

ACKNOWLEDGMENTS

I want to thank each and every one of you who have read my work and supported me in my endeavors. As a writer you spend so much time in solitude as you create these characters and their situations and that in itself is personally fulfilling. But it's made even more so when you bring your work out from the shadows to present to readers and the story strikes a chord with them. Again, I thank you and look forward to continuing the journey with you. Keep the emails coming—I truly appreciate them.

Blinding Mirror

Praise for Blinding Mirror:

What a wonderful and great experience I have had reading "Blinding Mirror" a novel by a soon to be literary star Shelley Halima. It was like watching a soap on television, I couldn't wait to get to the next page! Continued success as you are truly a gifted and talented individual, I look forward to your future works. **E'lyse Murray, ELYSE GROUP 7, AGENT to the STARS**

Shelley Halima's latest novel, Blinding Mirror, is three hundred and twenty one pages (previous edition) of sheer bliss. I think a mark of a good book is a writer's ability to make the reader understand why the characters do what they do. Halima has definitely mastered this technique in her work. I would highly recommend Shelley's work to any patron especially those who would like a change from the usual fare offered by many of her contemporaries. ~ **Stacie Brisker, Librarian at Cleveland Public Library**

Blinding Mirror is an exceptional thriller by Shelley Halima. Halima expertly weaves a multi-generational, multi-ethnic tale of suspense and intrigue. This novel takes you on an emotional journey as you see how Olivia grows from an impoverished teen to a selfish, gold-digging socialite. This novel is a sensational start to the Mirror series. **5 out 5 books ~ From Radiah Hubbert of Urban-reviews.com**

Blinding Mirror is splendid. A dark, page-turning gem, this rags-to-riches saga tosses happily-ever-after to the wind. Vivid characters propel an authentic saga, illustrating such ugly behavior as it fuels a desperate hunger for the beautiful life at a tragic, human cost. The climax stays with you long after you put Blinding Mirror down. It's a novel you can't wait to tell your friends they just have to read. **- Dwight Hobbes Mpls/St. Paul Magazine, Pulse of the Twin Cities**

In her third novel, "Blinding Mirror", author Shelley Halima continues writing about race and class struggles. This time the beautiful Olivia Valente tosses aside family and racial identity to strike out on her own to find wealth, and happiness. Halima's novels are reminiscent of those crafted by Harold Robbins, Jacqueline Susann and even Jackie Collins. We love Halima's hot mestiza characters in this page turner with a twist. Where is the mini-series? ~ **Charlotte Morgan, author, "Judgment in Goshen, Taxonomy of Ordinary Murder" and Editor of Intangible Magazine**

IG
Indie Gypsy
P.O. Box 511002
Livonia, MI 48151
http://www.indiegypsy.com

This book is a work of fiction. Names, characters, places, and incidents are products of the author's imagination or are used fictitiously. Any resemblance to actual events, locales or persons, living or dead, is entirely coincidental.

Prologue

She looked into the wild, enraged eyes of her daughter and winced as she felt the sharp point of the knife being held just beneath her chin.

"How could you do this to me?! I overlooked all of your lies, Mother! I made excuses for them! But this—I'll never forgive you! Do you hear me?! Don't you realize what I've done?!"

She exhaled sharply as the tip of the knife punctured her skin slightly but she didn't try to fight. One of her biggest deceptions had been revealed and the effects were nothing short of horrendous. All she wanted at that very moment was for her daughter to sink the knife in because death would be welcome. Neither of them would recover from her deceit and she would not be able to live with herself knowing she could have saved her daughter all this anguish.

"Just do it," she whispered. "Please."

As her daughter drew back the knife, she closed her eyes and waited for an end so she would no longer bear witness to the madness she had caused.

Shelley Halima

Part One

Chapter 1

Oliva Magdalena Delgado was born May 14, 1961 in Fresno, California to a mother whose ancestry was Afro-Mexican and a father who was Mestizo of Spanish and Amerindian descent. Her mother Inès's family was originally from Veracruz and her father Alphonso's family was from South Tehuacàn. Both sets of her grandparents escaped their impoverished lives in Mexico for slightly better yet still impoverished ones in the United States. The American riches they dreamed of proved to be out of their reach and poverty was the unwanted heirloom passed to their children. Not only did Oliva's parents have to contend with financial struggles but familial ones as well.

Alphonso's father was against his relationship with Inès. He disapproved of his son being involved with a woman he referred to as a mayate. Out of hurt pride, Inès's family countered by saying they didn't want their daughter with the son of a Pi-Po-Pe – a *Pinche Poblano Pendejo*.

They ended up running away to get married when Inès found out she was pregnant with Oliva. Though she didn't voice it to Alphonso, Inès never had the desire to be a mother and the only thing that pleased her about her pregnancy was it gave her the upper hand over the rival for Alphonso's heart—a young woman named Gloria. Inès was sure of Alphonso's love for her yet he was still fooling around with other women whenever the opportunity arose. She didn't know at the time Alphonso wouldn't let a wedding ring or a pregnancy interfere with his involvement with other women.

Alphonso desperately wanted a son and was so disappointed when Oliva was born he left the hospital before the umbilical cord was even cut. He went to a friend's home and drank until he passed out on the living room floor. There were three subsequent pregnancies which all ended in miscarriage. The miscarriages devastated Alphonso who felt each one was a missed opportunity for a son, but to Inès it was a relief. Any maternal feelings Inès possessed were more freely expressed to various pets she had throughout the years than to her only child.

A rumor got back to Inès that Alphonso had another child courtesy of an affair with a married woman over in San Benito. Alphonso denied it until they were in the heat of an argument he broke down and told her he had the son he always wanted. The resentment grew between them over the years and eventually the main thing that held them together was the sheer enjoyment of making each other as miserable as possible. Each blamed the other for whatever they hadn't accomplished in their lives. Somehow arguing was a good distraction from their dire circumstances.

When they weren't in a verbal battle, Alphonso blew away disappointments in clouds of marijuana smoke courtesy of the marijuana plants he grew in their backyard. He continued despite warnings from his doctor to stay off of drugs and alcohol because of his heart problem. Meanwhile Inès swallowed her disappointments with any calorie-laden food that was in the fridge or cupboards.

Considering the circumstances which her family lived, Inès had an odd snobbery about her. She believed her family to be better than most of the other families in the area. She was mindful to speak well and not use slang outside the confines of her home. This was a trait she passed on to her daughter.

Oliva's parents treated her as if she were an unwanted visitor in their home. At first her parents' lack of love and attention hurt Oliva. But from an early age the hurt was replaced with hatred. She despised her parents for not giving her what she deserved, not only love but material things. She resented that she had to wear shoes that were either extremely scuffed or were stuffed in the bottom with cardboard because they had worn through. Until she was fifteen and earned money from babysitting the neighbor's youngest child, she'd never had an outfit that wasn't worn by someone before her. To Oliva, her parents were pathetic and in her eyes they saw an additional mirror of their failings. While at first she was treated by her parents with complete apathy, it was when they saw the disdain she had for them that they began to direct some of the anger they felt for each other towards her. The only time Inès and Alphonso showed unity as a couple was when it was to gang up on Oliva.

By the time Oliva was in her mid-teens she'd not only acquired contempt for her family, but those in her neighborhood as well. Although she wasn't a very attractive child–skinny to the point she almost looked emaciated and all teeth and ears–by the time she hit her teens she'd developed into quite a beauty. Compliments from her parents were non-existent. It was when she began to notice the jealous stares of other girls and lustful ones of the boys that she became aware of her attractiveness. The wall she built around herself with her family extended to the outside world. She made no effort to nurture friendships with other girls or entertain the interest of young boys and kept to herself. When walking down the street, she'd grown accustomed to hearing, "apretada!" shouted in her direction from passing cars or a group of boys angry over their spurned advances.

Her teachers were amazed that she displayed a maturity and intelligence that far exceeded her peers. A few commented when they spoke with her, it was as if they were conversing with a colleague. She had the opportunity to advance a grade ahead a couple of times but her parents wouldn't allow it—they weren't concerned she might not make the adjustment; it was simply out of spite. To the disappointment of her teachers, Oliva decided to drop out of school right after she began her senior year. She simply found school a complete bore and knew some of the subjects better than many of the teachers. The majority of her time was spent in her room reading poetry, novels and books about places she wished to visit. Her world was a completely solitary one—until the day she met Pilar Machado.

Chapter 2

Oliva met Pilar two weeks after her eighteenth birthday. She noticed a moving truck unloading items at the old Garcia house but didn't take further note. A few days later as she was walking past on her way home from the library when she heard a female voice greet her with a hello. Oliva turned her head and saw a beautiful young woman waving to her. Her skin was fair with just a hint of copper and her auburn-colored hair fell past her shoulders. Her frame was tall and lithe. She was wearing a snug pair of hip hugger jeans, a plaid shirt tied just beneath her breasts and platform shoes. She looked a great deal like the actress Verònica Castro from the telenovela "Los Ricos Tambièn Lloran." To Oliva, she appeared terribly out of place in their neighborhood. She seemed more the type who would be sunning by the pool in the backyard of a swanky home in Beverly Hills. Oliva didn't say hello, she just waved back to her.

The next day when Oliva was walking by, she saw the young woman watering some flowers in front of the home. They weren't there before so Oliva supposed they'd been planted that day. She had her back to Oliva. Oliva paused for a moment then found her voice to speak.

"Hello."

The woman didn't respond. Oliva cleared her throat and tried again.

"Hello."

The woman turned around at the sound of the voice behind her.

"Oh, I'm sorry," she answered. "I thought I heard someone say something but I was in a bit of a daze. How are you?"

"Fine," Oliva replied with a tentative grin.

The woman bent the hose to cut off the flow of water and walked over to Oliva, offering her hand.

"I'm Pilar."

"My name is Oliva. I live just down the street."

"Pleasure."

"I see you're already sprucing up this old place. The flowers alone make a big difference."

"Oh yes, I'm trying. You should see the work I had done inside. I had someone come in and paint and put in carpeting and flooring so now I'm in the middle of the daunting task of unpacking boxes."

"Do you—would you like any help?"

"If you'd like to assist me it would be great. Actually, I need the help as much as the company. I don't know a soul here."

"Can I start tomorrow? This is chore day for me at home."

"Tomorrow is fine. Thank you, Oliva."

"No problem. Well, I guess I'd better get home now. I'll see you tomorrow."

"It's a date. Don't eat before you come because I'm going to make us some dinner, okay?"

"Sounds great. Later."

"Bye, Oliva."

She didn't know what it was but something about the way Pilar said her name sent a shiver through her. Oliva began her trek home wishing the next day had already arrived.

Chapter 3

Oliva arrived at Pilar's house and knocked on the door. She could hear music coming from inside as well as the inviting smell of food. She smoothed the edges of her hair around her ponytail one last time. A moment later Pilar opened the door and greeted her with a smile. She was wearing another shirt that was tied just under her breasts like the day before and high-cut blue jean shorts. She was barefoot and her toenails were painted bright red.

"Oliva! Come on in. I just put dinner on. I had to pick up a few things at the market so I got started a bit late." She moved aside to let Oliva in. "I've got a couple of fans going. It's hotter than a deuce today. I have to get some air conditioning in here."

Oliva stepped into the living room and took in the hip decor. It looked as if everything for that room was already unpacked. The furniture looked so new like no one had even sat on it yet. The thick shag carpeting felt plush beneath her feet. She decided to step out of her sandals so not to sully the new carpet. She was impressed with what Pilar had accomplished on her own with putting her home in order. A painting on the wall caught her eye and she walked over to it.

"That's a reproduction of a painting by Paula Rego called, 'The Firemen of Alijo'," Pilar informed her.

"It's kind of disturbing but I like it."

"Yeah, she's one of my favorite artists behind Lourdes Castro whose work I have in storage."

Pilar walked toward the dining room and began unpacking one of the boxes. Oliva followed and went to one of the boxes on the dining table.

"Oh, that's stuff for the spare bedroom. Instead of unpacking everything at once, I've been unpacking the boxes for each room and doing them one at a time. It took me all night to do the living room and kitchen. Right now let's unpack anything marked 'dining room'."

"Okay," Oliva replied. "Where are you from? I detect a bit of an accent."

"Portugal. I've lived in the states since I was a child but I go back to visit as often as I can so I guess that's why there's still a touch of an accent."

"Can you tell me about what it was like while we unpack?"

"Sure! I was born in the Madeira village Câmara de Lobos... "

Later Oliva sat at the kitchen table as Pilar prepared their plates. From the moment she stepped into Pilar's house she couldn't help but think how drab and shabby her family's was in comparison. The carpeting at her house was nothing like the spanking new shag carpeting she'd just walked on. It was so worn down until it was one with the wooden floor beneath and her mother had run out of rugs to cover holes. She looked over at the dish drainer filled with pretty dishes. The one at home contained a few plates but was mainly filled with used TV dinner and store bought pie foil plates for dinnerware. The kitchen floor was pretty, shiny linoleum. The linoleum at home was peeling, worn and so soiled it wouldn't come clean no matter how hard her mother made her scrub it. While Pilar had brand new harvest gold colored appliances, theirs looked like they could've been used on the I Love Lucy show. And Pilar added nice decorative touches like the ivy plant hanging over the sink in the macramé plant holder. Oliva was stirred with a mixture of jealousy and admiration. She would do anything to live in a home like this.

"This music is really cool. What kind is it?"

"It's called *fado*. I can listen to it almost non-stop. But I also like Elton John and Leif Garrett too."

"I adore Leif Garrett! He is so handsome."

"He is isn't he?"

"I wrote him a fan letter and he sent me an autographed photo. It's a rubber stamp signature but I still treasure it."

"That was cool of him. You'll have to bring it over and let me see it."

She brought over two plates and set one in front of Oliva.

"This is *arroz de maraisco*. It's one of those dishes I could eat every day."

"It looks great."

Pilar sat down, and then got back up to get the wine. She took her seat again and poured the wine. "Hey, how old are you?"

"I just turned eighteen. Why do you ask?"

Pilar tilted the wine bottle in her direction as an answer.

"I didn't want to contribute to the delinquency of a minor. I hope I'm not boring you with stories of Portugal but I have to tell you this. We have this ugly black fish there called *esprada preta*. It looks a sight but it's oh so good! When I'm there I usually cook it with *vinho e alhos*. Heavenly."

"Can you have some shipped over here? I'd love to try some."

"No, it doesn't transport very well. If you don't get it when it's fresh out the water, it's no good. Maybe one day you can go back with me when I visit and it'll be the first thing we put into our bellies."

"Are you serious?"

"Yes, sure. Why not?"

"Well, for one thing I don't have the money to go there..."

"Oh please. I'd take care of that. I'll probably go next year sometime so be prepared."

"Pilar, I would love to go there!" She had barely left the confines of her county much less the country and the possibility was exciting. "Thank you. I wouldn't even know how to repay you."

Blinding Mirror

Pilar waved her hand. "Don't even think about it. Do you have a passport?"

"Nope," Oliva answered with a note of dejection.

"That's okay. We have plenty of time to have that taken care of."

Oliva took another bite of food and thought over Pilar's offer of a trip to Portugal. They'd only met yesterday, yet here they were planning a trip together. It was strange but at the same it felt so right. She hoped Pilar wasn't just talking and really did intend on taking her to Portugal.

"I don't mean to be rude by asking this but are you rich?"

Pilar covered her mouth so that her laughter wouldn't cause food to fly out.

"You're very much to the point. I like that because you never know the answer to a question unless you ask. Let me just say I'm not hurting financially. My family has done pretty okay plus I married well."

Oliva felt a twinge of disappointment. "So you're married."

"Not anymore. Here's the story: my parents wanted me to come work at my brother's business—Carvalho Enterprises. But I didn't want to do that. I have no interest in working and why should I? So I met Jerry Machado and once I found out how loaded he was I got him down the aisle as fast as I could. Once my grandfather kicked the bucket and I received my inheritance it was bye-bye Jerry. Now I'm living off of what my grandfather left plus my alimony."

"With all your money, what made you want to move to this neighborhood?"

"My ex-husband refuses to accept that it's over and to let me go. I thought I'd go somewhere he'd never look."

"I see." For some reason Oliva didn't believe her. She had a feeling there was more to the story.

"It feels so good to be free of him. I'm only twenty-four. I have my whole life ahead of me. He served his purpose, now it's time to move on. I'm going to have fun as a single gal for a while before hooking another big fish. The alimony and inheritance is good but why continue to settle for good when I can have great?"

Oliva stared at Pilar with awe.

"I can see why your ex-husband has a hard time letting you go. You're amazing."

"Oh, aren't you sweet? My cousin Lori says I'm a gold-digging hussy."

"She's probably just jealous."

"Tell me about it. May I ask you a question?"

"Sure."

"I've been dying to ask this all day. What exactly are you? From the makeup of the neighborhood I'm guessing Mexican."

Oliva slightly squirmed in her seat.

"I'm mixed with Spanish and Indian."

"Ah, Mestiço. Spanish, Indian and what else?"

"What do you mean?"

"You look like you might have something else in you. Like Black for instance. Just a touch."

"What difference does it make what I have in me?"

"No reason to get testy. It was just a question. I mean there's nothing wrong with it if you are. We have some Moor blood in our background."

They fell into a strained silence for a few minutes.

"Oliva, don't think for a minute that I'm prejudiced in any way. You could be purple for all I care. Okay? I was simply curious, is all."

She cleared her throat. "My mother is a Black Mexican."

"I see. Well, I was only guessing really because you could pass for a dark Greek with your olive skin and that long and black straight hair. *Senhorita muito bela!*"

"What are the last two words?"

"Very beautiful."

Oliva blushed at the compliment.

"I actually considered taking Portuguese but took French instead. My parents never wanted me to speak Spanish. And only speak a little here and there themselves."

"I'll have to take you under my cultural wing then and teach you my language."

"Since you're Portuguese, are you considered Hispanic?"

"No darling. That's a term we don't use. That's an American thing," she sniffed. "I'm a white European—Moor blood or not."

"Do you think I could pass for Portuguese?"

Pilar tilted her head as she studied Oliva.

"Yes, you could as a matter of fact." Pilar took a long sip of wine and glanced at the clock. "I know you probably have to get home soon." She reached across the table and took Oliva's hand in hers. "When will I see you again?"

Oliva was taken aback by the affectionate gesture—yet pleased.

"I can come by tomorrow if you'd like."

"I'd like that. I'd like that a lot."

Chapter 4

Oliva entered her house to see her mother on the couch watching "Hart to Hart" and eating a Marathon bar. A box of Cheese Nips was propped against her hip and a can of Tab was between her ample thighs. Her eyes never left the television. Her ratty dog Pumpkin was lying at her feet. Pumpkin looked up at Oliva and moved to a spot between Inès's feet and the couch. Her father and his friend Carlos were sitting at the dining room table playing cards. Even though her routine was to come home and go directly to her room, no one seemed to take note or care of her whereabouts for the last few hours. Carlos gave her a lecherous grin and wink. Oliva shuddered in disgust and went to her bedroom, closed and locked the door. Ever since she'd begun to develop physically, she endured Carlos's unwanted attention and advances. She found him repulsive. He smelled of cheap cigars and musty body odor.

She pushed the unpleasant thoughts of Carlos out of her head went and stood before the mirror propped on her dresser. She turned her face from side to side and studied herself, as she'd never done before. She reached up, removed the rubber band and shook her head, letting her hair fall. She tilted her head to the side, formed her mouth to a sexy pout and struck a pose.

"Muito bela."

Oliva turned and took off her clothes and changed into a pajama top. She went over to the window and propped the box fan in front of it, and turned it on medium. She would've turned it on high but she didn't want to hear her parents bitch about it. They thought turning it on high translated to a higher electricity bill and would have made her turn it on low but fortunate for her, the low setting didn't work. She fell on the bed, stared at the ceiling and replayed the day with Pilar. Pilar was extremely fascinating. Even her name was engaging. Pilar Machado. She had such flair and personality–the likes she'd never seen. Oliva admired how she not only went after things she wanted, but she got it. She was beautiful, desirable and confident. Before meeting her, Oliva thought all the things she dreamt of being or having was just that-a dream. Now it had a glint of a possibility to actually happen. Perhaps Pilar could help her out of her shitty existence.

She thought of when she was leaving and Pilar gave her a long, lingering hug. She felt so good, so soft. Oliva could still smell the sweet scent of her perfume. When she inquired about it Pilar told her it was Chanel No. 5 and that it was her favorite fragrance. The only fragrance she owned was the Love's Baby Soft that she lifted from a nearby store. She turned on her side and put one of the pillows between her legs and rocked softly against it.

Later that night Oliva was awakened by the sound of her parents in the midst of yet another argument. Their voices rose above the hum of the fan. She wiped away the perspiration on her face, got up and left the bedroom to get something to drink. As she walked through the living room to the kitchen she didn't even look at either of her parents.

"All you do is sit on your fat ass all day! You do nothing but feed your fucking face yet you want me to buy this and buy that!"

"I don't ask for much, Alphonso! All I want is a decent couch for the living room. You'd think I asked you to buy a vineyard! I thought you could at least be man enough to provide something nice for the house. Stupid of me to think that! You can't stop smoking your yerba long enough to do anything that resembles what a man would do!"

"Who keeps the lights on? And the gas? Who pays the rent? And who pays for all the food you stuff in that big mouth of yours? That alone almost requires a second job! And you wonder why I don't touch you anymore. Look at you!"

"I don't wonder about that at all! I wouldn't want you to lay a finger on me anyhow! I don't care if you never pull that *chilito* out ever again!"

"Chilito, huh? It was enough to have you screaming and begging for more, baby! At least back when we used to do something! I bet I couldn't even find your stuff under that belly now."

Inès let out a laugh devoid of mirth.

"I always wanted a career on the stage and I should've done just that! Because if you think for one minute that I actually ever enjoyed having that pencil you call a dick inside of me, I should have an Oscar!"

"*Chingate!*"

"*A viente!*"

Oliva walked to the dish drainer and retrieved a glass jelly jar, shaking her head in disgust at their vulgarity. She rinsed out the jelly jar and went to the refrigerator. Pumpkin was curled up asleep on folded up old blanket and was awakened by the stirring in the kitchen. When she saw Oliva she quickly got up and timidly walked towards the living room, keeping a wary eye on Oliva. Oliva gave her a swift kick causing Pumpkin to yelp and scurry out of the kitchen. Oliva retrieved the apple juice bottle filled with water and poured a glass.

Inès stomped into the kitchen carrying her dog.

"What did you do to Pumpkin?!"

"I didn't do anything." Oliva took a sip of water as she put the bottle back in the fridge.

"You must've done something! Why did she cry out?!"

Alphonso entered the kitchen and stood behind his wife.

"I heard her cry out, too. What the hell did you do?"

Oliva shrugged her shoulders. "I accidentally stepped on her tail. I didn't see her."

"Well, watch where you're walking, stupid!" her mother spat.

Oliva casually took another sip of water. She looked on as her mother rocked the dog and planted kisses on her. She slightly winced at seeing the same dog that buried its face in its own shit lick her mother's mouth.

"Yes, mommy's baby. It's okay," Inès cooed. "That silly girl wasn't watching what she was doing. My baby's poor tail is going to be just fine. Yes, yes it is."

Oliva walked past her mother and father and back to her bedroom. She finished the rest of her water and placed the glass on her nightstand. Her parents resumed their arguing and she fell into a fitful sleep. About three hours later she woke up again. The house was quiet except for the snoring sounds coming from her parents' bedroom and the hum of fans. Oliva went into the kitchen and turned on the light. She went straight for cabinet underneath the sink. After fumbling a little, she found what she was looking for. She took a plastic fork from the dish drainer, went over to Pumpkin's dog dish and mixed rat poison in with the leftover dog food. She planned on tainting Pumpkin's food for the next couple of days. Then she figured it might not even take that long though because with her mother's other dog, Sheba, it took only a day for the poison to take effect and that dog was much bigger than Pumpkin. Oliva put the poison back under the sink, tossed the fork in the garbage and went back to her room. This time she was able to fall into a deep slumber.

Chapter 5

Before Oliva even entered her house she could hear voices from inside. She recognized one as that of Carlos. She let out an irritated groan. After having another great time at Pilar's, the last thing she wanted was to come home and see that pervert. She opened the door to see her mother being comforted by Carlos's wife Maribel. Oliva saw a box by the door with what looked to be Pumpkin wrapped in a blanket inside of it. It took all she had in her to suppress a smile. She didn't acknowledge anyone and headed to her bedroom. She didn't close the bedroom door like she normally would because she wanted to hear the conversation in the living room.

"She was fine until the day before yesterday," Inès tearfully explained. "Then she began to look weak. She was always good about letting me know when she had to go potty but the last few times she didn't and I noticed blood in her urine. And she had nosebleeds too. Why does this keep happening to me, Maribel? First, Tootie and Princess just disappeared, and then both Sheba and Pumpkin up and die. I'm afraid to get another dog! I couldn't take this happening again! It hurts so bad."

"Good," Oliva whispered. "And what dog 'goes potty'? What an idiot."

"Can you just take her away now? I can't bear seeing that box."

"Sure, I'll take her where we buried Sheba," replied Carlos.

"Thank you."

"Ines, you should really go lie down. You look so wiped out."

"I am, Maribel. You have no idea. Of all my dogs Pumpkin was my favorite. We just connected."

Oliva listened in disbelief at what she was hearing.

"I'll sit with you until Carlos comes back. I'm sure that daughter of yours won't be a bit of help to you. She's so rude the way she just walks into the house without speaking to anyone. I could just take her over my knee."

Oliva smirked at the comment.

"I tried to tell you. She's a very selfish child. She thinks only of herself."

"I'm going to use your bathroom real quick before I go."

Carlos was already in the hallway when Oliva heard him. There wasn't enough time to close the door so she pretended to primp in the mirror.

"Hello, gorgeous."

Oliva's eyes never left her reflection. Carlos leaned against the doorframe. He was a few feet away but

Oliva could already smell his rancid, unwashed scent.

"Funny how your mother's pets always meets a bad end," he spoke in a conspiratorial whisper.

"Yeah, funny."

"If I ain't know better I'd say someone poisoned little Pumpkin. I mean she had all the symptoms. But I wonder who would do that? Who could be so vicious as to kill an innocent little doggy?"

Oliva responded with a nonchalant shrug.

"I didn't tell your mother this because I ain't wanna upset her anymore than she already was. But uh, me and my friend Earl was out looking for Princess when she disappeared and we found her. Oh yeah. In the park all beat up and inside a plastic bag. There was a bloody bat lying nearby. Somebody had whooped that po' doggy to death. Now I ain't no educated man or nothing so I could be wrong. But it seems to me somebody got it in for your mother's little pets. Maybe it's someone who's mad because she's giving the dogs more attention--"

Oliva turned swiftly to him.

"You shut the hell up old man," she hissed. "As much as you pass out drunk in the park, maybe someone will creep up on you and take a bat to your head and put you into a permanent sleep. Now get away from my room. Or I'll walk in that living room right now and tell your wife how you offered me money to sleep with you."

The look in her eyes startled him a bit. There was a cold, evil glint to them. As a fifty-six year old man he felt silly being scared of a teen-aged girl but he couldn't help it. He knew what she said about him getting his head bashed in wasn't an empty threat. Nor was her telling his wife about his proposal. At that moment he knew she was more than capable of doing just about anything. He backed into the hallway as if he didn't want to turn his back to her. He then went into the bathroom.

Oliva looked back to the mirror and brushed her hair.

Chapter 6

Over the next few weeks Pilar and Oliva were inseparable. When they weren't at Pilar's home hanging out, they were at the park or the movies. Oliva quickly became used to going different places with Pilar instead of leading her solitary life in her room. But Pilar's affectionate nature wasn't something Oliva was accustomed to. Oliva could count on one hand the hugs she received from her mother and she never had one from her father. However, once she did get comfortable with Pilar's affection, she realized how much she enjoyed it.

One day when they were both lounging in the living room and listening to music, Pilar decided to make a confession.

"Darling, I have to tell you something."

"Shoot." She couldn't help but smile. She loved it when Pilar called her that.

"Remember when I told you the reason I was hiding from my ex-husband because he wouldn't let go of our relationship?"

"Yes, I remember."

"Gosh, how do I say this? That wasn't entirely true."

Oliva had been lying in her lap. She then sat straight up and turned to her friend.

"What do you mean?"

"The real reason is I took something from him."

"What was that?"

"Even though I get a good amount of money in alimony, I got a little greedy. My ex-husband Jerry does side work for some pretty connected people back east and has money stashed in a safe that he doesn't want to keep in the bank—that along with some other items. I hope you get what I'm saying without me having to spell it out."

"I think I understand."

"Well, I found out the combination to the safe. Instead of memorizing it the dumb oaf actually had it written down. I came across it by accident right before we separated and kept it handy until just the right time. When he was out of the country doing more work for his bosses, I let myself into the house and helped myself to some of the stash. I thought 'why not'?" He'll just end up spending it on his floozy on the side or at the racetrack so why shouldn't I get a little extra pay off? I heard he thought maybe one of his bodyguards had taken it but a nosy neighbor informed him they saw me coming out of the house and that fingered me."

"Do you think he'll hurt you?"

"No, he won't. But I'm sure he'll have one of his henchmen do the dirty work for him. They wouldn't kill me I don't believe. Just try and teach me a lesson by roughing me up. Maybe I should go back to my maiden name,

Carvalho. It's probably not too wise to still use his name. But his name opens even more doors than my family's."

"Why don't you give up the money, Pilar? You said you have some from your inheritance and alimony. It's not like you need it."

"No, but I want it. And I'm going to keep it. I always get what I want. Always."

Oliva saw the stubborn set of Pilar's face and knew it was futile to try and convince her further.

"I'll just continue to ride out the storm. I'm also lying low from someone else, too. I had a little affair with a man and it was nothing serious. However, it was serious enough for his wife. She is completely psychotic. I didn't find out she was until after she broke the windows out of my old car and slashed the tires. She was following me around town. I'd be doing some shopping and I would look up to find her staring at me from an aisle away. She didn't do anything but stare at me but after she did that a few times it creeped me out so bad I just wanted to get away. I needed a reprieve from the stress for a while. Anyway, it feels good to have told you that. It's like a load off, you know?"

"I'm glad you trust me enough to have told me."

"Now let's talk about you."

"What about me?"

"You've never invited me to your house and I wondered why, so I asked someone which house was yours. Once I saw it I understood. Most of the homes in the area are somewhat rundown but yours is especially so."

Oliva's cheeks were touched with the hot fire of embarrassment and anger at Pilar's words. She stared down to her lap.

"Don't be mad at me, sweetheart. I'm only bringing this up because I have a plan for you. When I'm free to leave here I want you to come with me."

Oliva's head shot up and she looked at Pilar. She wasn't sure if she'd heard correctly. Pilar saw the question in Oliva's eyes and answered. "Yes, I want to take you with me. From the moment I saw you, I could tell you were different from many around here. It's almost as if fate has played a cruel joke on you because you don't belong in this world. You deserve so much more and I want to help you get it."

"How?"

"You're going to reinvent yourself for starters."

"How will I do that?"

"I know how you feel about your parents. Do you think you would be able to leave all that you know now–including them, to start over as someone else?"

Oliva didn't even have to think about the question. Leaving all she knew was what she dreamt about.

"In a heartbeat. I'm willing to do whatever it takes."

Pilar beamed at Oliva. It was just the response she was hoping for.

"Remember when you asked if you could pass for Portuguese? I think that's what your new identity should be. You know that I don't give a fig what you are. Unfortunately, there are people who do. They will not be accepting of your Mexican or Black heritage but Portuguese is a different matter. As a White European it'll be easier for you to move in certain circles. I've thought about this over the last few days and I've already started forming plans. For starters, make a slight change to your name. Change it to Olivia because the pronunciation of your name—O-leeva sounds way too ethnic. And I've always like the name Olivia anyway. We'll come up with a last name later on."

"Olivia. I like it!"

"This is out of sight. Trust me on this, Oliva—I mean Olivia, and you won't regret it."

"I'm so excited about this. I've always wished I could have a brand new life. But how do I handle getting a new name?"

"Oh, that's simple. There are always people who can work that out for a price. You can change your name legally but since you're looking for a whole new identity you'll have to go outside the law. Acquaintances told me about an LA connect named Jojo. He hangs out around Mann's Chinese Theatre. Once we head out there we'll look him up."

Oliva stared into space. She was entranced by the new possibilities being presented to her.

"When it's safe for you to leave here that's where we'll go?"

"Yes, darling."

"So you're just going to pack up all this stuff all over again?"

"Yes."

"You certainly went through a lot of trouble to just be here temporarily. The new carpet..."

"Money. With money this is nothing."

"And nothing is exactly what I have."

"Not for long. I'll take care of you until you find money in the form of a sugar daddy. Olivia, women like us call the shots in this world. Forgive the tawdriness of what I'm about to say, but what we have between our legs is worth more than gold. There are men who run corporations, destroy nations and yet can be brought to their knees by pussy."

"There's this old guy that's a friend of my dad's who actually offered me money to go to bed with him."

"Did you do it?"

Oliva made a face. "Of course not. He's disgusting."

"And if he's from around here I'm sure that was a piece of change."

"Two hundred dollars."

"As I said, a piece of change. Don't ever sell yourself short. There are too many men in this world who will gladly keep us in the lifestyle we deserve to waste precious time with nickel and dime men."

"I can't wait to live that lifestyle. But let's talk about this some more tomorrow, okay? I have to be getting home."

"Chores again?"

"My father's birthday is today and my mom wants me to help with getting everything ready. He always wants to make a big deal about his stupid birthday. It's so fake the way they try and act like this loving couple in front of friends when they hate each other's guts. I'm sure most of them have heard those two screaming at each other through open windows. I guess I'd better get to the waste of flesh convention."

"Do me a solid."

"Sure, what's that?"

"Try and come over as early as you can. I'm going to do some shopping and I want you to come with me. The day after tomorrow my brother is coming and I want us to spend as much alone time as possible in the next day before he gets here."

"Cool."

"Plus, we need to confab some more on how you're going to snag a millionaire."

"I can hardly wait."

Pilar gave her their usual good-bye hugs followed by a soft, lingering kiss on the lips.

Chapter 7

Oliva put the various foods into the serve ware borrowed from Maribel for the occasion. She'd spent the last hour and a half tuning out her mother's cussing and fussing.

"You're off spending all this time with some friend that you haven't even introduced us to and have the nerve to just casually walk up in here two whole hours after you were supposed to be here! You act as if whatever the hell you're doing is more important! You're such a selfish little bitch! One day you're going to realize your family is all you have."

Oliva's foot hit against something under the table. She stepped and looked under the table to see what it was.

"You'd better be telling the truth about spending your time with a female friend by the way. Your father and I will kick you to the corner in a heartbeat if you're messing around with some boy and come up pregnant."

Oliva reached down under the table to get the item her foot made contact with.

"It's already a struggle with the three of us much less adding a bastard child to the mix."

"What do you want me to do with this?" Oliva asked as she held up one of Pumpkin's old food bowls.

A surge of glee coursed through her at the wounded expression on her mother's face.

"Jus-just throw it away." Her bottom lip quivered and her eyes welled with tears. "You finish up the rest. I'm going to lie down for a minute before people start arriving."

As soon as her mother turned to leave, Oliva broke into a grin. Instead of throwing it out as her mother requested, she put the doggie bowl back under the table and went back to readying the food dishes. She started singing. "I was made for dancing, all, all, all, all night long. Yes, I was made for dancing, all, all, all, all night long…"

Oliva gave herself one last once over in the mirror before joining the party. Everything she wore was courtesy of Pilar; her mint colored Dittos jeans with a matching colored halter-top, Cherokee wedges, hoop earrings and bangles. Her favorite item was the mood ring Pilar gave to her. Pilar bought it a few years before and was about to toss it out one day when Oliva stopped her and asked if she could have it. Oliva knew she would always cherish it because it was something once worn by Pilar.

Pilar decided her image needed a major overhaul. She told her that although she turned heads, with the right clothes and attitude she could command a room. She decided that tonight would be the test. Pilar gave her a few make-up lessons. She didn't need much but what she used accentuated her already beautiful features. Her hair fell down her back and was scented by "Gee, Your Hair Smells Terrific" shampoo. After tonight ponytails would be worn only on rare occasion. She was about to go after the life she always wanted and from tonight on she would look the part.

She fluffed her hair one last time and took a deep breath.

Oliva walked down the hallway to the living room where everyone was congregated and stood inside the archway. An album by Herb Alpert was playing on the stereo. As soon as one person noticed Oliva, it caused a ripple effect throughout the room and all chatter and laughter ceased. The men gave her appreciative stares and most of the women, jealous ones. She even noticed her mother appear uncomfortable as she self-consciously smoothed out the bottom of her blouse. Her father was already so high that if she were an alien exiting a spaceship, she doubted he would have even noticed.

She sauntered through the room over to the dining room where the punch bowl was and ladled some punch into a plastic cup. Her back was to everyone and though light chatter picked up again, she could still feel eyes burning into her. She threw her hip to the side and put her hand on it and sipped the punch.

"Hi, Oliva."

Oliva turned to see Carlos's nephew Ricardo.

"Hey, Ric."

He reached for a cup and didn't take his eyes off of Oliva except to pour.

"You look—wow!"

Oliva flipped her hair over her shoulder and gave him a winning smile.

"Thanks. Nice of you to notice."

"Yeah, I'm not only one. You have a modeling shoot or something?" He teased.

She used to have a crush on Ric when she was a freshman, though she never let him know it. He was always nice to her, even in her awkward looks stage. He even stopped some of the kids from picking on her whenever he was around. If he had any money she would have targeted him. But he was as poor as her family. Flirting was all he was going to get from her. But before she could work more of her charm on him, his girlfriend Sherry interrupted them.

"Ric, come sit back with me," she whined, as she glanced at Oliva suspiciously.

Oliva looked her up and down, taking in her competition for Ric's attention. *She's cute but nowhere near as beautiful as I am. If I were her I'd be jealous of me too.*

Ric reluctantly let Sherry lead him back to the couch, throwing backwards glances as he did so.

Inès sidled up next to her a moment later and opened up a bag of chips to pour into a bowl.

"Who do you think you are strutting up in here like some slut?" She asked in a lowered voice.

"What do you mean, Mother?"

"Don't play innocent with me. You know exactly what I mean. Where do you get off walking up in here with those tight and revealing clothes? How dare you embarrass us like this? You go into your room and change into something more decent right now."

Oliva turned to her mother. "No," she replied defiantly.

Inès struggled to remain composed in front of the guests. She stared Oliva down for a minute before walking away.

Oliva was sure she would be in for a huge scream-filled verbal barrage later, but she didn't care. This was her moment—her debut of sorts. She wasn't going to let anyone, especially her mother ruin it for her. She went and sat down in a chair not too far from where Maribel, her sister Yolanda and friend Susan were sitting. Even over the music that was playing she could hear them talking about her.

"It's just shameful the way these young ladies—and I use the term ladies very lightly—are dressing these days," huffed Maribel.

"No, common decency or self-respect," Yolanda added. "I'm surprised she can even sit down in those tight pants." She looked over at her husband whose eyes were trained on Oliva, as most of the men were. As if he felt his wife's burning gaze, he quickly averted his eyes.

Oliva listened to the comments with cool detachment. *If you hags had my youth and body, you'd be dressing the same way. Jealous old bitches. And that goes for dear old Mother, too. She just can't stand it that I'm getting of this attention and she looks even more of a cow compared to me. This is only the beginning. I'm about to set the world ablaze.*

"Oliva!" shouted Ric from across the room. "Come take a picture!"

Oliva saw him holding a Polaroid camera. She walked over and stood in front of Ric and posed with her hands on her hips. Ric took two more pictures of her.

"Ricky, don't waste all the film on one person," said Sherry, exasperated. "Try to get some of other people, too."

"Mr. and Mrs. Delgado, come get into the next one. I want a family photo."

Oliva was not happy about doing that in the least. She folded her arms and waited for her parents to get into the picture. Her mother stood on her right with her arms folded as well. Her father stood to her left with one hand in his pocket and holding a beer with the other.

"Why don't you all put your arms around each other?" Ric suggested.

Silence was their response. Ric took three photos before Oliva abruptly walked away and sat down.

A short time later she grew bored. The room was already hot even with two fans going and all the added body heat didn't help matters. She didn't understand why they didn't hold the party outside. She went over to Ric and asked for one of the photos of her standing alone to give to Pilar. After he gave it to her, she went to her room.

Chapter 8

Later that night, Oliva was jolted awake by the light being turned on. She sat up and saw her father standing in the doorway and her mother going through her closet.

"What are you doing?!"

Her mother swung around, her face contorted in anger.

"I'm here to teach you a lesson you little tramp! The next time you refuse me and tell me no—you'll be breathing your last breath!" She turned back to the closet and began pulling clothes off their racks and onto the floor.

Oliva got up and ran towards the closet to stop Inès. Alphonso lunged forward and with both hands, and pushed her backward on the bed with such force it temporarily knocked the wind from her. She slid from the bed down to the floor. As she was trying to catch her breath felt a mighty slap from Inès.

"Who gave you all of these clothes?! I know you're not making that much money from babysitting to afford all of these things! Answer me!" She screamed.

Oliva had her hand to her chest and was still trying to catch her breath. "M-my, my fr-friend P-P-Pilar bought- bought them."

"Your friend Pilar my ass! Why would she buy you all of these clothes? You're whoring yourself to some man to get these—I just know it!"

"Who is it?!" Alphonso demanded. "I'll find him and blow his brains out whoever it is!"

"I'll bet its Ric," Inès suggested. "I saw the way he was ogling her at the party."

"There is no man!" Oliva answered, finally catching her breath. "I swear my friend bought me those clothes!"

Inès turned back to the closet and resumed emptying it out until only an old jacket, a skirt and blouse remained on hangers. She looked down and began throwing pairs of shoes onto the pile. She then picked up an armload and left the room.

"Grab the rest of it!" she shouted to her husband from the hallway.

Alphonso did as he was told and began scooping up the remaining clothes and shoes. Oliva stood up to follow them out.

"You stay here!" Alphonso commanded. "Don't move!"

Oliva sat back on the bed. Her body shivered from fear and anger.

A few minutes later, Inès returned to Oliva's room.

"Come here."

Oliva looked up at her but didn't move.

"Now!"

Oliva got up and followed her mother. They went to the kitchen and Inès walked over to the window with a view to the backyard. Oliva felt sick. Inès pulled her in front of the window and stood behind her.

"You see what happens when you have a sassy mouth? You come walking into the party like you were belle of the ball. Not so full of yourself now, are you?"

Oliva looked out the window and for the first time in years began to cry as she watched her father throw her remaining clothes into a tin garbage pail that was lit ablaze. She was so entranced by the fire she didn't notice her father had come back inside. Suddenly she felt a violent pull of her hair as her mother snatched it and pulled her by it towards the back of the house. When they got to her parents' room, her mother pushed her on the bed on her stomach and pounced on her back and straddled her. All the weight from Inès instantly took Oliva's breath away. With one hand Inès mashed Oliva's face into the mattress. She leaned over to the drawer of the nightstand and fumbled in it until her hand came upon what it was looking for.

Out of the corner of her eye Oliva saw something shiny and in a horrifying instant realized it was a pair of scissors. She knew what was coming and began to struggle to get up but she was no match for the massive poundage of her mother holding her down.

"Be still!" shouted Inès.

"Mom, no! Please! I promise I won't do it again! I promise! Mom, please!"

"Shut up!" She leaned down and held the sharp points of the scissors to Oliva's face. "If you don't be still I swear to God I will cut your face. How would you like that?"

When Oliva heard this, she stopped moving. She couldn't bear it if something happened to her face. She quickly resigned herself to what was about to happen and she became perfectly still. The tears from earlier didn't make a reappearance but went back to where they normally resided—locked deep within. She all but physically removed herself from what was happening and became almost like a slightly interested bystander. She saw her father standing in the doorway with his arms folded. She listened to the snipping sound of the scissors as they ate through her long beautiful hair and watched as the strands of hair were tossed in an ever-growing pile next to her.

It was four-thirty in the morning and guilt interrupted Inès' quest to fall asleep. It had been years since she had laid a hand on her daughter. The last time was when Oliva was twelve-years-old. Inès was already angry over finding out about another one of Alphonso's women—this one an old friend of hers, when Oliva accidentally dropped a pot of spaghetti as she was taking it to the refrigerator. It was during a particularly rough period when Alphonso was in between jobs and money was even more scarce. Inès had planned to stretch out the spaghetti to have for dinner the rest of the week. When she saw the contents of the pot splattered on the floor she lost it. She picked up a broom that was nearby and beat Oliva with it until the broom broke in half. She then started in on her with her fists; punching her until Alphonso came in and pulled her off Oliva. She got up later and looked in on Oliva who had gone to bed. That's when she saw the bruised face, arms and legs. Luckily, Oliva didn't appear to have any broken bones because that would've meant a trip to the hospital and a bunch of questions from the doctors and nurses. She made Oliva stay home from school until the bruises were no longer visible. She told herself from then on she wouldn't lay a hand on her daughter again and she'd kept that promise until now. One of the reasons she was so anxious to leave her family in Chula Vista was to get away from her brutal father who beat her mercilessly on a regular basis.

She never wanted to abuse her daughter the way she was but there were those few times that she couldn't help it; like tonight for instance. When Oliva strutted into the party a storm of jealousy began to brew. She'd certainly taken note of her daughter's burgeoning beauty over the last few years but it hit her smack dab in the face earlier. She walked into that room as if she owned the world. Every head in the place turned in her direction. Oliva had command of the room and displayed an air of confidence Inès had never seen in her before and she saw all the promise of what she herself never had nor would ever attain. And she hated her daughter for it. She had to teach her a lesson and put her in her place. Especially when she saw the way *he* looked at her. He even had the nerve to say Oliva was the sexiest woman he'd ever seen. He won't think she's so sexy now.

Chapter 9

Pilar opened the door to greet Oliva and was stunned by what she saw. Oliva was wearing an old skirt and blouse with a scarf on her head. Pilar was about to ask why she was dressed the way she was when she noticed the dead look in Oliva's eyes. She pulled her inside the house and took her in her arms. She then guided Oliva to the couch.

"Sweetheart, what happened?"

"My parents burned all the clothes you bought me," she replied in an almost robotic tone. "They even burned some of the clothes I'd bought for myself. All I have is what I've got on right now."

Pilar stared at Oliva, not believing what she was hearing.

"They burned—why would they do that?!"

"That's the kind of people they are. I told they were horrible. I figured you thought I was exaggerating but now you see. And that's not all they did." She slowly reached up and slid the scarf off her head, revealing her haphazardly chopped locks that were now about three inches long in some spots and four inches in others.

"Jesus Christ, Oliva!" She leaned her head into Oliva's and rocked her gently. She lifted her head and looked at Oliva who was staring straight ahead. She was lost to her at that moment. She was somewhere closed off emotionally. Pilar placed her finger under chin and turned Oliva's face to her. The eyes staring back her were without a hint of its former spark.

"I'm so sorry, baby," she whispered. She leaned in and pressed her lips into hers. Oliva was unresponsive to her kiss. Pilar pulled away from the kiss and stroked Oliva's back. She knew other than telling her what happened Oliva didn't want to talk about it any further and decided not to ask more of the questions swimming in her head. The main one being what kind of monsters was her parents? She noticed Oliva holding something in her hand. It was a photograph.

"What's that?"

Oliva handed it to her. "It was taken at the party. It'll be a while before my hair is like this again."

"You're so photogenic. Don't worry. Your hair will grow back before you know it. Can I have this?"

"Yes. I brought it for you.'

"Thank you. It's going to be okay, baby. I promise." She stood up and grabbed Oliva's hand. "Come on. Let's go."

"Go where?"

"Just come on."

Oliva sat in the beauty chair as the hairstylist tried to correct the damage done to her hair. She wasn't the least bit optimistic. She was devastated that her long locks were gone. "Oliva, I think you're going to love what Frances has done with your hair."

Oliva glanced up at Pilar, not believing her. The stylist Frances then twirled the chair around to face the mirror. Oliva was a little pleased. It looked much better than it did when she first sat down in the chair. Frances cut it into a very nice style. Still, it couldn't compare with her former flowing tresses.

"Sweetie, you look like Dorothy Hamill! It's simply adorable!"

"It is quite cute."

"Quite cute?" repeated Pilar. She went and stood directly behind Oliva and their eyes met in the mirror. Pilar put her hands underneath Oliva's chin and caressed the sides of her face with her thumbs. "Baby, you look beautiful. This style makes you look so classy and mature. It may be your mother did you a favor."

"Thanks," Oliva mumbled. She squirmed a little in the chair, uncomfortable with Pilar's public display of affection and endearments.

"Now let's go replenish your wardrobe."

Oliva's face finally brightened.

"Really?"

"Yes. I thought that would perk you up."

"But what if they did what they did last night."

"You'll keep them in the closet of my spare room."

"Sweet. Thank you, Pilar."

Chapter 10

Carlos furiously stroked himself as he moved closer on the verge of orgasm.

"Carlos!" Maribel shouted from the top of the cellar stairs. "I need you to help me hang this picture! You know I can never hang it evenly like you do!"

Carlos stopped masturbating at the sound of her voice. *It's like she knows what I'm coming down here to do. She never bugs me until she sees me heading down here. I've been upstairs for four hours and the moment I...*

"I'll be up there in a minute, Mari!"

Maribel stood listening for a moment.

"Well hurry up!" She turned to go back into the kitchen. "Dirty beast," she mumbled under her breath.

Carlos looked back at his new Playboy magazine featuring Miss August, Dorothy Stratten. Other than Oliva, no other woman brought forth the lust in his loins like Dorothy. What a beauty she was—full mouth, shiny blonde hair and curvaceous body. Maribel was painfully thin and though he loved her, her lack of curves did nothing to inspire him to make love to her. He began to massage himself again. This time he thought of the other object of his desire. *Oh, that Oliva is a hot one. Those small but firm tits and perfect ass. Mmmm, I bet her chocha's just as good as her mother's. Actually even better—nice and tight. Last night I couldn't keep my eyes off her. She could be a Playboy model too if she wanted. I've never seen her look more beautiful. Even though there was something scary about her, I'd still fuck the hell out of her. Old Inès didn't like it when I whispered to her how sexy her daughter was. I had too many beers and didn't know better. She gave me such an evil look I hope she'll still meet me at the motel tomorrow. Yeah, when I bang that fat pussy I'm going to be picturing Oliva. Oliva. You sexy little wench. You try and pretend you don't want this dick but I know you do. I'm going to give it to you, too. I'll be covering your mouth to stifle your screams when you come, just like I do Inès. I'll—I'll—*

Carlos swallowed the groan bubbling in his throat as his seed oozed out and dripped down his hand. After a few moments of collecting his thoughts he reached over and picked up an old rag next to the milk crate he was sitting on. He used the same rag to clean himself the last two visits down to the cellar. He pulled up his pants and started for the stairs.

As Carlos entered the kitchen, Maribel eyed him with distaste.

"The picture is sitting against the wall in the living room," she informed him. "When you go to visit your cousin in El Segundo you'd better not forget to bring back those sconces she promised me. I'll put them on either side of the picture."

Carlos walked to the living with Maribel close on his heels. She certainly knows how to finagle things out of people, he thought.

"You won't believe this."

Carlos stifled a sigh. Maribel enjoyed filling his ears with the latest *chisme*. She always prepared him with the opening phrase, "You won't believe this."

"What won't I believe now?"

"I saw Oliva today at the salon."

Carlos's ears immediately perked up at the name.

"And?"

"All of her hair was gone!"

He almost dropped the hammer he'd just picked up from the table.

"What do you mean her hair is gone?!" He hoped he either misunderstood or his wife was wrong. One of the sexiest things about Oliva was her waist-length hair. He always fantasized about what it would feel like to trail over his body.

"I saw it with my own eyes. I went to Ruby's Salon with Sherry while she got her hair done and I saw Oliva with that young woman who moved in the old Garcia place. I found out her name is Pilar. I don't think Oliva saw me though. Anyway, she came in looking like her hair got caught in a meat grinder or something."

"What?"

"Yes, all of that long hair was gone." Maribel's reply was accompanied by a self-satisfied smirk. "Frances sure didn't have much to work with. Oh, and she had on some old rags," she added with a touch glee. "She didn't have on those hot mama clothes she had on last night. Without the clothes and the hair she's nothing special at all really."

Carlos didn't say anything but doubted that to be true. He knew her comments stemmed from envy. Oliva still had the same body and face so she was still a beauty. But there was no doubt the hair and clothes were a nice addition to the package. I wonder what the heck happened. Inès! I know she's behind this!

"Something funny is going on between Oliva and that Pilar," said Maribel.

"Funny how?"

"It was the way she was touching Oliva. It was, I don't know. The way a man touches a woman." She glanced at her husband sharply. "You know. The way you used to touch me."

"Oh come on, Mari. I still touch you!"

"Right. You mean like on our anniversary or my birthday? Anyhow, it was like that. You don't think they're *marimachas* do you? As far as I know Oliva has never had a boyfriend and she's 18-years-old. I was married at that age. She's an odd girl so I wouldn't be surprised if she was—you know—that way. Poor Alphonso and Inès. I would die if one of our kids were queer."

Carlos hammered the nail into the wall and tuned out his wife. *Oliva can't be a pata! Mari has it all wrong and is reading into things. But what if she isn't? That would explain why no matter how sweet I am to that girl she turns her nose up at me. I know I'm not the young buck I used to be but there's still crowing left in this rooster. If she's what Mari thinks she is, one night with me would set her right.*

"I'm going to take Señora Sanchez something to eat. She's still laid up from her surgery. I'll probably sit and visit with her for a few before coming back home."

Maribel waited for a response from her husband but there was none. He looked like he was in another world. With an exasperated cluck of her tongue, she turned on her heels and walked back to the kitchen.

Shelley Halima

Chapter 11

Oliva felt good for the first time that day as she hung up her new clothes. It was only a band-aid for the wound she suffered the night before yet it was an effective one. Pilar had gotten out her charge card and replaced all the clothes she'd bought for Oliva before and then some. She had a wide assortment of jeans, skirts and blouses. When things died down at home she would bring some of the clothes home. Although she was starting to like her short hairstyle more every time she looked in the mirror, she still missed her hair. The new hairstyle did make her look older and a little more sophisticated but it didn't compare...

After she finished hanging up the clothes she joined Pilar in the living room. She was standing by the record player, pulling her most played Amàlia album from its sleeve. Soon the room was filled with voice of the singer Oliva had also come to love. Pilar sat on the couch and patted the space next to her for Oliva. When Oliva sat down she reached for one of the wine glasses Pilar had set out on the table.

"Thanks again for the clothes. I don't know how I'll ever repay you."

"You don't repay gifts, my love. Your happiness is enough for me. Now let's talk about our future plans. I think it'll be safe for me to get back on the scene in another few months."

"A few months?" Oliva asked, disappointed. "I was hoping we could leave sooner."

"Patience, darling. I need to make sure my situations have cooled. I'm just as anxious to leave here as you are–trust me. But it's all about timing. Now here's my plan. In Los Angeles there's a good mark for you. Valente Construction is a company headed by Anton and Gino. I've done my homework on them and these guys are loaded. They own buildings across the country and they've been building malls like crazy. Now how are your secretarial skills such as typing and filing?"

"I've taken typing in school. I've never filed but I know my ABC's so that should be no problem. Why?"

"From what I've heard Gino would be the better target because he's more a soft touch. It's kind of known that any woman with a sob story will get his sympathy and money. If you can get in his secretarial pool and try to get as much time as you can, I guarantee you he'll be yours before you know it. What's the faraway look for?"

"I'm going to have to sleep with him, aren't I?"

"Eventually," Pilar replied with a laugh. "You've never been with a man before have you?"

"Nope. I wouldn't know what to do."

"You have to do everything, just not all at once. You want a man to think you haven't been around too much even when you've gotten experienced. Therefore you have to be coy in the beginning and gradually loosen up into this wild beast they think they've unleashed. Men want to be the one to stake the flag in the bedroom. They love to hear, 'I've never felt this way before'. Or 'no one has ever made me feel this good'. Did you read those manuals I gave you last week?"

"Yes, I don't know if I can do those things, Pilar."

"You will if you want to keep your rich man happy and living the good life. Do you want that?"

"More than anything."

"If you want that more than anything you have to be willing to do anything."

"I understand."

"Good. Tomorrow is going to be a busy day with my brother."

"I can't wait to meet him."

"He's a character all right—a real ladies man. I don't know how but he is."

"What makes you say that?"

"Let's just say he got short-changed on the looks genes in our family. He's not ugly by any means, just nothing special. I guess his smooth words and money help him out in the women department."

"What does he do?"

"He has a company that imports and exports goods to and from places all over the world. Our father actually had to go to him for help in an investment venture. Oh! This song is so beautiful! I can hear a million times and never get tired of it."

Oliva tilted her head as she listened to the song "Meu Amor, Meu Amor". Pilar stood up and grabbed her by the hand.

"You've got to dance with me to this song."

Pilar and Oliva wrapped their arms around each other and began to slow dance. Oliva closed her eyes and laid her head on Pilar's shoulder. The trauma she felt from the events of the night before were temporarily suspended while she was in Pilar's arms. There was no place she would rather have been than where she was at that moment.

As Maribel walked briskly down the street going back home, she thought of the many chores she still had left to do before her head hit the pillow. She would have to find the strength to complete them thanks to her visit with Senora Sanchez. *That woman is such a little vampire. She sucks the life right out of you. I went over there out of the goodness of my heart to feed her and she wanted me to do a million things. Wash a load of clothes, put another in the dryer, wash the dishes, and change her linen. Aye dios mio! As if I don't have enough to do at my own house. I'd better*

have a nice reward for me when that old woman croaks. She knows how much I've been coveting that silver and the Blue Willow dish set. And the painting she has in the dining room would be perfect for my home. It would take the place of that cheap piece I had Carlos hang today. Speaking of the devil I wonder what he's up to now. He's probably downstairs with those dirty magazines doing something I don't even want to think about. Humph! He said he built that cellar to store wines. I knew that was a lie from the start because the only liquid that passes those lips is beer. Men are so filthy—minds always in the gutter. I should've burned those magazines when I found them. But what good would that do? He would just get more.

When she got near Pilar's house she slowed her pace. She could make out two shadowy figures near the window. Her eyes never left the house as she walked past it. Suddenly she stopped in her tracks. She looked around to see if anyone was out. When she saw that the coast was clear, she went to the house toward the side window. She maneuvered around the shrubbery until she was right at the window. There were sheer curtains hanging at that window which gave her a good view inside. Her eyes widened as she saw Oliva and Pilar in a close embrace, dancing. *I knew it! Wait until I tell Carlos this.*

Maribel was disgusted at what she was witnessing, yet found it hard to stop looking. She finally tore herself from the display and headed for home. Before she got to her house she decided to make a quick visit elsewhere first.

Chapter 12

Oliva paused on the porch before going into her house. She took the scarf from her pocket and tied it on her head, covering her new hairstyle. She then walked up the steps and entered her house. As soon as she stepped inside she knew something was wrong. Something told her to turn around and run but she closed the door behind her. Alphonso and Ines were both sitting on the couch as if they were waiting for her. *God, what now? I just want them to go back to ignoring my existence.*

"Where have you been?" demanded Alphonso.

Since when do you care? "I've been over my friend's house."

"What friend? The one who bought you all those clothes?"

"Yes."

Alphonso got up and walked towards her until he was inches from her face. Oliva was instantly frightened. He looked as if he were extremely angry.

"Are you a fucking queer?"

"What?!"

"Are-you-a-fucking-queer?!" he shouted.

"No!" Oliva took a step back.

"Your mother and I found out something is going on between you and that woman that moved in down the street! I've been worried you were messing around with some man and here you are fooling around with a woman! You freak!"

Alphonso spat in her face. Oliva quickly wiped the warm saliva from her face with the back of her hand. She started towards her room when she felt her father's hand viciously grab her throat.

"I will not have some pervert living in my house!"

He slammed her body back against the wall. Oliva furiously tugged at his hand, trying to loosen his grip around her neck. After a few moments he finally let go. Oliva gratefully breathed air into her lungs in huge gulps.

"Maribel said she saw you and that woman rubbing your hands all over each other and kissing!"

"No!" It was Oliva managed to say. She decided to try and seek refuge in her room. She knew it was futile when she heard her father's footsteps following close behind her. She felt a push from behind and fell to the floor in the hallway. She looked behind to see her mother push Alphonso to the side and look down to her.

"We are a good, upstanding family and you've brought shame to us! I'd rather you be a prostitute on the street corner than–than what you are!"

Oliva got up on her knees in an attempt to make another run to her room. Ines grabbed the back of Oliva's blouse to pull her back and in the process buttons popped off from the force. Somehow Oliva's scarf came off and Ines saw the new hairdo.

Alphonso grabbed her by the legs and pulled her in further back into the hallway. He removed his belt and jerked his head to the side, signaling Inès to move out of the way. He began beating Oliva, each lash fueled by the heat of raging anger. Oliva cried out and again tried to crawl away. Ines moved in front of her blocking her way.

"I'm going to make sure you're not a sick pervert!" Alphonso shouted. "Because I will beat it out of you!"

Other than him pushing Oliva the night before, he'd never laid a hand on her. But that night he made up for all the years he had never whipped her as he tried his hardest beat out the demon he feared resided in his daughter.

Chapter 13

Oliva woke from an exhaustive slumber. She was on her bed lying on her stomach and in the stickiness of her body's perspiration. She instantly wanted to regain the refuge of sleep, away from the pain throbbing throughout her backside. She not only felt it from her neck down to her ankles but also on her arms and hands when she had curled up in a fetal position during her father's attack. With great care she eased off the bed and walked to mirror on her dresser. She unbuttoned the sole button left on her shirt and gingerly removed it. She turned her back to the mirror and looked over her shoulder and surveyed the darkening welts. She then stared in the mirror and wondered how everything could go so wrong. The weekend had started with the promise of it being one of the best of her life and instead became one of the worst. She had gone from being mostly ignored for years by her parents to receiving two straight days of their brutalizing attention.

I can't believe they did this to me. I wish that they were dead. "Good, upstanding family." What a joke. They're nothing but trash. This whole neighborhood and everyone in it with the exception of Pilar is trash. I can't wait until I'm far away from here. I swear to God that once I leave I will never look back. I've always detested Maribel and I hate her even more now!

She walked into the hallway to the bathroom. She wanted to take a bath but she knew it would be too much to bear so instead she washed up as best she could in the sink. After going back to her room, she pulled out an old t-shirt from the bureau and put it on. It was big on her and didn't cling too much to her sore skin. After going through the house and seeing that no one was home, she went to the phone in the kitchen and dialed.

"Hello?"

"Pilar, it's me."

"Oliva? You sound different. Are you okay?"

"Look, I won't be able to come over later. In fact I probably won't be able to come down there for a few days."

"Why?! What happened?"

"I can't talk right now. I'll tell you whenever I see you."

"Tell me something! You can't let me just wonder like this. What did they do to you now?! I know they did something! Bastards! I'm coming down there."

"No! Please, Pilar. Don't do that. If you care anything about me you'll just wait until I can come see you. I'm begging you," she said, her voice choked with emotion. "You'll just make everything so much worse for me. Be patient. Is your brother there?"

"No, he had to delay his trip but he'll be here next week."

She heard the loud motor of her father's Ford Pinto pulling into the driveway. "I have to go. I'll see you soon."

"I love you, O—"

Oliva hung up the phone and as fast as she could move walked back to her bedroom. She turned the box fan on and went and lay on her side. She blocked out everything from her parents to even Pilar. She closed her eyes and fell asleep. Except for getting up to use the bathroom she slept for a day and a half.

Chapter 14

Maribel was giddy with excitement as she made her trek home from Señora Sanchez's. She decided to not make Maribel wait until her death to inherit one of the pieces from her Blue Willow set. Maribel held on to the Blue Willow meat platter like a child with a long wished for toy. Señora Sanchez estimated the piece to be from the 1800's. Maribel planned to keep it for as long as she possibly could before selling it. She knew exactly where she wanted the platter to go; in the middle the top shelf of the curio cabinet that held other dishes she'd been collecting over the years.

As she did the week before, she slowed down as she neared Pilar's house. There seemed to be no one at home and therefore nothing to see and gossip about so she quickened her pace once more. When she got to her house she went around to the back door and saw the light in the back of the house was out. *Why must I always remind Carlos to turn on the lights once it's dark? He's probably busy being filthy in the cellar.* She fished her keys from her pocket with one hand as she held the platter close to her chest with the other. When she put the key in the lock a deafening blow hit her right ear. As pain from the blow to her ear vibrated through her head, the quiet early evening was broken by the sound of the prized Blue Willow platter shattering as it hit the ground. Maribel felt something like a scarf cover her mouth. She was forcefully yanked backward and dragged behind the garage. There she was pummeled and kicked by her assailant until she nearly lost consciousness.

Over the next few days Oliva was relieved when things went back to normal and unless it was a command, her parents barely spoke to her. One day they left to go to the flea market and to the store to replace her father's black slacks and shirt that had come up missing. Alphonso accused his wife of leaving them behind at the coin laundry.

Oliva decided it was a good time to go see Pilar. She knew her parents would spend hours at the flea market alone so they would be gone for a while.

The closer she got to Pilar's house the more she looked about. She darted up the sidewalk to the porch where she rang the bell.

Come on, Pilar. Hurry.

A moment later the door opened but instead of Pilar there was a young man standing there.

"Yes?" He looked Oliva up and down.

"Is Pilar here?"

"No, she's gone shopping."

"Do you know how long she will be?"

"There's no telling. My sister is a master shopper."

"Sister? You're Tony?"

"Yeah," he answered with a raised brow. "Wait, are you Oliva?"

Oliva nodded.

"Well, well, well. So you're the girl she's been worried about."

Oliva looked about quickly. "Can I come in, please?"

"Of course. Excuse my manners." He stepped aside to let her in. He tried to assess her figure under her shabby, loose clothing. Even though she didn't have on a stitch of makeup and touseled hair, she looked quite a beauty. *I can see why my sister is so enthralled. She's definitely a diamond in the rough.*

"Would you like something to eat?"

"Um-no. Well, what do you have?"

"I have some leftovers heating in the oven," he informed her as they walked to the kitchen. "I told Pilar to get with the program and buy a microwave. Anyway, I'm heating up some lamb chops, wild rice and vegetables. Sound good?"

"Very." Almost as if on cue Oliva's stomach began to growl with hunger. She hadn't eaten much since the last incident with her parents but suddenly her appetite was back with a vengeance.

Oliva took a place at the table while Tony set out dishes and silverware. Oliva covertly gave him a once over. He was well-groomed and was wearing designer jeans, suede Adidas shoes and shirt. *Pilar was right—he isn't much to look at but he does have a certain appeal. He's just like Pilar, so cool and self-assured.*

Tony took his place at the table opposite Oliva, sitting in the chair sideways. He crossed his legs and propped an arm on the table and drummed his fingers. He then averted an intense gaze to Oliva. She shifted a bit in her chair as she became uncomfortable being under scrutiny.

"You're very beautiful, you know that?" Tony asked as he placed his hand under his chin.

Oliva looked down in her lap. It wasn't that long ago she would've answered, "yes" but the confidence about her looks was no longer there.

Tony instantly picked up on her lack of confidence and decided to lay it on even more thick. Nothing appealed to him more than a woman who was insecure. Getting women like that into bed was a shoo-in and, since tomorrow would be his last day in town, he didn't have much time. He knew he was no Shaun Cassidy or John Travolta but if there was one thing he did well besides make money, it was getting a woman into bed. Oliva was on his radar and he was determined to have her. He didn't care what was going on between her and his sister. He'd bedded models, actresses as well as almost every woman who'd graced the inside of Studio 54, so getting an insecure, poor-as-dirt girl would be cinch. He was getting aroused just looking at her.

"You are, Oliva. You literally took my breath away when I saw you standing there when I opened the door. My heart almost jumped out of my chest." He smiled and shook his head. "I can't believe that just came out of my mouth. I've never said that to a woman before." In reality it was the standard line he used. "Let me check on the food. I don't want it dry out in the oven." He got up and removed the dishes from the oven and put them on top of the stove.

"You know you saved me from being a pig. I heated up enough for two or three people." He got a plate from the table, took it back to the stove and put food on it. "Here you go, my lady." Tony put the plate in front of her.

Oliva picked up her fork and was about to dig in but didn't want to be rude so she waited for Tony.

"Want something to drink?"

"Yes. What's in the fridge?"

Tony set his plate down then went to the refrigerator. He opened it and bent down to look inside.

"Let's see. We have Tab, orange juice, Cactus Cooler--"

"Cactus Cooler, please."

He opened the soda and poured her a glass. He sat down and poured himself a glass of wine and took a sip. Oliva noticed the look on his face.

"You don't like your wine?"

"Pilar has always been terrible at picking out wines. She's practically surrounded by vineyards and still can't pick a decent Cabernet Sauvignon to save her life."

Oliva cut into her lamb chop and ignored the comment. She didn't like him criticizing Pilar.

"Tell me about yourself. I'm surprised some man hasn't swept you off somewhere."

"There's nothing much to say except I'm ready to leave this town."

"I can't say I blame you. There's not much around here. Where do you want to go?"

"Everywhere. Anywhere but here."

"You're pretty vague. What's your life here like?"

Oliva stopped eating and looked him square in the eye.

"I have no life here," she stated firmly.

Oliva intrigued Tony because there was obviously much more to her than she let on. He saw a lot of pain and anger in her eyes. And he also saw even more determination. He had no doubt her talk about leaving her hometown was not just talk. She would leave it all behind and probably not think twice about doing it.

"I wish you could've come by here sooner. I'm leaving for New York tomorrow afternoon. I would love to have spent more time with you. I want to get to know you."

"I wanted to come for a visit your first day here but I couldn't. If I can, I'll come by to see you tomorrow before you leave."

"I'm looking forward to it. What happened to your hands?"

Oliva looked at her bruised knuckles. "I was working out in the yard."

Tony took her hand in his. "A woman like you shouldn't be doing manual labor."

Pilar never made it back in time to see Oliva before she had to leave for home. Tony spent the time they had together wooing Oliva enough to where she'd do whatever it took to come see him the next day. Oliva looked at the clock and decided she'd better get back home. Tony walked her to the door.

"You're not going to stand me up tomorrow and have me leave for New York without seeing you again are you?"

"I'll do everything I can to make it back over to see you. What time are you leaving?"

"Not until later in the afternoon, so the earlier you can come over the better. If you can, try and be here around 12:30."

"All right."

"Pilar told me a woman in the neighborhood was attacked a couple weeks back. Do you need me to see you home?"

Oliva chuckled lightly. "No, I'll be just fine."

Tony stood in the door watching her walk away and wondering what she found so humorous about his offer.

Chapter 15

Oliva was not the least bit experienced when it came to men, yet she was savvy enough to know when one was trying to get her in the sack. She knew not only from what Pilar told her about her brother that he was a slick one, her instincts told her that as well. Still, Tony was fascinating, charming and worldly. He had traveled to even more places than his sister. She had a strong inkling he would play an even more important role in her life than Pilar.

Oliva knocked on the door and within seconds Tony had opened it.

"Hi!"

"Hello." This time Oliva didn't wait for him to invite her inside. She just stepped in and brushed past him. "I hope Pilar's car is in the garage and she's home."

"Nope, she's not," Tony said as he closed the door. "I'm glad you were able to make it."

"Did you tell Pilar I was going to try and come over?"

"Yes, I did. She had to take care of some things." He in fact didn't tell Pilar that she was coming over and didn't even tell her she'd stopped by the day before. He'd cleaned up the dishes and any other signs of Oliva's visit. He sent Pilar off on some errands and did not let her know of Oliva's plans to come over to say good-bye. He didn't want anything to interfere with his plans to bed Oliva before he left for New York.

"Remember yesterday when I was talking about my sister's lack of finesse in picking out wines?"

"Yes," Oliva answered as she sat on the couch.

"I spoke too soon. I found a very nice Riesling and I thought we'd have some fruit and cheese with it." He wanted to loosen her inhibitions and Cactus Coolers was out of the question.

Tony poured both he and Oliva some wine.

Since Oliva hadn't eaten anything since the day before, she almost immediately felt a buzz from the wine. Tony engaged her in his normal witty conversation while keeping an eye on the clock. He knew the window of time he had to seduce her was closing.

"I'd love take you on my yacht. I just bought it a few weeks ago. It's tremendous if I say so myself. If I sent you a ticket would you come back east and visit me?"

"Sure!"

Pilar and Tony both were offering her opportunities she'd never before been presented. But she was tiring of hearing about places to visit and new lifestyles to live—she was ready experience it firsthand and now! Quickly weighing the options in her head she felt Tony was a better bet. There was really no telling how much longer Pilar wanted to hide out and Oliva was ready to escape as soon as possible.

"Can I call you sometime?"

"Young lady, I'd be hurt if you didn't call me." Tony grabbed his jacket that was hanging on the back of the couch and pulled a business card from the inside pocket. "Here you go. I want you to feel free to call me any time," he said as he handed her the card.

Oliva glanced at the card before sliding it into the pocket of her skirt.

Tony slid closer to her until their legs touched and poured more wine on top of the little she had left in her glass. After she took another sip he slipped his arm around her waist.

"I can't wait for you to visit me. I'm going to show you all the best New York has to offer; Tavern on the Green, 21 Club, and maybe we'll spend a couple of nights at The Algonquin."

A surge of excitement coursed through Oliva at hearing about The Algonquin because she'd read it was one of the haunts of poet, Dorothy Parker. She was so lost in the thought of finally seeing the places she'd only read about it took a few seconds before she realized Tony was kissing her neck.

"Pilar, she could be back any time now."

"No, my sister went on quite a few errands. She'll be gone for a while."

Oliva knew exactly what he wanted and she was ready to give it to him in exchange for what she wanted. She sensed some guilt because she felt like she was betraying Pilar. But she needed an escape and she needed it immediately. So she leaned back on the couch and let Tony kiss and caress her body before he took her by the hand and led her to the guest bedroom.

Oliva lay naked on the bed and though she tried to remember all the things in the book Pilar had pointed out to do in bed to please a man, it all faded in her memory. She was about to give up her virginity to a man she barely knew. Also, she was scared about the pain that was coming. Once, she'd overheard the conversation of some girls at the next table during lunch. They were talking about their first times. All of them said the first time a man entered you was painful and a couple of the girls said they had bled some.

"Ow!" Oliva cried out as Tony bit one of her nipples.

"I'm sorry, baby."

Tony nudged her legs open with his. He reached down to finger her vagina and was dismayed at her lack of wetness. *What's wrong with this girl? Usually women are screaming their heads off before I even put it in but this one is just lying here looking at the ceiling. I'll give it to her good and change that.*

Tony spat on the tips of his fingers and ran them across the head of his penis. Oliva tried her best to hide her distaste.

"You want it now, lover?"

"Yes." Oliva had to suppress a laugh at him calling her "lover". It sounded so strange to her.

When she felt his hardness pressing against the opening of her vagina, she braced herself for the pain. She felt a tiny pinch and then he was pumping his hips and panting wildly. He was raised up on his elbows and Oliva looked down between her legs. *He's in. But I barely felt anything. Maybe he's not in all the way.*

Oliva tried her best to lose herself in the moment and to enjoy the experience as much as possible but she couldn't. The women in the photographs in the book Pilar had given her all had looks of ecstasy on their faces. She wasn't even coming close to feeling anything to make her feel that way. She kept waiting for the pleasurable sensations like the kind she got the times when Pilar demonstrated to her what a man does in the process of making love to a woman. Pilar's touch was gentle and smooth while Tony's was rough and clumsy. Within two to three minutes he let out a loud moan and fell off to the side of her on his back. Oliva surreptitiously glanced over at his penis.

My God. No wonder I didn't feel anything. It's four inches if that. Four slim inches in fact. It certainly didn't compare with the sizes of the men in the sex book.

"I'll be ready to go again in a minute," Tony said, still breathing heavily. "I'll finish you off, I promise."

Finish me off? You have to get me started first.

Oliva just continued to lie there, feeling the small warm pool of wetness between her legs left courtesy of Tony. A few minutes later he was back on her, sucking at her breasts and stroking her body. Soon he was back inside her pumping away in rhythm-less fury. This time Oliva began to play the part. She moaned in feigned delectation, grabbed his back and moved her hips.

*Ah, that's it. I knew you would come around to this good coc*k. "You're getting it good aren't you?" He looked down at her as she licked her lips.

"Oh yes! Don't stop!"

"I won't stop, baby. I'm slamming it! I'm slamming it!"

What on earth is the deal with this "I'm slamming it" stuff? Do women actually enjoy this? Just shut up and get this over with.

She received her wish five minutes later when Tony let out a sound oddly similar to that of a wolf baying at the moon, then collapsed on top of her as she waited patiently for him to get off of her. A noise from the next room caught Oliva's ear. There was definite movement. She pushed Tony off and sat up.

"Did you hear that?"

"Hear what, baby?"

As if to answer, Pilar appeared in the doorway of the bedroom. There was a hardness glinting in her eyes that were wet from tears.

"Oliva, you have two minutes to get out of my house," she stated simply before walking away.

Oliva sat stunned for a moment. The sound of her heartbeat pounded in her ears so loudly it took a few seconds to make out what Tony was saying.

"She'll be upset for a while but I'm sure you two will be, uh, friends again soon."

She swiftly got up from the bed and put her clothes on. She didn't say anything to Tony before leaving the room. Pilar was in the living room on the couch, drinking wine from one of the glasses. There were two filled garbage bags at her feet.

"So how was it fucking my brother?" She asked without looking up.

Oliva didn't answer.

"I had no idea you were such a slut. You told me you'd never been with a man before yet you walk up in here and screw Tony the minute you meet him."

"We met yesterday..." Oliva's voice faltered at her own flimsy attempt to explain herself.

"So you were over here yesterday?"

"Yes."

"Why would you do this?" She finally looked up at Oliva.

"You told me to not give myself to someone who was poor, remember? You said to set my sights on someone who could provide me with the best." Her voice brimmed with a plea for Pilar to understand her actions.

Pilar got up and walked to Oliva.

"And you actually think my brother is going to give you that? You stupid little girl. I told you what he was about, didn't I? He won't give you a damned thing other than what he just gave you in the bedroom."

"He gave me his number and said I could call him. He wants to take me around New York and on his yacht."

"Tony only squires around the crème de la crème of women on his arm. There's no way in hell he'd been seen in his crowd with piece of poor trash like you."

Neither of the incidents that happened to Oliva that horrible weekend with her parents compared to the pain of Pilar's words. Somehow she didn't let the tears fall.

Pilar walked over to the two bags, picked them up and held them out for Oliva.

"It's the clothes I bought you. You don't deserve it but I want them out of my house. Take them!" She demanded when Oliva didn't make a move to grab the bags.

Oliva took the bags and headed for the door. Pilar walked up behind her as she got to the door.

"I was going to give you everything, Oliva. I was going to groom you and make sure you had nothing but the best. You won't get that now. I guarantee if you call my brother he won't take your phone call. I don't ever want to talk to you again. If you see me on the street I don't even want you to look in my direction. You are going to be here in this pathetic place with pathetic parents living a pathetic life forever."

Oliva left Pilar's home for the last time, carrying the two garbage bags filled with clothes back to her house. She'd never felt such desolation and despair. What she believed were the only options to leave her miserable existence had slipped from her in a matter of minutes.

Shelley Halima

Chapter 16

Oliva sank into a deep depression and didn't leave her room for weeks except to bathe and that wasn't very frequently. She never made an attempt to call Tony because she couldn't take the rejection she knew awaited. Even her parents were a bit concerned. They had never seen her so despondent and withdrawn. She always kept to herself and was distant–but this was different. Her mother even brought a plate into her room and left it on her dresser, which was something she'd never done before. When she went in Oliva's room the next day the food was untouched except by flies and ants. Oliva was curled in a ball on the bed and Ines noticed the bones starting to show through the thin t-shirt she had on and dark circles under her eyes. Ines didn't voice her concern or offer words of comfort to her daughter, she shooed the flies and ants off the plate and left the room with it.

Besides melancholy, the only other emotion residing inside Oliva was hatred, hatred of her parents, Tony and herself for messing up the course of her life. *I have nothing and I never will. All I have in this world is in two bags stuffed underneath my bed.*

One day as she was lying in bed, she was hit with a wave of nausea. Soon she felt so violently ill she had to rush to the bathroom. She'd only had a piece of toast that morning so the only that came up was a minute portion of bread mixed with bile. This happened for the next few mornings and was noticed by Inès. She went to the hallway closet where she and Oliva kept their feminine products. When she looked at the boxes she saw that Oliva's box of sanitary napkins had not been opened. She knew it was the same box she bought her daughter a few weeks back because she tried a different brand than she normally bought. She went to tell Alphonso of her suspicions.

For the first time in weeks, Oliva was out of her room for more than a few minutes and was sitting at the kitchen table drinking some iced tea. Inès and Alphonso entered the kitchen and sat down at the table.

"Are you pregnant?" Alphonso asked bluntly.

Taken aback by the question, Oliva didn't respond right away.

"Are you?" asked Inès.

"No, I'm not."

"When was the last time you had your period?"

Oliva bristled at the question her mother asked. She didn't like talking about such matters in front of her father. She shrugged.

"When was the last time, Oliva?" Inès asked again.

"I don't know, maybe a couple of weeks ago."

"Liar! Your napkins haven't been touched since I bought them! If you had your period I sure would like to know what the hell you were using for it! Besides, I can smell a pregnant woman a mile away."

"So I guess you been with a man?" Alphonso inquired.

"What a stupid question, Al! If she's pregnant of course she's been with a man!"

Again, Oliva didn't answer right away. Her first inclination was to refute it but though she tried not to think about it because the unexplained queasiness paired with the missed period, she knew she was pregnant. There was no way she could continue to deny it and since the truth would be evident soon, it was fruitless to say otherwise. Something else came to mind. This would be a great opportunity redeem herself from her parents' allegations about her.

"Yes, I've been with a man. My friend Pilar–the one you accused me of being with, I'm really her brother's girlfriend. He's a big time businessman in New York and he comes here to visit me. He's really the one bought me all those clothes."

"If he's such a big time businessman, why is his sister living here?" inquired Inès.

"She's just hiding out here for a little while from her crazy ex-husband who tried to kill her. But if you've seen what she's done outside to that house, you'd know she's got money too. And the inside is spectacular, it has all new carpeting, appliances and expensive artwork."

Inès and Alphonso both weighed what their daughter had just told them. The possibility of her being pregnant out of wedlock was not something they ever wanted, they were both relieved that she was involved with a man.

"Well, since he's a big time business man as you say," began Inès, "then he should be contacted so he can do right by you." *And us. If he's indeed what Oliva says he is, he will certainly want his child to live a better lifestyle and its grandparents. Oliva getting pregnant could be the best thing to happen to us. She'd better not be lying.*

The wheels in Alphonso's head were spinning in the same direction as his wife. Hearing his daughter was pregnant by a rich man had him seeing dollar signs. His daughter could for once in her life be of some use.

"I think you should call and let him know of your predicament," suggested Inès. "He needs to know so he can take care of his responsibilities."

Oliva was mortified. She had backed herself into a corner. Inwardly, she cursed herself. She needed to buy herself some time. "He's out of the country until next month. I'll call him then and tell him."

"Are you sure he's got money?" asked Alphonso. He wanted to be sure before he got his hopes up.

"Yes. He owns a huge business and he has a yacht and everything."

Inès and Alphonso exchanged looks. They could barely contain their glee. They were about to hit the big time.

Oliva got up from the table.

"I'm going to lie down. I don't feel so good."

"Yeah, yeah," said Inès. "You go lie down. I'll bring you some food in a few minutes. You need to start eating again, honey. You're eating for two now."

Oliva nodded and left the kitchen.

God, how I hate them! I know the only reason they're being nice to me is because I told them Tony was rich. Honey. That witch has never in her life called anybody but her fucking dogs "honey". How am I going to get myself out of this? Tony couldn't care less that I'm pregnant. What am I going to do?!

Chapter 17

The next day while her mother was visiting Maribel and her father was at work, Oliva dug out the card from the pocket of her skirt and made a call to Tony. She didn't bother making the call collect.

"Carvalho Enterprises. May I help you?"

"I'd like to speak to Tony."

"He's tied up at the moment. May I ask whose calling?"

Oliva noticed the tone of the secretary's voice immediately changed from super friendly to coldly formal.

"Can you interrupt him, please? This is urgent. Tell him it's Pilar."

"Pilar? Oh, I'm sorry. I didn't recognize your voice. You sound different. Please hold the line a moment."

A minute later Tony was on the line.

"Pilar? I'm surprised to hear from you. I thought you were still mad at me."

"It's not, Pilar. It's me, Oliva."

"Why did you lie to my secretary?"

Oliva caught the sudden change in his tone as well.

"Because you wouldn't have come to the phone if you knew it was me."

"What do you want? I'm a busy man and I don't have time to chat."

"Right. But you had time to sleep with me though. I'm calling to let you know I'm pregnant."

"And? What does that have to do with me?"

"It's your baby!"

"Really? And how do you know that?"

"You're the only man I've been with—ever!"

Tony let out a laugh. "Hold on a minute."

Oliva could hear the sound of a door closing then the phone being picked back up.

"You're a funny girl. Did you just tell me that I'm the only man you've been with as in you were a virgin when I screwed you?"

"Yes," Oliva replied through clenched teeth. She was getting angrier by the second at his mocking tone.

"That bastard you're carrying–if you are actually pregnant, could be anyone's. I don't believe for a second you were some snow-white virgin. First of all, you let me in your panties after only talking to me for a few hours tops and, secondly when I first put it in, you didn't even flinch! You didn't say 'ouch' or anything. You took it like a pro. You've been around the block and then some. You may have fooled my sister and have her thinking I took advantage of you but I run into broads like you all the time. Different pussies but the same lies."

"I'm not lying! If I didn't yelp and cry out in pain when you put it in is maybe because..." Oliva stopped herself from saying what she wanted to. She knew Tony had the upper hand. However, she was going to have to play it as if she did. "It's yours. I don't want this baby anymore than you do. You can take care of this now and you'll never hear me again or I'll carry the baby full-term, we get a paternity test that proves you're the father and you'll be paying for a child for eighteen years. It's up to you."

Tony was quiet for a few moments as he let what she said sink in.

"Damn you. Fucking you wasn't nearly worth all this headache."

"Trust me. I feel the same way."

"How much do you need for an abortion?"

"This isn't just for an abortion. I want enough so that I can start a new life somewhere. I want fifteen thousand dollars."

"Fifteen thousand dollars?! You're out of your mind! I'll give you a few hundred and that's it!"

"No! You will give me fifteen thousand dollars for the abortion and for me to never contact you again, or I'll get a lawyer who would love to get as much money as they can out of someone like you. Fifteen thousand is pocket change to you and in the long run you'll come out much cheaper."

"Like I said before, how do I know you're even pregnant? A man like me has to deal with money hungry sluts all the time."

"Fly me there and we'll go to the doctor of your choice to prove I'm pregnant."

Tony let out an exasperated breath. He had a strong inkling the tramp was telling the truth. This was all he needed right now. He and his secretary were getting pretty serious. She would flip out if she knew he'd gotten some girl pregnant. He just wanted this girl gone and out of his hair for good.

"Give me your address and I'll send you a check. But so help me God if I ever hear from you--"

"You won't. I promise. I'll get rid of the baby and I won't ask you for another dime. Can you send cash? I don't have a bank account."

"Cash? I can't send cash through the mail!"

"Send it through a courier. And please listen. This is very important. I want you to send it in a box with some made up name of a book company and put a few books in it."

"What?! I'm not doing any ridiculous mess like that!"

"Just do it! Please, Tony. When can you send it?"

"I don't know–I have some money in the safe at home and I'll have to draw the rest from the bank. You'll get it in a couple of days. What's your address and last name?"

Oliva cringed. She was pregnant by a man who didn't even know her full name. She gave him the information and he slammed the phone down. Until she received the money she would be on pins and needles. Best-case scenario, she would get the money and get out of town as fast as she could. Worst-case scenario–her parents would find out about the money and take it–closing off another avenue for her to escape and start a new life.

Chapter 18

Three days later, Oliva was a knot of wrangled nerves. Between that and battling morning sickness, she was a mess. She found the term "morning sickness" to be a misnomer since it hit her at times outside the a.m. hours as well. She sat on the porch and waited for the package and planned on being out there every day until it came. After she was out there for a while, she was overcome with the urge to throw up. She left her stake out on the porch and went inside to the bathroom. As she was splashing cold water on her face she heard it—the pounding knock on the door. Without even drying her face, she raced out of the bathroom and to the front door. Her heart almost stopped. Her mother was writing on a clipboard and a young man handed her the package. Everything seemed to be moving in slow motion. Her mother closed the door and inspected the package.

"Is that for me?" asked Oliva.

"Um-hmm. It's from New York but it looks like it's from some book company. That rich boyfriend of yours doesn't work as a publisher does he?"

"No, these are some books I ordered."

"Ordered with what? You haven't babysat for weeks so where did you get the money?"

"I meant Tony actually ordered these for me." She held out her hands for the package.

"When Mr. Tony gets back into the country he's gonna be spending that money of his on far more important things than some stupid books."

To Oliva's relief, Inès handed over the package. She went to her room and closed the door. She tried to open the box with her hands without success. She picked up a fork from the plate on the dresser and pried open the box. She tossed aside books until she got what she was looking for. At the bottom of the box was paper brown bag. Oliva took it out and tore it open. She almost cried from joy. Inside were five bundles of money in one hundred dollar denominations. Quickly she closed the bag back and stuffed it in her pillowcase.

She did so just in time as Inès opened the door a mere seconds later. She stood in the doorway and looked into the room.

"So what books did lover boy buy you?"

I knew you were going to bring your nosy fat ass in here. "A mix of everything." Oliva went through the books. "There's Harold Robbins, Danielle Steele, Gore Vidal, and Fay Weldon. Do you want to read any?"

Inès wrinkled up her nose in response.

"I'm going to check on Maribel. I'd better take that bat again since that lunatic is still out there somewhere. I'll be back later." She closed the door.

Oliva immediately began to plot when she would make her getaway.

Blinding Mirror

Later that evening, Oliva was awakened from a nap by the urge to use the bathroom. When she was coming out of the bathroom she heard her parents talking in their bedroom. She paused in the hallway at the mention of her name.

"And what if that man of Oliva's doesn't take care of his responsibilities, huh? Then I'll have three mouths to feed plus mine!"

"Shut up, you fool! We'll make sure he takes care of his duties."

"I don't care what you say! I was excited at first but nothing good has ever come out of that girl and nothing will. *Puta la madre, puta la hija!*"

"I tell you what. When the money does start coming in, I'm going to remember this! I'll take Oliva and the baby and we'll go living the high life without you!"

"Ah, high life my ass! I'm still not sure I believe her story about this so-called rich boyfriend. If he has so much money why would he want her when he could have any woman? Even if it is true, what if things don't work out the way you want? Then what?"

"If for some reason we can't get what we want then she and the little bastard will be out in the streets. She can move in with that friend of hers. I'm not going to have any screaming kid around here if there's nothing in it for me."

"That's the first bit of sense you've said tonight."

Oliva went to her room and closed the door. She sat on the bed and mindlessly caressed the pillow that contained the money.

"Oliva! Oliva!"

Oliva woke to her mother shouting her name. She jumped up and when she got to the hallway, she saw her father on the living room floor sprawled on his back and her mother by his side on her knees.

"What's wrong?"

"He just started grabbing his chest and fell to the floor. Go get his pills! Hurry!"

Oliva ran to her parents' bedroom and came back to the hallway a minute later.

"Where are they? They're not on the night stand where they usually are."

"Keep looking, you idiot! I'll call emergency!"

Within minutes Oliva was letting the ambulance crew into the house. They worked on Alphonso for a few minutes before putting him on a stretcher and carrying him out to the ambulance. A tearful Inès got her purse and went in the ambulance with her husband. She said a prayer for him to be all right. She desperately needed his income to get by. If they couldn't get money from that Tony person, she didn't know how she would survive.

Once the ambulance drove off, Oliva went to the hall closet and pulled out a beat up suitcase. She went and packed the clothes Pilar had bought her that were still stuffed in garbage bags under her bed. She went to her drawer and got a stack of papers that she kept together–her awards for excellence in school, birth certificate, etc. She put most of the money in the suitcase as well and then called a cab. As she waited by the doorway for the cab, she noticed a picture on the console near the door. It was one of the pictures taken by Ric the day of her father's birthday party. Someone had written her and her parents' names and date of the picture at the bottom. She slipped it inside her purse, not out of any sentimentality, but to have as a symbolic reminder of where she came from and an incentive to make sure she did everything in her power to never have to come back.

Chapter 19

Oliva stepped off the Greyhound bus cloaked in a mixture of fear and excitement. As she made her way through the terminal to the bathroom, she saw a young man snacking on a sandwich and it made her hunger pains even more intense. She hadn't eaten since she left Fresno hours before. And then she only had a bag of chips and soda from the vending machine. She was also exhausted. She didn't allow herself to sleep on the bus because she was paranoid someone would rob her of her suitcase or purse. She wouldn't put it in the carriage underneath the bus nor even leave it to use the toilet. She entered the bathroom and went into the one empty stall, bringing the suitcase with her. The person before her had for some reason thought it unnecessary to flush away their waste. Oliva's bladder was not allowing her to be picky and wait for another stall, so she hit the flush handle with her foot, hurriedly covered the toilet with tissue and sat down. She heaved a sigh of relief since she was close to having an accident.

She went to the sink to wash her hands and splash water on her face. She reached in her purse, took out a comb and went through her hair. As she was putting the comb back in the purse she took out her father's prescription bottle of his heart medication and threw it in a nearby receptacle.

Oliva walked out of the bus terminal and back outside. She ignored the catcalls from the unsavory looking men loitering about and hailed a cab. The cab driver stepped out to put her suitcase in the trunk.

"That's okay," said Oliva. "I'll put it on the seat next to me."

The cab driver shrugged in a "suit yourself" gesture and got back in the driver's seat.

"Where to?"

"Take me to a hotel near Mann's Chinese Theatre. A good one like a Hilton."

Chapter 20

Oliva devoured the last French fry from hamburger deluxe plate she ordered from room service. She was so famished she almost ate the parsley garnish. She put the tray on the dresser and got under the covers and went over what she would have to do over the next few days. Whenever she went out she would have to get some bare necessities like shampoo, conditioner and soap. The little complimentary items supplied by the hotel weren't nearly enough. She would also have to find a reasonably priced place to live. She paid in advance for a week's stay at the hotel. She figured that would give her enough time to find out exactly what she was going to do.

After giving it much deep thought while on the bus, she decided she wasn't going to have an abortion. She would've gotten rid of Tony's baby without a second thought but one thing made her decide not to go through with it—Pilar. She would not be able to bring herself to destroy something that was her only connection to her. Despite the horrible things Pilar said to her the last time they saw each other, Pilar had gotten to a place inside her no one else had. And she knew deep down Pilar's words were out of hurt and anger. There were so many things they were to do together and it was not going to happen because of her foolish mistake. She knew Pilar would never have anything else to do with her and the baby was the only thread that held them together. Being pregnant could be a definite disadvantage in landing a rich husband but somehow she would work it out. Oliva stroked her still somewhat flat belly. *No, I can't get rid of you. I just can't. I'll find a way to take care of you. I know this money isn't going to last forever so I'll have to come up with something. You're not going to live like I did. I'm going to give you everything you need and then some. Whatever it is, if you want it, it'll be yours. Even if I have to kill for it, you'll have it.*

Blinding Mirror

Chapter 21

Since leaving Fresno, Oliva's luck took a turn for the better and everything was falling into place. A few days after she arrived in Los Angeles she finally hooked up with Jojo. She'd asked around about him and one day a young lady pointed him out. She went over to him, introduced herself and let him know what she was looking for. After he gave her the once over and assessed she was too young to be a cop, he suggested they go to a restaurant down the street for some coffee.

She told him she wanted I.D. and a birth certificate in her new name that said she was twenty-one. When he told her it would be five hundred dollars she almost choked on the juice she was drinking. He informed her he was actually cutting her a deal. She didn't know whether or not to believe that, but she needed what he could provide. She supplied him with the information she wanted on the documents. He gave her his phone number. She didn't know the hotel number so she gave him the name, location and her room number. When she received the documents, she knew she had gotten a good deal because they looked so authentic. Everything was just as she wanted—place of birth, fake parent names, year of birth, etc.

All of it came in handy when she answered a rental ad for a furnished garage apartment for rent and it was just walking distance from her target location. Her landlords were an older couple, the Andersons. Seeing that she was young, they let her know the minute she threw a wild party or caused any disturbance she was out. She told them she'd just moved to the city and had a job all lined up. To be on the safe side because she didn't have job references for past employment, she had to put up three months rent plus security up front. It was worth it because Oliva loved her new digs. The apartment was much better than her old home. It was small but it was hers and she felt like an adult but most of all, she felt free. She bought dishes, silverware and glasses as well as towels, linens and cookware. Her biggest extravagance was a nineteen-inch color television.

She never had one of her own. The television back home was in the living room and she could only watch what she wanted when her parents weren't there.

She sat on the bed and surveyed the room. Her apartment was one big area and from where she sat she could see the living room, dining nook, kitchen and bathroom. It was her very own piece of heaven. But it was time to start going for an even bigger chunk for her and her baby. She reached for the telephone directory and flipped it to the V section. She picked up the phone that had just been connected earlier that day and dialed.

"Valente Construction. How may I direct your call?"

"Hi. Will Gino Valente be in the office tomorrow?"

"Let me connect you with one of his secretaries. One moment please."

A few seconds later another voice was on the phone.

"Gino Valente's office."

"Hi. Will Mr. Valente be in the office tomorrow?"

"No, he won't be back from Philadelphia until Thursday. May I ask who--"

Oliva hung up the phone.

Good. That'll give me an extra day to prepare. I'll go and get my hair and nails done and buy a professional outfit. Plus, I can swing by the library and see if there are some articles I can read up on about the Valentes. Any information in addition to what Pilar already told me will come in handy.

Chapter 22

Oliva sat outside in the lobby just outside of Gino Valente's office. It was ten-thirty and she had been waiting for two and a half hours. She saw three secretaries enter the office when she first arrived. She found a photo of Gino Valente and his brother in an article about them in *BusinessWeek* so she knew who to keep an eye out for. He was nowhere near the kind of man she found attractive. He looked to have a medium build, was balding with a prominent nose and thin lips. The photo was black and white so she didn't know what color the hair he had left was or his eyes. Her patience was rewarded when she spotted Gino coming down the corridor. She stood up and walked up to greet him. He was about 5'10", with sandy brown hair and light brown eyes.

"Hello. Mr. Valente?"

"Yes?"

"I know you're a busy man but could I have just five minutes of your time?"

"What's this about? You're not trying to sell anything are you?"

"No, sir. I just need five minutes and I'll tell you everything."

Gino looked at the pretty young woman trying to find out if perhaps they'd met somewhere before but nothing rang a bell. He had a very hectic day ahead of him but he decided to take a few minutes to find out what she wanted.

"Just five minutes."

"Thank you."

He walked to the door and held it open for her. He greeted the women in the office. The older woman of the three regarded Oliva with curiosity and suspicion. Oliva nodded to them with a frozen smile on her face and followed him to his inner office. He sat in his chair and waved her to the seat in front of his desk.

"Now what's this all about?"

"I want to work for you."

He let out a sigh tinged with slight exasperation.

"Miss, we have a Human Resource office down on the first floor. They handle all job inquiries."

"I need a job badly and I want to work here. I don't have any job experience so I know my application will go straight to the trash. That's why I wanted to make my pitch directly to you. I'm a fast typist and I can file, answer phones and run errands. Well, as long as it doesn't involve driving because I don't know how. I promise I'll be a hard worker. You won't regret hiring me."

"To be frank, all of my secretaries are experienced and have been doing this for years. The head secretary, Betty, has been with me since my brother and I took over from our father."

"Was she experienced when you first hired her?"

Gino hesitated for a moment.

"Well, no. But she caught on quickly."

"So can I if you give me a chance."

"Listen, I wish I could help you out but I do know most of the jobs we're hiring for are out in the field or administrative positions that call for a degree plus experience." He stood up. "I'm sorry I couldn't help you out. But there are other businesses around here that I'm sure you'll have better luck with."

Oliva forced herself to cry. Gino glanced around his office for a box of tissue and when he didn't spot any he took out a handkerchief from his jacket pocket. He leaned over the desk and handed it to Oliva who took it and heartily blew her nose.

"I'm sorry. I know I'm not leaving a very professional impression on you. But it just seems like nothing is going right for me. I don't mean to be so emotional but ever since I lost my mother and father it seems my life has gone downhill. It's been just one thing after another one."

"You lost your parents?"

"Yes." She sniffled and pretended to struggle to gain composure. "You know about Flight 182?"

"You mean the one that crashed in San Diego last year?"

"Right. They were on that flight. I would've been on the plane with them but I stayed home because I wasn't feeling well. So many times I've wished that I was on that plane with them. I don't have anyone else—no brothers or sisters, aunts or uncles. I was staying with my dad's friend until he, uh, began making advances. So now I'm renting a place not too far from here. My parents didn't have much to leave me and my money is dwindling which is why I need a job desperately." She dabbed the handkerchief at her nose. "This is going to sound silly but the other reason I want to work with you so bad is Dorchester Plaza."

"Dorchester Plaza?"

"I know you and your brother built it. My parents and I used to go there every Sunday to window-shop and have lunch. I still go there and pretend they're with me. My father was an admirer of a lot of your work. He was a bit of an architectural buff and he showed me many of the buildings you did in the area: the Lyndon Building, Century Mall. I'm sorry I didn't mean to go on and on."

"That's quite all right. My brother is the one who is responsible for the designs of the building. I handle the construction end. In any case, I'm sorry to hear about your parents."

"Thank you. I apologize for taking up your time." She rose from her seat. "I just had to give this a shot."

"Wait. I'll talk with the girls and see if maybe they could use some extra help around here. Perhaps we can start you off part-time."

Oliva's face lit up. "Really? I won't let you down. I will work so hard, Mr. Valente!"

"Hold on a minute. I can't make any promises but I'll look into it for you."

"Okay. I'll keep my fingers crossed. It would be great if something good finally happened for me."

Gino picked up a note tablet and a pen and handed them to her.

"Write down you number so I can get in touch with you."

She took it and wrote her phone number.

"And your name. What is it by the way?"

She looked up from writing.

"Olivia. Olivia Machado."

Chapter 23

Oliva, now Olivia, walked to her place feeling she had accomplished her mission. She knew it was only a matter of time before she heard from Gino. She put on a convincing performance and the job was as good as hers. How could he add another twist of bad luck to her already heart-wrenching sob story? Finding out his parents died in a boating accident was just what she needed when she was coming up with a tale to spin. Pilar told her once that one of the things that could connect total strangers was a similar tragedy. She owed everything to her. Before she met her, Olivia only dreamt of what she was now well on her way to attaining. Pilar showed her it could be done. That's why she chose the last name Pilar held onto. Her life and all she was about to achieve would be a dedication to Pilar and her own way of making up for her betrayal.

In five minutes she was able to push the right buttons in Gino to get what she wanted. She had no doubt given even more time with him she could have him wrapped around her proverbial finger.

The call Olivia was waiting for came the next afternoon. She was just getting ready to take a nap when the phone rang.

"Yes?"

"Miss Machado, please," said a female voice.

"This is she." Olivia sat up in the bed.

"Hello. This is Betty St. James from Mr. Valente's office. He told me to call and inform you he has a part-time position here in the office if you're still interested."

A smile that would make a Cheshire cat proud spread across Olivia's face.

"I'm very much still interested."

"Good. You can begin Monday. Your hours will be from eight to twelve, five days a week. Before you come to this office, stop down in Human Resources in 108 to fill out the necessary paperwork. Be sure to bring at least two pieces of I.D. And, I guess that's it. Any questions?"

"No, not that I can think of. Thanks for calling."

"Certainly. And Miss Machado, Mr. Valente told me this is your first job so I feel I should let you know I oversee all that goes on in the office and I run a pretty tight ship. That means no tardiness, no personal phone calls unless it's an emergency and always, always be professional. Anything less than that and I'll take it up with Mr. Valente. Are we clear?"

"Yes, I understand."

"We'll see on you Monday."

Blinding Mirror

Olivia heard the line click and she hung up the phone. She sat back against her pillows and began thinking of all she had to do to set her plan in motion once she started to work at Valente Construction. Near the top of her list was coming up with a way to get rid of Betty St. James.

Chapter 24

Olivia's confidence in her plot to win over Gino took a hit. She had been working at Valente Construction for three weeks but only had two opportunities to engage him in conversation and both times were interrupted by Betty telling her about a task that needed to be completed. The time slot that she worked also went against her in finding some time to spend with him. He normally came in late in the morning and stayed late at night. The person who often worked late to assist him was Betty. Olivia thought at the rate she was going she would never find a way to get close to him.

One thing she detested about the job was being under the constant watchful eye of Betty. She scrutinized everything Olivia did and once lectured her for half an hour over the importance of filing correctly because Olivia mistakenly filed a document in the folder behind the one it should have gone in. Olivia didn't know it but Betty's scrutiny would be the key she needed to get closer to Gino.

Betty had never been pregnant but if there was one thing she could do it was spot when someone else was. There didn't have to be the obvious bump either. There were a few instances that she informed women of pregnancies they weren't even yet aware of. Only one time was she wrong. However, she was sure the new girl Olivia was expecting. She didn't like Olivia from the start. She had a brash confidence that irritated Betty to her core. She walked into the office as if she was the boss. Betty had been there for fifteen years and she would be damned if the young upstart was going to come in there with that attitude. She tried to talk Gino out of hiring the girl but he was insistent. Who the hell did she think she was to just walk off the street and appeal for a job to him directly? No, Olivia had to go. During one of the late nights she worked with Gino she let him know her suspicions in the hopes that along with her complaints about Olivia's work would make him consider letting her go.

Olivia was typing up a memo when Gino walked in.

"Good morning, ladies."

"Good morning, Mr. Valente," they all chimed.

He walked over to Olivia's desk.

"Olivia, may I speak to you in my office for a minute?"

Olivia looked up at him puzzled.

"Of course."

She got up and followed him into his office. As she passed Betty's desk, the smug look on Betty's face let her know she was behind whatever talk Gino was about to have with her. She entered his office and he closed the door behind her. She sat in the chair in front of his desk and he leaned against the desk facing her, arms folded.

"Olivia, I have a very delicate question to ask you."
"Sure, what is it?"
"Um, are you, uh, are you with child?"
The wheels began to spin furiously in her head.
"Why do you ask?"
"Please answer the question."

Now Olivia knew for sure Betty was behind him asking the question. The day before, she made a remark to Olivia about her having that glow that many pregnant women have. Olivia ignored her but now...Then it hit her. The nosy witch had really helped her out. She already had the story ready for Gino whenever the opportunity presented itself—and here it was. Olivia covered her face with her hands and worked on the tears. When she felt the tears come, she removed her hands.

"Yes, I am pregnant. Remember when I told you about my Dad's friend that I was staying with until he began making advances?"

"I remember."

"Mr. Valente, he did more than make advances. He-he-he raped me."

"Dear God!" As he did before, Gino handed her his handkerchief for her tears.

"Yes, he raped me." With as forlorn a look as she could muster she turned her head up to Gino. "I was a virgin. I was saving myself for my husband and he took that away. Now I'm just soiled and dirty and no one will want me."

"No, don't say that, Olivia. It wasn't your fault." His heart went out to her. To have gone through the tragedy of her parents being killed was bad enough but to then be raped and impregnated by the only person left to turn to was terrible beyond words.

"I was going to have an abortion. I couldn't do it. I don't want this baby to not have a life because of that monster. It's not the baby's fault."

"I understand. You're so brave. I had H.R. send me a copy of your application and saw that you just turned twenty-one this year. I'm truly in awe that you've managed to survive all you have at such a young age and to be so strong. I'm sorry for prying and asking you about this." The reason he wanted to know was he was a bit taken with Olivia. He tried his best not to show it but he actually looked forward to seeing her face when he came in every morning. Still, after Betty told him she thought Olivia was pregnant, he was surprised at the jealousy that arose in him. He figured she must have had a boyfriend. And that jealousy was strong enough for him to cross the professional line and ask such a personal question.

"I'm glad you did. It feels so good to talk to someone about it instead of keeping it bottled up. Am I going to lose my job though?"

He looked shocked at the question.

"Come on, Olivia. Do I look like some heartless shrew? Of course I'm not going to fire you. Just be sure to take it easy. I'm going to tell Betty not to have you picking up those boxes of old files and taking them down to storage anymore. And don't worry about medical expenses or anything. We have a great benefits package that you'll be eligible for soon. And if you need some prenatal care before then, just tell me and I'll pull some strings. Let me know if I can be of help in any way, okay?"

Olivia stood up and hugged him tightly. She then stepped back and pretended to be embarrassed by her gesture.

"I'm sorry, Mr. Valente. It's just that being shown such kindness makes me feel like I'm not so alone, you know?"

"You're not alone." He held her gaze for a few moments and then broke it. *I'm one second from taking this girl in my arms. I've got to get ahold of myself.*

There was a knock on the door. Betty didn't wait for a response to her knock and opened the door.

"Mr. Valente, that call from Illinois you were waiting for is on line 1."

"Thanks, Betty."

Betty stood at the doorway as if she were waiting for Olivia to come out.

"Thanks again," Olivia said to Gino.

"You're very welcome."

Olivia turned and walked out past Betty. Betty went back to her desk and sipped on her coffee and looked at Olivia as she went back to typing the memo. She tried to read something past the self-satisfied smirk on Olivia's face. She wondered what Mr. Valente said to the girl but it didn't look as if she would finally be out of her hair anytime. Olivia looked up from her typewriter and their eyes met. Betty didn't know why but she was unnerved by the look Olivia was giving her. She turned away and shuffled some papers on her desk.

Olivia knew she had to find a way to get rid of Betty as soon as possible. She found the ideas she had come up with were far too involved and she needed something relatively simple. Even though today was the first time she and Gino spent any time alone since she first approached him about a job, she could tell he was beginning to like her. Why else would he send for information on her and ask about her pregnancy? Olivia thought at first she was imagining that certain look in his eye when he greeted her but after the tension she felt from him in his office; she knew she wasn't imagining it. Now she needed to spend time with him to work on him some more. Betty was the only secretary able to work the late nights with Gino since the other two secretaries Desiree and Valerie had kids they had to attend to when they got out of school. Once Betty was out of the way there should be no problem with her being chosen as the one for the late work nights. Sure she was still inexperienced but despite Betty's comments about her work, she knew she caught on to many things quickly. Yes, Betty was about to be taken of.

Blinding Mirror

As Olivia was about to leave for the day and Desiree and Valerie to lunch, Betty announced she needed to speak to them for a minute. They all covertly rolled their eyes and walked over to where she was standing by her desk.

"Girls, on Friday we are going to have some very important clients from Japan come in. Actually, they're not clients yet but we're hoping they will be. Desiree, I'm going to need you to arrange a catered lunch and set up the conference room, and Valerie you're going to be in charge of arranging transportation from the airport and making hotel reservations. I'm going to need your desks to look extra spiffy with not a pen out of place." She looked at Olivia as if she were specifically directing her last comment to her. "So wear your best outfits and an eager smile. It's very important we make the greatest impression possible. That's all, you may go."

The three of them left out of the office and as soon as they were out of earshot of Betty they began grousing.

"I cannot stand her sometimes!" exclaimed Desiree as she pushed the elevator button. "She can be cool one day then the next she's Cruella DeVille. 'You may go'," she mocked. "Just dismissing us like little schoolgirls." She pushed her long dark hair off her shoulder as they got on the elevator.

Olivia couldn't help but feel a little envious whenever Desiree wore her hair down because it reminded her of her long locks that were still in the beginning stages of growing back.

"We've been working here long enough to know how to conduct ourselves," Valerie chimed in.

"She was probably just saying that for my benefit," said Olivia.

"Psh!" Desiree waved her hand. "She shouldn't have to tell you either. I couldn't believe it when I heard this was your first job. You conduct yourself like you've been doing this for years, Olivia."

"Thanks," Olivia blushed. She liked Desiree and Valerie. They were the closest she had to having friends. Though she spared the details, she confided in them that she was pregnant. They didn't seem to judge her and were quite supportive.

"Yeah, you really do," agreed Valerie. "Don't you just love it when she decides to make these announcements right when it's time for us to leave for home or lunch? She was sitting right there at her desk for a full hour before she called us over but she waits until we're about to leave out."

"Okay, we'll see you tomorrow," Desiree told Olivia.

"Bye," said Valerie.

Olivia waved to them both and began her trek to her apartment. She had to call JoJo when she got home because she needed his help again. She didn't know if he could supply what she needed but she was pretty certain he would know someone who could.

Blinding Mirror

Chapter 25

Gino was giving his potential new clients a tour of the building. His brother Anton was still out of town overseeing a project in Philadelphia so Gino introduced Anton's staff and showed off some models of projects in the works. He and the Osakis struck up an even better rapport in person than over the numerous telephone conferences. Everything was going well but when they got back to his office, all hell broke loose.

As soon as he walked in and saw the looks on the faces of Olivia, Desiree, and Valerie, he knew something was wrong. Desiree came up to him, did a quick, awkward bow to the Osakis and whispered to Gino.

"Mr. Valente, something is terribly wrong with Betty."

"What? Is she sick?"

"I don't know she just started acting really strange and ran out of the office--" She looked over his shoulder and gasped.

Gino whirled around to see Betty, his secretary of fifteen years who even though could be overbearing at times had never once caused him a moment's embarrassment, standing in the doorway topless with her bra in one hand and blouse in the other. She appeared dazed and disoriented. Her face, neck and pendulous breasts glistened with sweat. She looked around the room as if she were seeing it for the first time.

The Osakis stepped back and furiously whispered to each other in their native language. Gino was so stunned he couldn't move for a minute.

Betty dropped her bra and held up her blouse to her face as she intently studied the pattern and texture. She lost consciousness of everything but the blouse. She no longer noticed those in the room looking at her in astounded silence nor did she notice that her bladder released urine that traveled down her legs and formed a puddle on the carpet at her feet.

Gino finally moved and took off his suit jacket. He went over to Betty to cover her nakedness. As soon as Betty saw Gino come towards her, she dropped the blouse and attacked him with her fingernails, scratching his face.

"Get away from me! I'll kill you! Don't touch me!"

Gino got behind her and tried to hold her arms down but with almost superhuman strength she freed herself from his grasp, turned around pushed him so hard he was sent tumbling from the office to the hallway.

Desiree dashed to the phone and called down to the front desk.

"This is Gino Valente's office. You've got to send security up here immediately!"

Betty walked over towards Desiree who dropped the phone and ran to huddle in the opposite corner where Olivia and Valerie were. Gino got up and made another attempt to subdue Betty. They wrestled with each other for a few moments before Betty broke away yet again and ran out of the room.

A minute later two security officers were at the doorway.

"Mr. Valente, we were told you have a situation up here," said one of the officers.

"One of my employees," he panted, out of breath from the tussle with Betty. "I saw her run down towards the conference room. She's out of control–crazed. I've never seen her like this. I think you should call emergency and get medics over here."

The two security officers went to the conference room. One called for medical backup on his radio. Everyone in the office was so overcome with curiosity they followed behind. All made sure to sidestep the wet spot of urine in the carpet.

Betty was found sitting cross-legged on the conference table, calmly eating by hand the salad meant for the clients' lunch. The security officers approached her with great trepidation on either side of her. To the officer on the left of her, she held out a piece of lettuce in silent offering. The officer slowly removed the lettuce from her hand and placed it on the table. Betty was no longer aggressive and let them lead her off the table and handcuff her.

While everyone was engrossed in the scene with Betty, Olivia slipped away and back to the office. She went to Betty's desk and emptied the small remainder of her coffee into a nearby potted plant. She opened Betty's desk drawer and placed the contents of her pocket into Betty's purse.

Chapter 26

The whole building was abuzz with the antics of Betty St. James that fateful day. Talk was so rampant a memo was sent out warning that gossip about the incident would no longer be tolerated. Of course that only stopped the chatter out in the open. Secretly, it was still the main topic of conversation for weeks over lunches and after work cocktails. The story, as most stories are, was blown out of proportion with more salacious, almost comical details added. Instead of Betty taking off her bra and blouse, scratching Gino Valente, urinating on herself and sitting on the conference table eating salad it became she was completely naked, tried to hump Mr. Valente, and defecated in a salad bowl.

When she was taken to the hospital, doctors surmised she showed all the classic symptoms of someone under influence of a hallucinogenic drug. Betty was never known to imbibe in anything but the occasional glass of champagne so this was surprising. The *coup de grace* to Betty's reputation was when a small amount of cocaine and some uppers were found in her purse, hinting to a very well hidden drug problem. When the effects of the drug wore off, the police confronted Betty about the drugs. She emphatically denied knowing anything about it and swore she had no idea how they got in her purse. She was promptly placed under arrest and charged with possession.

With the bad publicity that resulted after the story made the local papers and losing hundreds of thousands of dollars in potential revenue when the Osakis walked, Gino had no choice but to let Betty go. It was doubtful she would even have the courage to face her co-workers again anyway. But since she was such a loyal employee who'd been with him for years, he supplied her with a generous severance package and had one of his attorneys assigned to her case and paid her legal expenses.

Olivia couldn't have been more pleased with the way things turned out. She was a little worried that she might not get the desired effects from spiking Betty's coffee. She didn't tell JoJo's friend Bobby who supplied the drugs what her intentions were. But she did ask him about the possible effects; if it could make a person act crazy. Thinking that's what she was looking for and not wanting to lose her business, he told of course it would. However, when she asked JoJo the same question later he said it depended on the person and the effects varied. Some people just appeared to be mildly intoxicated. That was definitely not the effect she was looking for in Betty or else planting the drugs on her would be a waste of time. Fortunately, things worked out even better than she planned. Desiree took over Betty's position as lead secretary. As Olivia hoped, she was offered a full-time position and began working many late nights with Gino when Desiree had to leave.

Gino grew more and more enamored with Olivia. To him she was a sweet, virtuous and hardworking young woman who was robbed not only of her parents but her innocence. He didn't know how she could survive losing both her parents at such a young age. He was thirty when his parents perished ten years before and he still felt the devastating effects from losing them. Even though he and Anton were better business partners than brothers, he could at least somewhat lean on him and other family members for emotional support during that time. This girl had no one but the monster who ended up raping her. Every time he thought of what happened to her he became irate. Something in him called out to protect and shield her from any further danger or heartache. She and her baby needed someone to look after them. What was burning in him to do made no sense but it was there nonetheless.

One night they were working late and having dinner that was delivered.

"Olivia, I want to ask you a question and I need you to answer it honestly."

Olivia instantly felt on guard and wondered if he found out something about her or the incident with Betty.

"Sure, what is it?"

"Am I working you too hard?"

Olivia almost audibly sighed with relief.

"No, of course not. Why would you ask that, Mr. Valente?"

"Wait a minute. I thought we agreed that when we're alone you can call me Gino."

"I forget sometimes—Gino," she said with a smile.

"I know we've been pulling a lot of late-nighters. I don't want to put you or your baby through any stress."

"Not at all. And that's the truth. I look forward to working late because otherwise I'd just go back to an empty apartment."

"I hate to hear that. Don't you have any friends to hang out with? You seem pretty close to Desiree and Valerie."

"I am, here at work anyway. But they both have husbands and kids to go home to and they don't have time to really hang out. I don't know anyone else. Now that I'm starting to show I'm scared of trying to make new friends."

"Why is that?"

"I know we're about to move into the eighties but I don't like having a child out of wedlock and I think people will look down on me. This isn't the way it was supposed to be." She bit her lip and made a tear fall. "It's not the way I was raised."

"Olivia, you were taken advantage of in the worst way. You can't help that you ended up pregnant." He reached across the desk and took her hand in his.

"I can't wait for the holidays to be over with. I can make it through most of the year pretty okay—except for on their birthdays. But Christmas and New Year's is going to be unbearable without my folks."

"I have a suggestion. Would you like to spend the holidays with me? I have a place up in South Lake Tahoe that I like to go to during the holidays. I can't stand the thought of you being alone during this time of year."

Olivia put her other hand on top of his.

"You have no idea how much that means to me. I don't know what to say."

"I want you to know that you can trust me. I know you had a terrible situation with your father's friend but I promise you'll be safe with me."

Another tear rolled down Olivia's face. Yet to her surprise it was real. She was genuinely touched by Gino's gesture.

"I'd love to spend the holidays with you."

"Good. I'll call ahead have one of the spare bedrooms ready for you. I know I can't make up for your parents not being here, but I'm going to do my best to make sure you have an enjoyable time."

Chapter 27

Gino and Olivia left for their destination on the company plane. Olivia didn't expect her first plane ride to be so scary. She held Gino's hand for most of the quick trip. She tried to look out of the windows but was nauseated at the sight of the clouds. All she could think of was the many miles that separated the plane from the ground.

When they finally arrived at Gino's place she was even more flabbergasted. She'd never seen anything so breath-taking. The home was on the lakefront and was tremendous in size. They got out of the car and the driver began taking their bags inside. She slipped her arm through Gino's as they walked into the home.

"This is—I can't even describe it."

"Thanks. I built this a few years ago."

They entered the home and Olivia was even more awed. There was a big fireplace in the living room, the interior was a mixture of stone and wood and a high ceiling with a view to the second floor. The home she grew up in could fit into the living room alone. An older woman with bleached hair walked into the living where they were standing.

"Mr. Valente," she greeted. "So nice to see you."

Gino and the woman exchanged a quick but warm embrace.

"Same here. I'm glad to see you're up and about so soon after your accident."

"I've had worse tumbles on those slopes. Although now I have to be extra careful because the bones don't want to set back into place like they used to."

"Oh, Mrs. Winters, this is Olivia Machado. She's going to be my guest for the holidays."

Mrs. Winters extended her hand to Olivia.

"Nice to meet you."

"Hello."

"I hope you both are hungry because I went a little crazy on some new recipes."

Gino let out a laugh. "So we're guinea pigs are we?"

"Has my experimenting ever gone awry? That last pheasant dish notwithstanding."

"I was about to remind you of that. Do you mind showing Olivia to the guest bedroom?"

"No, not at all. Follow me, please."

Gino touched Olivia's elbow. "I have to make a few phone calls. I'll meet you in the dining room in about half an hour."

"All right. That will give me time to freshen up."

Mrs. Winters led Olivia up the stairs to her room. The room was substantial with a view of the lake and mountains. There were glass sliding doors that led to a small balcony just outside her room. Against one of the walls was a king-sized bed with the covers already turned down for her. She could see a connecting bathroom to her left.

"I hope everything is to your liking."

For Olivia, it was the most absurd question in the world.

"Yes, it's perfect. Just perfect."

She took off her coat and went to the closet to hang it up.

"Oh no, Ma'am. Let me get that for you."

Mrs. Winters took her coat from her and hung it up. When she turned back around from the closet she spied the now visible bump protruding from Olivia's belly. Mrs. Winters was already curious as to the nature of the relationship of Mr. Valente and the young woman. Now even more questions arose.

"Once you've freshened up just take the stairs opposite the ones we came up and turn left. You'll see the dining room there."

"Thank you."

Mrs. Winters gave her a nod and left the room, closing the door behind her. Olivia went to the doors leading to the balcony, slid them open and stepped outside. She folded her arms against the cool, brisk air. She surveyed the splendid scenery and was suddenly overcome with emotion. She became afraid she would wake up in her old bed back in Fresno and find this was just a dream. She reached out and grabbed the ice-coated banister with both hands. After a few moments she removed her hands and looked at her damp and pale palms and was satisfied everything was real.

At dinner, Olivia was a knot of nerves. She was trying her best not to look so much like the fish out of water that she was. All the glasses and silverware confused her. The casual dinners with Gino at the office and the ones with Pilar left her ill-prepared. She could barely concentrate on her dinner because she was watching Gino for guidance on what utensils to use. She was also used to all the food being brought to the table at once. It was an adjustment getting used to the different courses Mrs. Winters brought out. She was thankful artichokes weren't part of the menu. She remembered seeing a character on television who was as completely befuddled by the vegetable. Still, she was confident she would have it all down pat after another dinner or two.

After dinner, Gino and Olivia retired to the living room. Opera music was playing on the stereo system and it was driving Olivia nuts. She was all for broadening her cultural horizons but she simply did not like the music. She would've much preferred hearing Meatloaf or Jefferson Starship.

"Are you comfortable? Do you need anything?"

"I'm just fine," she said with a smile. "You and your staff have been treating me like a queen."

"Good! You deserve to be treated as such. Do you like this?" He nodded toward the stereo.

"Yes, it's fine."

He grinned. "What would you like to hear?"

"No, really this is fine."

"It's all right if you don't like opera. I listen to it from time to time because it reminds me of my mother and father."

"I don't want anything reminding me of my parents, " she said before catching herself. "I-I mean is I don't want anything more reminding me of them at this time of the year."

"I see. Opera was the music of choice for my folks. When my father retired, he and my mother moved to Georgia. I mostly saw them during the Christmas holidays and it's all the music I heard. I guess this is my connection with them at holiday time." He paused for a moment before looking back at her. "You know what kind of music I like?"

"What kind?"

"Promise you won't laugh?"

"Sure."

"Although I prefer Mel Torme, Ella Fitzgerald and rock music such as the Rolling Stones, I like disco music too."

Olivia looked away as she suppressed a grin. Finally, she couldn't contain the giggles that came spilling out of her mouth. Gino joined her in laughing.

"I'm sorry, really I am. I just can't imagine you liking Donna Summer."

"Oh yeah, I like Donna Summer, Gloria Gaynor…I know it's funny that an old guy like me listens to that but I do." He got up and walked over to the stereo. He took the opera album off and put another one on the record player. Soon the Bee Gees filled the room with the song Too Much Heaven. He walked and stood in front of Olivia and held out his hand.

"May I have this dance?"

As soon as she took his hand and they began dancing, she had flashes back to the last person she danced with and the incident that followed. Without being consciously aware of it, she drew closer to him, seeking comfort in his arms.

"A business associate paid for these guys to play at a private function. They were even better live. I'm going to keep an eye out for their next concert so I can take you—that is if you like their music."

"Mm-hmm. I do."

A minute later Mrs. Winters interrupted their dance.

"I'm sorry to bother you, Mr. Valente."

Gino looked over his shoulder, an arm still wrapped around Olivia.

"Your brother is on the phone. He said it was important."

Gino inhaled deeply and looked upward. "Thank you. I'll pick up the line."

When Mrs. Winters left the room Gino turned back to Olivia. He put both hands on her shoulders.

"I'll make sure to keep it brief, all right?"

Olivia nodded and offered a smile. As he gazed into her eyes he resisted the urge to kiss her lips and instead gave a peck on her forehead before leaving to take the call.

Olivia thought back to when she first saw the picture of him and his brother and how she wasn't impressed by the looks of either of them. Gino wasn't her type at all. Ideally her husband would look like either singer Rex Smith or her heartthrob Leif. Gino was a little more than twice her age, balding, with a completely ordinary face. But there were qualities about him that gradually made him appealing. He worked out every morning and as a result his body was quite toned. His voice was very sexy. It had deep timbre with a hint of huskiness. But what was most attractive was his money. That was the aphrodisiac that stirred her feelings for him. She and her baby were about to be set without a single financial worry. She could feel it. It was time to take things up another level.

A few minutes later, Gino reentered the room and took a seat next to her. This time he sat even closer to her.

"Something just clicked a minute ago."

"What was that?"

"From the moment I saw you, you reminded me of someone. I just couldn't think of who it was. Then I thought about what I said earlier about liking the Stones and it finally connected – Mick Jagger."

Olivia's eyes widened. "You think I look like Mick Jagger?"

Gino let out a hearty laugh. "No, no, no. You remind me of Mick's wife Bianca—the one he just divorced. You look like a younger and even prettier version of her. I read she was Nicaraguan. Are you of a similar background?"

"My parents were from Portugal."

"Really? That's fascinating. What part?"

"Madeira."

"Which village? I have an old friend who moved to Portugal with his wife and I think that's the island they live on."

"Câmara de Lobos." She wanted to change the subject before he asked a question she couldn't answer. "Um, what about your family? Where are they from?"

"My mother was Maltese-Scottish, born in Australia and raised here in America. My father was from Malta—which is where they met when my mother was visiting relatives one summer as a teen. It's also where they died. They were on their way back from a visit to Malta Island." His gaze moved to the fireplace where it settled as he became lost in thought.

Olivia took his hand in hers. He looked down at their entwined hands and then to her. He slid closer to her and stroked her cheek with his other hand. He leaned in and gave her a gentle kiss. The gentle kiss then segued into a more passionate one with Gino and Olivia's arms wrapped around one another. Gino caressed Olivia's body, her thighs and back. His hands were finding their way to her breasts when he stopped himself. He broke from their kiss and rested his forehead on hers.

"I'm sorry."

"Sorry for what, Gino?"

"I was getting a little carried away."

"We both were."

"I made a promise to you and I want to keep it."

"What if I don't want you to keep your promise?"

He looked at her, searching her eyes for confirmation he hadn't misunderstood.

"Gino, I've never felt this way before in my life. Being with you makes me forget all the bad things that have happened to me. I love the guest room you've set up for me but what I really want is to stay in your room tonight. I don't want to be alone."

"Are you sure? I don't want to pressure you in any way."

Olivia took his face in her hands and gave him another kiss. "I've very sure. Unless you don't want me..."

"You're kidding, right? It's taken all the willpower I have in me to not ravish you right here and now."

Olivia rose and took his hand. He stood and gave her a quick kiss before they went upstairs to his bedroom.

Chapter 28

livia sat on the edge of the bed and watched as Gino stoked the wood in the fireplace with the poker iron. She began to pull up her sweater to take it off when Gino turned around and stopped her.

"Don't, Olivia."

She pulled her sweater back down and gave him a questioning look. He put the iron in the holder and went to her.

"I want to do that."

He knelt and slipped her shoes and socks off her feet. Placing one foot at a time on his knee, he gave them a soothing rubdown. When he was done his hands traveled up her leg with lazy sensuality before resting for a moment on her hips. He unzipped her slacks and Olivia lifted her hips so he could slide them off. His hands and lips explored the soft skin of her thighs. He took her sweater off and tossed it on the floor.

Gino then scooped up Olivia and laid her in the middle of the bed. He proceeded to remove all his clothes before joining her. Olivia glanced at his rigid penis. It was only about one or two inches longer than Tony's but was twice the girth. Gino lay beside her. He kissed her long and fully, bringing forth a passion within her that she wasn't expecting. He moved his mouth to her neck and nibbled and licked which elicited a low moan from Olivia. His mouth then turned its attention to the swell of her breasts. He reached his hands underneath her, and with deft unhooked her bra and removed it. He ravished her nipples with his lips, tongue and teeth. Unlike Tony, Gino knew how to use his teeth without hurting her. Olivia's moans increased in volume and frequency. Gino moved his kisses down her body. When he got to the crook of her arm he sucked and flicked his tongue at its center. Olivia's eyes flew open from the shock of the sensation. She was astounded that having that spot kissed could feel so incredible. Gino moved down to her belly and planted soft pecks all over it and slid her panties off. He was irresistibly drawn back to her pert breasts that were slightly more swollen from her pregnancy.

He lightly nibbled on her hardened nipples; alternating between swirling his tongue around it's engorged center and sucking it. His hand went down between her legs and his middle finger sank into her wetness and he began to stroke her.

Olivia moved against his hand. She was in a state of erotic bliss. She now understood the looks on the faces of the women in the books Pilar gave her. She wanted more. She wanted Gino inside of her. As if he read her thoughts, he moved between her legs and positioned himself for entry. As he got the head of his penis in, Olivia cried out.

"I'm sorry," he whispered in her ear. "I'll go slowly."

"Okay."

With ease and precision, he worked himself inside her without causing more discomfort. Olivia was disappointed that the intensity of what she was feeling was beginning to wane. Then she began experience a different type of sensation as Gino made love to her. He was an adept lover and he made sure each thrust made contact with the right place. After her experience with Tony, she thought the whole idea of women enjoying intercourse was a fluke and any of them who proclaimed it pleasurable to be either liars or delusional. As she relished Gino's lovemaking she forgot all the advice Pilar gave her as far as not letting a man know she was enjoying it right away. Her whimpers, moans, sighs and grinding hips let Gino know how he was making her feel.

Gino lifted his head to look at her. Her lips were parted and her eyes were half-closed and she appeared to almost be in a trance-like state. It turned him on even more than he already was. He was trying his best to hold back and not orgasm too soon but the friction from her tight vagina enveloping him made it difficult. He couldn't remember the last time he'd had sex this gratifying. He wanted to put her legs up so he could go deeper but he was wary of doing so for fear of possibly hurting her unborn child. He put his mouth back to her ear. Olivia gripped his back tighter.

"You feel so good," he whispered. "So good."

He felt the build up leading to orgasm and tried to pull out but he didn't do so in time. He grabbed Olivia's buttocks and cried her name as his body shook from an intense release. Moments later he showered her face with kisses.

"I'm sorry, sweetheart. I tried to stop it and wait for you…"

"Gino, you don't have to apologize." She wiped away the perspiration beading on his forehead. Though she wasn't very experienced, she knew from pleasuring herself and her experimentations with Pilar that she didn't have an orgasm. But the experience was so pleasing it didn't even matter.

Gino moved from on top of her and on his side, facing her. She turned and faced him as well. She reached out and lightly stroked his cheek.

"Thank you," she said softly.

"What on earth are you thanking me for?"

"For helping to erase the memory of my terrible first time." That wasn't a complete lie. Her experience with Tony was like a bad dream or joke. Despite the baby growing inside her as proof of their sleeping together, she didn't consider him her first. As far as she was concerned Gino took her virginity.

He was touched not only by her words but the sincerity that rang from them. He caressed the curve of her hip.

"I'm happy to hear that. I want to try and erase as much of the pain you've been through as I can."

"There's not an eraser big enough for that," she replied in a slightly sardonic tone.

"I want to give it a try—if you'll let me. I'll be there for you and your baby."

"You want to make it official and be my boyfriend?"

"No. I want to make it official and be your husband."

Olivia sat up on her elbow. "What did you just say?"

He grabbed her and turned over on his back, bringing her on top of him. He held her hair back that fell to her face.

"This isn't exactly how I planned on asking you. Will you be my wife?"

She was too flabbergasted to speak. She didn't expect for things to fall into place this soon. She had still been formulating plans to get him to this point.

"I've been thinking about this for a while now. Ever since you told me about what happened to you. Especially when you said how you felt about having a baby outside of wedlock."

"So essentially you're taking pity on me."

"Not at all. I want to take care of you."

"Do you love me?"

He stared at her for a long time before answering. His long pause provided her with the answer before he spoke.

"I care a lot about you and I know I can and will fall in love with you."

She rolled off of him and on to her back. Though she wasn't in love with him either, it stung her ego that he hadn't fallen for her.

Gino turned towards her.

"Look Olivia. I'm a forty-year-old man who has never been married before and doesn't have any kids. I've wanted to settle down for a while now but I've been tied up with work so much it's left me little time to socialize. I think we can make each other very happy. I'll be the best father and husband possible. This can work for both of us if you're willing. What do you say?"

"Yes, of course. I'll marry you."

A huge grin spread across Gino's face and he gathered her in his arms.

Olivia closed her eyes and relished her victory. She managed to do what more experienced women couldn't do, especially in such a short length of time. She conceded she'd arrived on the scene when Gino was in the mindset to settle down with a family. If she weren't pregnant she would be asking for a glass of champagne. She had snagged one of the richest men in town in a matter of weeks and therefore was about to become one of the richest wives in town.

Chapter 29

Within two weeks, Gino and Olivia were married. Gino was prepared for his bride-to-be to plan a spectacular wedding like most women and was stunned when Olivia suggested a quickie wedding in Las Vegas. And she told him she wanted it right away because she couldn't wait to become his wife. He was flattered that she wanted to marry him as soon as possible and said instead of going to Las Vegas, they would have a private ceremony in his home. Olivia would have loved nothing more than to have a big, extravagant wedding but she was afraid Gino would change his mind. She convinced him they could have a celebratory function afterwards and invite his friends and family along with some people from work. The only sibling Gino had was his brother Anton and seeing their relationship was a strained one, he didn't think it was too big a deal for his brother to miss out on the wedding.

Gino did have his lawyers draw up papers for Olivia to sign before they were married stating that if they were to divorce she would be entitled to three million dollars and one of his homes. Gino intended to give the baby his name and make him or her rightful heir. To Olivia's ears, the offer of three million dollars was like someone told her she had hit the lottery. For her it was a win-win situation. Whether she stayed with Gino or not, she stood to be a rich woman. But Gino was a savvy businessman who wanted to protect the financial empire his family had spent years to build. Though he cared deeply for Olivia and was looking forward to their life together, he knew there was always a possibility things could go awry. And if that were to happen without a prenuptial agreement in place, he stood to lose a great deal from not only his stake in the business, but stocks, investments and property.

"I don't know how you did it," began Desiree. "But whatever you did to snag a man like Mr. Valente should be put into some type of how-to book."

Olivia sipped from her juice-filled champagne flute and beamed. She glanced around the room at the people who were invited to come over and celebrate her and Gino's marriage. The only people she knew were Desiree, Valerie and a few others from the office.

"I had no idea you two were even seeing each other," added Valerie. "Next thing we know Mr. Valente comes into the office and announces you two are married. Des, how did we ever miss this brewing right under our noses? You and I are always the first to get the scoop."

"I know!"

"Our relationship was a whirlwind. Things happened pretty quickly."

"Yeah, no crap," replied Desiree. "Are you coming back to work at the office?"

"You're kidding, right?" Olivia responded in a tone brimming with sarcasm.

Valerie and Desiree exchanged quick glances.

"In case you two haven't noticed, I'm with child. I need to stay off my feet as much as possible."

"I worked up until two weeks before I gave birth," said Valerie.

"And I had Jason a few days before I was to take some time off," added Desiree.

"What does that have to do with me?" Olivia asked.

"Nothing I guess," Valerie replied dryly.

"Look who's here," Desiree said pointing to the entrance of the living room.

Olivia turned to look and immediately she recognized Anton Valente. The girls were right when they said pictures of Gino's brother didn't do him justice. He wasn't a dashingly handsome man by any means but he was certainly attractive. More than anything he had a presence that Olivia could feel from across the room. Both left and right, heads were turning in his direction. Olivia observed that his face held a certain arrogance and self-importance. She could tell that he had a sense of entitlement for whatever he desired and he would stop at nothing to get it. That was the quality she admired so much in Pilar. At that very moment she knew she would fall in love with him.

"I finally get to meet my brother-in-law." Olivia tried her best to make sure her voice didn't betray what was going on inside her.

"Word back at the office is the reason he stayed in Philadelphia so long wasn't the project but some woman he met."

"Valerie, that doesn't surprise me one bit," Desiree replied with a giggle.

Olivia said nothing as the two bantered about Anton's supposed new love interest. She'd only spoken to him briefly a few times when transferring his calls to Gino so she was surprised she suddenly felt a pang of jealousy over his purported involvement with another woman.

Gino appeared by her side, slipping an arm around her waist. He nodded to Valerie and Desiree.

"Thank you for inviting us to your lovely home, Mr. Valente."

"You're more than welcome, Valerie. I'm glad you both could make it. I want you to know that you're welcome here any time. I know you all have become friends and since Olivia isn't coming back to work, feel free to drop by to visit."

"Thank you!" Valerie and Desiree responded.

Olivia didn't say anything. She had no plans on inviting them over. It was Gino who asked them over for the celebration. She liked them and thought they were nice but she was now on a different level. She would have to become acquainted with women of the class she was now a part of. Some of the women in attendance who Gino had introduced to her seemed a bit cool toward her. But that would change. She was now Mrs. Gino Valente and they would give her the respect she was due.

"Come, sweetheart. Let me introduce you to my brother."

Gino nodded at Valerie and Desiree and guided Olivia across the room to where his brother was now talking to one of the guests.

"Excuse me. I'm sorry to interrupt Mr. Signelli, but I want to introduce my bride to my brother."

"That's quite all right." With a slight nod, Mr. Signelli stepped aside.

"Anton this is Olivia."

"Olivia, it's nice to finally meet you." Anton took Olivia's hand in his. "It certainly didn't take long for you to capture my brother's heart. I thought he would join me in becoming a life-long bachelor."

Olivia's pulse quickened. What she had been feeling from across the room became even more intense. Anton was lightly stroking her hand with his thumb. That tiny gesture alone made her sexually aroused. Finally, he let go of her hand.

"Nice to meet you," was all Olivia could manage to say. She put her arm around Gino's waist and hoped her feelings weren't displayed on her face.

"You've certainly made my brother a happy man. I haven't seen him look this lively in years."

"He's made me even happier." Olivia gazed at Gino.

Gino kissed her cheek.

"I'm going to leave you with my brother a minute while I go and check on some things. I'll be right back." He kissed her on the lips before leaving.

"How do you like your new home, Olivia?"

"I love it of course. It's beautiful. And it's so huge I'm sure it'll be a while before I even see all of it."

"Quite a change from the garage apartment, I'm sure. This was our parents' home before they moved to Georgia and of course they left it to Gino. I heard you've been up to the South Lake Tahoe place. So far I haven't received an invite to check it out. Perhaps you'll be a kind sister-in-law and allow me to visit."

"Sure." She was still pondering how he knew she used to live in a garage apartment; then thought Gino probably told him.

"I see that you're expecting a little one. It's not my brother's is it?"

Olivia's face darkened in embarrassment.

"From my calculations of when you started work for our company and seeing the stage of pregnancy you appear to be now, I'd say you were pregnant beforehand. Not unless Gino was seeing you on the sly. But that can't be the case because I remember Betty complaining about how you just came in off the street asking for a job. So, who's the father?"

"If you must know my child's father was killed in an accident." She convinced Gino that it would be the best story to tell everyone, including her unborn child one day. She said she couldn't bear it if anyone knew her child was the result of a rape.

"An accident? Another one? Tragedy sure has touched your life. I heard your parents were killed in a plane crash. And you have no other relatives?"

Olivia struggled to maintain her crumbling composure.

"No, I don't." She didn't like what he seemed to be implying.

"I guess Gino only has your word on that. It has to be pretty convenient not having relatives around. No one to dispute you are who you claim."

Anton's eyes, filled with unspoken accusations, bore into her. Olivia became frightened. Something told her Anton knew all about her and he was going to ruin everything. She moved past him and left the room and went to the study. She closed the door behind her and lay against it. She cursed herself for not remaining calm. She spotted a decanter on the credenza that was half-filled with an amber colored liquid. She went and poured herself a glass and downed the liquor in one gulp. At that moment she gave no thought about the effect drinking could have on her unborn child nor of her distaste for hard liquor. She needed something to calm her frazzled nerves. A moment later there was a tap at the door. She quickly wiped away her lipstick from around the rim of the glass with the bottom of her blouse and went and stood in front of the desk.

"Yes?"

The door opened and just as she feared it was Anton. Looking at him she wondered how she went from desiring him to loathing him in a matter of minutes. He walked over and positioned himself in front of her. His hands were in his pockets and from the curve in his mouth she couldn't tell if it was a smile or a sneer. She averted her eyes from his concentrated stare.

"What's your real name?"

"Olivia Valente."

"Cute. What's your real maiden name?"

"Olivia Machado."

"Were your parents named Machado?"

"What kind of silly question is that?"

"Were they?"

"Y-yes."

"Then why wasn't there anyone with that name on the passenger list of the plane that crashed?"

Olivia leaned back against the desk for support.

"You look peaked, Olivia. Is it the pregnancy or knowing you've been caught in a whale of a lie? I'm willing to wager it's the latter. I'm not my brother. He's an absolute genius in his profession but he's always been a fool in his personal life. I did what I'm sure never even crossed his mind—I had you checked out. I know you're not who you say you are but I haven't found out the exact truth yet. The social security number you have listed on file at the office belongs to a woman from Seattle. You are a slick one, breezing into Valente Construction, finagling a position, getting close to my brother and convincing him to marry you in such a short time. All while being knocked up with another man's child no less."

He leaned into her until there was only an inch or two between their faces.

"You are deceitful and wicked, my little flower. Unlike Gino, I don't trust you at all."

He reached out and stroked her arm.

"You're trembling. As well you should. I have your fate in the palm of my hand and it's at my will whether I cradle it or crush it."

"Are y-you g-going to t-tell Gino?"

Anton looked at her long and hard before answering.

"That's up to you."

He put his mouth on hers, giving her a passionate kiss. Olivia didn't want to feel what his kiss was stirring inside her. But somewhere beneath her fear of him was still a yearning. To her displeasure he moved his mouth away from hers and walked to the door. He paused with his hand on the door. He glanced over his shoulder at her.

"I think you and I will get along just fine. We have a lot in common. Me calling you wicked and deceitful, I may as well have been talking about myself. I have to go back to Philadelphia to wrap up some things. When I get back we're going to get to know each other very well."

"Does what you have to wrap up include a woman?"

"That is none of your concern."

He opened the door and started to walk out. He turned around.

"I could taste liquor on your mouth. You really shouldn't drink while you're pregnant." With that he finally left.

Olivia went to the door to watch him leave. He jaunted down the hallway to the foyer. When he got to the front door she hoped he would know she was looking at him and would turn around and give her one more glance. But he didn't.

Chapter 30

Gino was standing behind Olivia with his arms around her stomach as they listened to toasts being given by various guests. Mr. Johnston, a middle-aged man from accounting had the floor.

"I want to wish you both years of wedded bliss or as many years are left in Gino."

Light laughter dispersed through the room.

"Hey, watch it!" Gino joked.

Mr. Johnston held up his glass to them.

"To Mr. and Mrs. Valente."

Olivia had a smile plastered on her face but she'd grown weary of all the well wishes. She was tired and wanted desperately to go to bed. Suddenly many in the room made a collective gasp. Having made her way through the crowd was Betty St. Griffin. She held a champagne glass up and tilted in the direction of Olivia and Gino.

"I, of course didn't receive my invitation. However, I just had to stop by and give my congratulations to Olivia."

She looked at Olivia with pure hatred and contempt.

"When you first arrived at Valente Construction, I didn't trust you. Not even a smidgen. I thought you had an agenda that had nothing to do with filing papers and answering phones. But I had no idea exactly the kind of person you were until after the day that changed my life forever." She looked around the room. "Some of you here tonight are under the mistaken assumption that I had some drug problem. I swear on the life of my mother that is not true. Other than aspirin I've never taken a drug in my life. What happened to me that day was someone slipped me something. Those drugs found in my purse were absolutely not mine. So after I had time to think I realized I was set up. The question became by whom? Who had access to my purse? Mr. Valente is not even in the equation. So that left the girls in the office. I know I'm not one of Desiree and Valerie's favorite people but could they do something so diabolical? No. So that only left one person. And it's to her that I raise my glass. Congratulations Olivia! You not only got me out of the way but you latched on to my Gi--, to Mr. Valente."

Gino signaled two men to take Betty outside. They went up to her and one removed the glass from her hand before they began to lead her away.

"I'm going to pray for you, Mr. Valente! I'm going to pray that you wake up and realize the monster you've married! She's not to be trusted!"

Olivia could feel all the eyes upon her. She closed her eyes and fell backward in Gino's arms in a feigned faint.

Olivia lay in bed and listened as Gino spoke with the housekeeper, Mrs. Petrova.

"Do you think we should call a doctor?"

"No, sir. I think she fine," she responded in her clipped English. "It probably shock of situation with lady. Just keep her lie down and get rest. I bring up some tea."

"Thank you."

"Gino?" Olivia called out in a faint voice.

He went to the bed and sat beside her.

"I'm here, darling. How are you? Still lightheaded?"

"A little. Is Betty gone?"

"Yes, she's gone. I've told the staff that she is not allowed on the premises."

Olivia felt an instant wave of relief. Gino obviously didn't believe what Betty had to say.

"Why would she say such horrible things about me? I wouldn't even know where to get drugs much less slip them to someone and plant them."

"I know, I know. She's probably still distraught over losing her job and the humiliation of what she did. I never wanted to bring this up but I've been told by a few that she had feelings for me. I never noticed until it was pointed out a few times. Then once I did notice I did my best to ignore it. I think it was at the core of what she did tonight. I still find the whole drug thing very odd. It was so out of character for her."

"She didn't have many people who liked her at work and I'm sure she rubbed those in her personal life the wrong way as well. Perhaps someone did slip her drugs and it didn't take effect until she got to the office."

"Who knows? I've sent the guests home so you don't have to worry about interacting with them."

"I wanted to make a wonderful impression on your friends and now they must think I'm some psycho."

"Don't worry about it. If they want to remain my friends they won't bring this up again and they'll accept you."

"You are too good to me, Gino. I don't deserve you."

Chapter 31

Over the next few months Olivia was on edge. Not only from the impending birth of her child but from not hearing from Anton. She found out he was working on yet another project in Philadelphia but she had no doubt he was making time for the floozy the girls were telling her about. She tried her best to take her mind off him by keeping occupied. Gino had given her access to some of his credit cards so she spent a lot of time shopping. She hated that she had the means to buy whatever outfit she desired but was limited to maternity clothes. However, she spared no expense when it came to buying items for the nursery.

When she found out Gino was looking for another secretary she insisted on coming in to interview and choose her replacement. She didn't want another woman getting close to her husband by spending late nights working with him the way she did. Any woman the least bit attractive had her resume trashed. She found the perfect applicant in Jane Wiesenthal. She was a fifty-six year old mother of three and grandmother of five who had no plans to retire anytime soon. She confided in Olivia that she believed the reason she was let go from her other job was because of her age. It was her age along with her plain appearance that won her a position as Gino's new secretary.

Gino didn't want to leave town, especially with Olivia so close to giving birth. But he had to fly to New York for a crucial business meeting. As luck would have it, it was during his business trip that Olivia went into labor. She was being driven to a luncheon hosted by the wife of one of the board members when she felt contractions in her back. They were so strong she couldn't talk. She signaled the driver by hitting the back of the seat. When he looked back and saw the expression on her face he immediately rerouted the car and headed to the hospital.

Gino was called and he rushed back as soon as he could. He arrived in time to be there for most of Olivia's labor. It was hard for him to see his wife in such pain. But he knew his discomfort was nothing compared to what she was going through. Before he left, Olivia settled on a name for the child. They had chosen one for if it was boy and one for it was a girl. Finally the moment arrived and the baby made its way into the world.

"Gino, what is it?"

"It's a girl. Honey, she's not even cleaned up yet and I can tell she's a beauty."

"Really?"

"Really."

Finally the nurse handed the bundled baby over to Olivia. She was relieved upon seeing her. The baby looked white. So far there was no hint of her ancestry. Olivia hoped the baby's complexion would continue to reflect its paternal lineage.

"Hey you," Olivia cooed. "You put your mother through a lot yet it was all worth it. Your father was right; you are a beauty. Just wait until you see your nursery. You're going to love it."

She looked at Gino. "I love her already. Look at how pale she is. Did you see her blue eyes?"

"Yes, but I'm not sure if they'll stay that color. My mother said my eyes were blue when I was first born."

"I hope they stay blue. Wouldn't it be something if she ended up with blonde hair, too?"

Gino gave her a half-smile. He didn't understand his wife's fascination with the baby's coloring. He was just happy she appeared to be healthy.

"You are going to break hearts one day," she said to her daughter. "Yes, you are. I can see it already. We will be fighting off a swarm of boys coming to the house to see Lourdes Pilar Valente."

Chapter 32

livia was checking in with Elizabeth, the nanny, to make sure Lourdes was taking her nap when Mrs. Petrova came to let her know she had a call.

"Who is it?"

"Mr. Valente."

She went to the nearest phone.

"Hello, dear. Please don't say you're calling to tell me you're working late again."

"Okay, I won't. I'm calling to hear your voice. It's been a while."

Olivia's pulse began to race. It was Anton.

"Can you hold on for a moment, please?" Without waiting for an answer she put the phone down and turned to Elizabeth.

"Elizabeth, hang this up for me when I get the other phone."

"Yes, Mrs. Valente."

When she got to her bedroom, she closed the door and picked up the phone.

"You can hang up now, Elizabeth."

Olivia waited until she heard the click sound.

"When Mrs. Petrova said it was Mr. Valente, I wasn't expecting it to be you."

"I don't think she knew it was me. My brother and I sound a lot alike."

"Your niece is almost two months old and you still haven't seen her."

"My niece?"

"Yes, your niece," she responded with mild irritation. "Gino has made her his legal daughter."

"Isn't that interesting? Did you receive my gift for her?"

"I did. Thank you."

"I heard I missed the spectacle Betty caused when I was there last. I guess I should've stayed a while longer and been entertained by the show."

"She made a fool of herself."

"So did you do it?"

"Do what?"

"Don't be obtuse. Did you do what she accused you of?"

"No! As I told Gino, someone at her house could've done it and it didn't take effect until she got to work. A lot of people disliked her therefore anyone could've spiked her coffee. She just pointed the finger at me because she wants Gino for herself and I have him."

"How do you know it was her coffee that was spiked?"

"I, um, I just guessed."

"That's an awfully good guess. It could have been anything like her breakfast, a glass of juice…"

Olivia became nervous. She didn't want Anton to have any more ammunition against her than he already did.

"Never mind that. I'm sure Gino has given you a vehicle. Jump in it and meet me at my place in thirty minutes. Get a pen and I'll give you directions."

"Excuse me?"

"You heard me. I want you here in half an hour."

"I don't know how to drive."

She heard him let out an exasperated breath.

"I'm going to leave for the Beverly Wilshire. Have your driver drop you off there. Tell him you're meeting someone for lunch and you'll call when you're ready to be picked up. Now I'll give you an hour."

He hung up the phone. She held the receiver for a moment. Just as when they first met, he managed to annoy and excite her at the same time. She hung up the phone and went over to the intercom.

"Mrs. Petrova?"

"Yes, Ma'am?"

"Have Mr. Calhoun bring the car around. I'll be ready to leave in twenty to thirty minutes."

"Yes, Ma'am."

Chapter 33

When she arrived at the Beverly Wilshire, she spotted Anton in the lobby. He saw her and began walking toward the elevators and she followed him. Once they got to the room, he closed the door behind her and pushed her against it. He took her purse and threw it to the floor. His hands roamed over her body.

"Not an ounce of fat from the baby. I do miss the fullness it gave your breasts though."

Abruptly, he removed his hands and went over to the bed. He picked up a piece of paper and handed it out to her.

"Beginning next week this person is going to come by your house to give you driving lessons."

"Why do I need driving lessons?"

"Look, I know you're content with being chauffeured everywhere but it's going to be a lot more convenient for you to be able to drive yourself around. Gino's employees are very loyal to him and it would be only a matter of time before they let him know you were being dropped off at my house. Since he and I aren't close it would raise red flags if it looked like you and I were. Understand?"

She nodded and looked about the room, not sure of what to do next. Without him coming out and saying it, he was letting her know they were going to embark on a relationship.

"Come here," he commanded.

She put the paper on the nightstand and stood between his legs.

"Down."

Olivia knelt before him. He unbuckled his belt and unzipped his slacks. He wriggled his hardened penis from his underwear.

"How do you and my brother screw?"

She was taken aback by the question and the coarseness of it.

"Do you suck his cock?"

"No!"

"Does he ever go up your ass?"

"Absolutely not!"

"Then that's how we'll do it."

"Do what?"

"For someone so cunning, you act as if you haven't a clue. We're only going to screw in the ways you and Gino don't. Now do you get it?"

Olivia's jaw dropped. It never even crossed her mind to make love in the manner Anton was suggesting. The thought of it disgusted her. Anton placed his hand on the back of her head and guided it toward him. She resisted until she felt the sting of him slapping her.

"Do it!"

Reluctantly, she put her mouth on him. She found the salty taste a bit repugnant. She moved her mouth up and down.

"Suck on it."

Olivia did as he said but noticed his penis getting more flaccid. Anton finally pushed her head away. He leaned over to the phone and began dialing.

"Who are you calling?" She asked, worried.

"Hello? What are you doing? Yeah, well I need you to get over here to the Beverly Wilshire right away. Let me give you the room number…"

Olivia sat on the bed in a bundle of nerves. Anton had refused to let her know who was on their way over. She didn't know if he called Gino or not and wondered if the whole thing had been a set up. She looked over at Anton and he was going through his briefcase getting out paperwork. A short time later there was a knock on the door. Anton went to open the door and let in a tall redhead. She looked like an actress Olivia had seen on television before but she wasn't sure. To her dismay, Anton grabbed the woman in his arms and gave her a long, ardent kiss. He moved backward to the bed and sat next to Olivia.

"This young lady doesn't know a thing about how to orally please a man. I thought if she watched you, she'd find out how it was supposed to be done."

The woman gave Olivia a dismissive smirk and knelt before Anton. Olivia watched as the woman took his penis into her mouth and expertly sucked it, moving her hand up and down it as she did. Olivia glanced at Anton's face and his face was contorted as if he were in a state of sexual ebullience. His moans grew increasingly louder. She hated to see another woman giving Anton such pleasure. She jumped up and jerked the woman's shoulder. She took her mouth off of Anton and looked at Olivia.

"Huh?"

"Move! Now!"

When the woman didn't move fast enough Olivia pushed her to the side. She then positioned herself between Anton's legs. He smiled down at her. Olivia placed her mouth on him and began to mimic what she'd seen the woman do to him. Olivia perked up with pride once he began moaning from her manipulations. A few minutes later she felt his body stiffen and her mouth was filled with his semen. She didn't want to show her repulsion so she just let it slide out of her mouth and down his penis. She took her mouth off him and sat back on her heels. She gave a triumphant glance to the still nameless redhead. Anton turned to the woman.

"Either you're a fantastic teacher or she's a quick learner."

"Do you need my services any more or do you want me to stay for some more fun?" She gave Olivia a seductive look.

"No, we're all set." Anton stood and pulled up his pants and reached to take out his wallet. He gave the woman a few bills.

"Oh, thank you baby. I sure needed the money. It's been a while between acting gigs. Call me anytime."

Anton glanced to Olivia.

"If I need your teaching services again, I'll be sure to call you."

Olivia knew it was meant as warning for her. If she didn't do something he wanted or didn't do it right, he would invite the woman back to try and show her up. She wasn't going to let that happen.

After Anton saw the woman out, Olivia sat back on the bed, anxious about the other way Anton wanted to have sex with her. He took his unbuttoned shirt completely off and slid off his slacks and underwear.

"Take off your clothes, Olivia."

She hoped he would be romantic like Gino and remove her clothes for her. Gino said he liked to do that because it was like unwrapping a gift he never tired receiving. After she was naked, Anton told her to get under the covers. He retrieved something from his briefcase and got in the bed with her.

"Lie on your stomach."

Olivia complied. She heard a squirting sound and looked over her shoulder. Anton was squeezing something from a tube and applying it to his penis. He stroked himself until he was erect again. She then felt something like a cool liquid being put on her anus. She buried her face in the pillow. This was not what she was expecting. She wanted to make love to him in the normal way. She felt his hardness pressed against her. She screamed in pain into the pillow as he entered her. Her cries didn't deter or give him pause. He continued until he was completely inside her. Gradually, Olivia's cries subsided after a few minutes as most of the pain went away. Soon, the slight pain became mixed with pleasure. All of the discomfort went away and she enjoyed the feeling of Anton moving in and out of her.

"You like this, don't you?" Anton whispered in her ear.

"Um-hmm."

"I knew you would."

He moved his hand underneath her and his finger found her wet clitoris. Almost as soon as he started touching it she let out a loud cry. He pulled out almost to the very edge and plunge back deep inside her. Olivia thought she would faint from the ecstasy. She had no idea such pain could give way to this much pleasure. She put her hand over Anton's as the crescendo of her oncoming climax rose through her body, finally exploding. Gino was a generous and skillful lover who pleased and brought her to orgasm many times but it was nothing like this. Anton wrapped both arms around her belly and pressed his mouth to her neck. He emitted a guttural moan as he ejaculated. She placed her hands over his, enjoying his warm body next to hers. Abruptly, he slipped out and off of her and got up to head for the bathroom. Puzzled, Olivia remained still. She heard the toilet flush and expected him to come back out but then heard the shower turn on. She rose from the bed and went to the bathroom door and knocked. She received no response and knocked louder.

"What?" Anton responded sharply.

"Can I join you?"

"No!"

Dejected, she walked back to the bed. He finally came out of the bathroom a short time later, still toweling himself off.

"You can go get your shower now. Hurry up; I've got work to do."

"I found this afternoon that you're a quick learner," said Anton. "I hope you pick up driving just as quickly."

Olivia said nothing and just continued getting dressed. She had just called Mr. Calhoun and he was on his way. She couldn't wait to leave because she was incensed at the cold way Anton treated her after their lovemaking. The way he jumped out of bed and wouldn't let her join him in the shower greatly annoyed her. As soon as she was finished dressing she grabbed her purse and went toward the door.

"Hey!" Anton called out.

Olivia stopped and turned around.

"What do you want?"

Anton got up from the chair and retrieved the piece of paper from the nightstand and gave it to her.

"Don't forget this."

She snatched it from his hand and continued to the door. He reached out and grabbed her arm, pulling her to him. He put a hand on her derriere and the other under chin. He stared deeply into eyes and he watched her angry demeanor melt away.

"I really enjoyed being with you today. I think this is the beginning of something special with us. We'll talk soon."

He gave her a quick kiss before sending her on her way. Once the door closed behind her a smirk spread across his face. Olivia wasn't the first of Gino's women he'd conquered. Unbeknownst to his brother, he'd slept with four of his past girlfriends. He could've easily flaunted his conquests to his brother but as long as he knew, it was good enough. Sleeping with his brother's wife, however, gave him the biggest thrill of all.

He enjoyed the power he had over women. Other than bedding them, the biggest joy he received was toying with their emotions. In a span of minutes he could have a woman on the verge of tears and then desire. When he had a background check done on Olivia, he thought maybe he'd met his match. Anyone as young as she and so devious would have to be more of a challenge. Especially since he was almost certain she had drugged Betty St. Griffin. Alas, she was no different than any other woman. Easily manipulated and fooled. Still he would enjoy Olivia to the fullest—at least until he was tired of her.

Chapter 34

Three months after her first rendezvous with Anton, Olivia found out she was pregnant again. She wasn't happy at first since she didn't plan on getting pregnant again so soon. Then she realized how happy Gino would be to have a child of his own. He cared for Lourdes as if she were his, yet she knew he would appreciate having children of his flesh and blood even more. For her, the child she was carrying was a gift and a form of penance to him for what she was doing behind his back. She cared for him but she didn't love him. Not in the way she could tell he loved her and she loved Anton. But she was grateful to him though. He treated her very well and gave her whatever she desired. He allowed her to have the lifestyle she always dreamed of.

She was even happier for the manner in which she and Anton had sex. It would be torture for her to have to wonder about whose child she was carrying. Her only concern was how Anton would take the news.

"Sweetheart, you look so deep in thought," said Gino.

Olivia turned from the window. She had not heard him enter the room. He put his briefcase on a nearby chair and came over to give her a brief kiss before sitting down to go through his mail.

"Has Lourdes already been put down to sleep?"

"Yes. Elizabeth said she was very active today and it must've tired her out because she went fast to sleep."

Gino didn't like that Elizabeth seemed to spend more time with their daughter than she did but he held his tongue.

"I have some news for you. I kind of suspected but today I found out for sure."

"And what is that, love?"

"I'm pregnant."

Gino didn't say anything. He dropped the mail and went over to her, taking her in his arms.

"Are you sure?"

"Yes. The doctor's office called me with the results."

"Here I was stewing all day because a deal fell through and I come home to hear this. It makes everything else seem so unimportant. I love you."

"I love you, too." She so wanted to say those words to him and mean it.

"You have no idea how happy you've made me."

"I'm glad."

"Are you excited?"

"Oh yeah. I am," she lied. "I'm very excited."

Olivia repeatedly knocked and rang Anton's doorbell. She knew he was home because all three of his cars were in the driveway and she heard footsteps of someone walking to and from the door. She went to a nearby window and saw Anton sitting on the couch calmly reading a newspaper. She rapped on the window to get his attention. He didn't glance her way, as if he didn't hear her. She knocked on the window again and shouted his name. At last he tossed the paper aside on the couch and walked to the door. She went back to the door and the second she did it flung open.

"What do you want?"

"I want to see you! Why were you ignoring me?"

"How did you get here? You weren't stupid enough to have your driver drop you off were you?"

"I took a cab. I'm going to finally take my driver's exam next week."

"Good for you. I'll call a cab to pick you back up."

"Why Anton? Why are you treating me like this?!"

"I'm busy right now."

"Busy? Busy what, reading the paper? Let me in."

"No!"

"Why?" she wailed.

"Because you're pregnant with my brother's child that's why! When you're no longer carrying his seed in your belly we'll see each other. Until then I don't want to talk to you and I definitely don't want to have sex with you. I'll have my needs taken care of elsewhere. I'll call for another cab." With that he slammed the door in her face.

After standing at the door for a few minutes she finally walked to the sidewalk. She stood in a daze until she heard a car pull up and saw it was a taxi. Her body stiff with leashed emotions, she got into the cab.

Anton peered from the window as Olivia was being driven off. He knew she was hurt but he didn't care. *How dare she give my brother a child? I didn't care about the first one with the unknown father but this is another story. I'll teach her such a lesson this will be the last time the silly bitch lets herself get pregnant.*

Chapter 35

Over the next few months Olivia sank into the depths of desolation. Adding to her melancholy was when the doctor informed her and Gino there were two heartbeats. While before she could find some joy in her pregnancy because of Gino, now she cursed the twins she was carrying. Until she gave birth, she could not see her beloved Anton. She even wrestled with the idea of making herself fall and causing a miscarriage but she was afraid she would jeopardize her life in the process. While she only had the one drink while pregnant with Lourdes, with this pregnancy she snuck a few drinks. Though she preferred wine, she chose hard liquor instead. She still didn't care for the taste of brandies and whiskies. She just wanted to punish her now unwanted babies.

"Olivia?"

"Yes, Gino." *God, I just want to go to sleep. I hope he doesn't want sex because I can't bear him to touch me right now. I know we were intimate up until my eighth month with Lourdes but that's not going to happen this time around.*

"Don't worry, I don't want that. I'm tired of being turned down. We need to hurry up and find a replacement for Elizabeth now she's moving out of state. I think Mrs. Hopkins would be a great choice. I'm going to call her back for a second interview."

"Mrs. Hopkins? Which one was that? Oh wait a minute. You don't mean that Black woman do you?"

"Yes I do. What's wrong with her?"

"Our children need a nanny, not a mammy."

Gino looked at her back that was turned to him, not believing what he'd just heard.

"For your information, she has excellent credentials. I think if she's good enough to have worked years as the nanny for a former mayor's children, she will be good enough for us."

"I don't want her. You know how those people are."

"No, I don't know how those people are."

"There's no telling what kind of bad influence she could have on our children."

"I'll tell you one influence I don't want our children to have and that's being a bigot like their mother."

Olivia turned over to face Gino.

"I'm not a bigot. But I call them as I see them and if that means I don't want my children growing up with nigger ways then that's too bad!"

Gino slightly shook his head at her.

"Unbelievable. How can you use that word and say you're not a bigot?"

"Oh, Gino get with it! Those people call themselves that all the time so don't look at me like I made up the word."

"I find it highly ironic that you're saying such horrible things about Black people when I've had a couple of my friends ask me if you had some Black in you!"

"Who? Who said that? Who damn it?!"

"Calm down, Olivia."

"I won't! Now who the hell asked you that?!"

"Never mind. I shouldn't have brought it up. It doesn't even matter. Not to anyone but you."

"I don't have a drop of Black blood in me! And whichever one of your friends said that can go to hell!" She snatched the covers off and stalked off to one of the spare bedrooms.

The next day she suddenly took it upon herself to choose a nanny. She was a young woman from London, Abigail Miller. She didn't have as much experience as others who applied for the position but Olivia thought she was perfect. To her it was quite classy to have a British nanny. Abigail was in a tight spot as far as her living situation and asked if she could move in immediately.

By the time Gino came home that evening, the young woman was bringing luggage into the house. He ignored Olivia because he knew he would lose his temper with her. As it was she had used up the last bit of his patience. Abigail Miller lasted three days before Gino let her go. He called the couple she had just worked for and found out the reason for her need to move in so quickly.

The husband informed him Abigail was let go for leaving her charges unattended. The couple came home early from their trip to Reno to find their children crying, hungry and alone. Abigail came traipsing in, boyfriend in tow a short time later. The husband gave her twenty-four hours to get out of their house. Abigail pleaded with them saying she had nowhere to go–her boyfriend lived with his mother and she wouldn't allow her to stay with them. The wife took pity on her and asked her husband to give her a few days to find a place. That's when Abigail came across the ad placed by Gino.

Even after hearing this, Olivia tried to make excuses and have Abigail keep her job. Gino didn't bend. He did give the young woman two weeks in severance pay but told her she had to leave immediately. Right after Abigail left, Mrs. Hopkins came in. Olivia was furious. She was used to Gino giving in to her but he was not going to this time. The welfare of Lourdes and their soon to be born children was of the utmost importance to him.

A short time after Mrs. Hopkins began her employment; Olivia was walking past the nursery. Mrs. Hopkins was walking back and forth with Lourdes, softly singing a tune. Olivia paused and stood at the doorway. She could find no fault with the way Mrs. Hopkins cared for the baby, still, she could not stand the woman. Especially the way she looked at her. It was as if the old woman saw straight through her skin to inside her and knew all her secrets.

"What song is that you're singing to my child?"

Mrs. Hopkins turned to her and put a finger to her lips to signal Olivia to be quiet.

"She's almost asleep," Mrs. Hopkins whispered.

"I asked you what song is that," Olivia demanded, not lowering her voice.

"It's an old Aretha Franklin song."

"Don't sing those types of songs to my baby."

"Ma'am it's just a gospel song."

"I don't care what it is. You keep those Negro spirituals to yourself and sing them to your *grandchirren*."

Olivia turned to go down the hall and bumped right into Gino. By the hardened look on his face she knew he'd heard the exchange. He took her by the arm and led her into their bedroom where he closed the door behind them.

"I know you don't care for my choice in a nanny. Other than your own hateful prejudice you have no cause to not want that woman to care for our children. I will tell you this and I'll tell it only once. I never again want to see, hear or even hear about your being disrespectful to Mrs. Hopkins again! Are we clear?"

"I can't believe you're talking to me like this."

"And I can't believe what an absolute witch you've been these last few months, not only to me but to everyone. I've tried to give you the benefit of the doubt and blame it on your hormones. But, I'm afraid that's not the case. I think this is the real Olivia finally making an appearance. And the sweet young woman I married was just an act you put on to win the part of my wife."

Olivia stood unmoving; still stunned by the manner in which he was addressing her.

"And another thing. Perhaps you can give Mrs. Hopkins a break and spend some time with your own child once in a while. I know you're disappointed that her eyes have turned brown and her hair isn't blonde, but try and be a decent mother. Put aside your Aryan mindset for a minute and love her because she is your child."

"I do love my child!"

"Show it for once. I'm going to meet a client for dinner. And don't bother waiting up for me. I'll be sleeping in one of the guest rooms tonight."

Blinding Mirror

Olivia tiptoed into the nursery and over to Lourdes's crib. She lightly stroked her baby's back, careful not to stir her. *I love my child. I'd do anything for her. Maybe I'm not in here fussing over her every five minutes, but that doesn't mean I don't love her. She is everything to me.* She leaned into the crib and kissed the top of Lourdes's head. *What a foolish thing for Gino to say! I don't spend enough time with you because of your coloring when you look like any other white baby. I'm still amazed that he talked to me the way he did. I guess I have been on edge since I haven't been able to see Anton. God, I can't wait until these babies are out of me. That Mrs. Hopkins can spend her time raising these two while I spend more time with you.*

Chapter 36

On June 30th, 1981, Sofia Gina and Isabella Cecilia Valente were born. Gino named both girls since Olivia offered no input. Before Olivia, Gino had been in love with a couple of women. With both of them he couldn't pinpoint the moment he fell out of love with them. It was a gradual process. But with his wife he could say the exact moment he was no longer in love with her.

She was back in her room when the nurse brought their daughters in. He took Sofia and signaled the nurse to give his wife the other child. When the nurse went to hand her Isabella, she tossed an uninterested glance at the nurse, shook and turned her head. Confused, the nurse looked at Gino. He told her to put the baby back down. Part of him wanted to believe she was just exhausted from the birth but he knew that wasn't the case. Though she initially seemed happy about her pregnancy, soon he saw otherwise. With Lourdes she enthusiastically decorated the nursery but for the twins she deferred all responsibility to an interior designer to decorate and arrange the nursery to accommodate them.

During her first pregnancy she never missed appointments, but this time, the nurse from the doctor's office called him because Olivia rarely showed up. Before Olivia went into labor, he received a call from Mrs. Petrova that she walked in on Olivia drinking some of the sherry he kept in his study. He was incensed and made plans to leave work early to go home and confront her but then he got another call. This time it was Mrs. Hopkins informing him that Olivia had gone into labor.

Now he sat looking back and forth between his precious twins and a wife who couldn't care less about their existence. He then wondered if it was the end of his love for her or his infatuation.

He thought maybe he was just enamored with the idea of having a readymade family fall into his lap right when he was most longing for personal stability. He wanted nothing more than to be madly in love with the mother of his children but that was not the case. He cuddled Sofia closer to him as he pondered the fate of his family.

Two weeks after the births of the twins, Olivia decided she needed some time away. She wanted to hurry and see Anton but she found out he was overseas for the next week. She didn't want an argument from Gino about her leaving the babies so soon. She had Mrs. Petrova pack her a suitcase and Mr. Calhoun whisk her to the airport before her husband got home. She went to a resort in Palm Springs where she relaxed, got pampered and of course, shopped. She was gone for a week and, during that time didn't call home once to check on her children, only to have Mrs. Petrova relay her whereabouts to Gino. She knew Gino would be livid but she was resigned to dealing with his anger upon her return. In the meantime, she enjoyed not having to answer to a husband or her children. She could just be herself. When she got back home she would put on the best act of contriteness she could for Gino. And she would be the best mother possible to the girls. She knew she could be that for Lourdes but she wasn't sure about the other two. Nevertheless, to placate Gino she would at least make a show of it.

Chapter 37

Olivia took in a deep breath before following Mr. Calhoun in as he took her luggage and packages upstairs. She went directly up to the nursery where she found Mrs. Hopkins changing the twins' diapers. Olivia went straight over to Lourdes's crib and picked her up into her arms. Lourdes giggled in delight at the sight of her mother.

"How's my baby been, huh? Did you miss your mommy? I sure missed you, yes I did. I brought you something back, too."

She sat down in the nearby rocker and bounced Lourdes on her knee. She looked over to where the twins were to find Mrs. Hopkins holding one of them, giving her a disapproving stare.

"Is there a problem, Mrs. Hopkins?" she inquired curtly.

"No, Ma'am."

After a few minutes of playing with Lourdes, Olivia put her back down to go over to the girls when Lourdes screamed in protest.

"Oh, it's okay, baby. I'm right here. I'll be right back."

Lourdes cried even louder prompting Olivia to pick her back up. She balanced the baby on her hip and continued to the twins. She looked at them, almost as if for the first time. *They are pretty babies. I had no idea babies could change in two week's time because I'd swear they were kind of ugly when I left. Neither of them is as beautiful as my Lourdes but still...*Olivia took turns rubbing their bellies with her free hand. She felt an inkling of remorse at having drunk liquor while carrying them. They appeared to be normal babies. She heard someone clearing his throat. It was Gino. He was leaning against the doorframe.

"When you get a moment can you come to my office?" His request was laced with ice coldness.

"Sure, Gino."

She took Lourdes back to her crib where she found a toy to occupy her while she slipped out of the room. She slowed her pace the closer she got to Gino's office. Olivia stopped as she got to the door and ran her fingers through her now below shoulder-length hair and entered the room.

Gino was sitting stone-faced, his fingers laced together. He looked like a boss about to fire an employee. Olivia slipped into the chair in front of his desk.

"And how was your vacation?" His inflection was pseudo jovial.

"Gino, I know you're mad but I needed some time away."

"Mad? Oh you don't know half of it, lady. How about disgusted, sickened and enraged at your lack of mothering skills. What kind of mother leaves her newborn babies who haven't even been in the world two weeks and without so much as a 'so long'?! And you call leaving a message about where you were without once asking about your children!"

"Please, please try and understand. It was just so overwhelming for me, I thought if I didn't get out of here, I would go crazy. But I've had a chance to clear my head. I promise you I'll be a much better wife and mother. I'll prove how much I love you and the children."

His response was a piercing gaze that showed he was unmoved by her words. He stared at her with such marked acrimony it made her shift in her seat.

"I saw something interesting on the insurance bill."

Instantly, she knew what was next. She braced herself for more of his wrath.

"Seems that during your hospital stay you instructed the doctor to perform a tubal ligation. It was so thoughtful of you to make such an important life-changing decision without even consulting your husband. But then again, that's your modus operandi isn't it? You didn't come to me when you decided to go leave our babies while you went to get pampered in Palm Springs. You certainly didn't come to me when you wanted to pour liquor down your throat. So why would you come to me with your decision to forgo the possibility of having any more children? By the way, I swear to God Olivia, if there are any problems with my kids from your drinking..." He moved his head from side to side, his eyes holding an unspoken threat.

"I'm sorry, Gino," was all she could manage to say. She had worked out a whole script in her head but being hit with two unexpected curve balls like him finding out about her drinking and the hospital procedure, completely threw her off. She had figured he or his accountant would just pay the bill and not actually go over it.

"Not that it would do any good but you can apologize about drinking and leaving your children but by God don't apologize for cutting off an avenue to have more babies. Because darling, I wouldn't want you to have another one of my kids for anything in the world." He leaned forward as he pointed at her. "You aren't even fit to raise a dog much less children!"

She was so rankled by his last sentence that she flinched. Gino rose from his chair and marched out of the room leaving Olivia there, too astonished to move. She grabbed on to the front of the desk as she inhaled deep breaths. Tears were threatening her eyes but she forced them back inside. A moment later Gino reentered the room.

"And so you know, from now on I'll be sleeping in a separate bedroom. I would go to the other wing but I want to be close to my kids."

"Your kids? They're my kids too," she responded without turning around to face him.

"Are they? You have a habit of doing things that make me forget. Anyway, the only reason I'm not filing for divorce is I want to at least try and give the girls as stable a home as possible. We will put on a united front for their sake since I don't want them growing up in a broken home. No matter how lousy a mother you are, it's better than them not having a mother at all. That's the only reason your bags weren't packed and waiting for you when you got back." He left the room for the final time.

Olivia stepped inside her substantial closet, turned on the light and closed the door behind her. She looked around and felt comforted by all she'd acquired. Her wardrobe could rival any movie star or First Lady. *No matter what's going on right now with Gino, I'm still on top. Look at all I've gained.* She went over to a hatbox on a shelf and retrieved a black velvet box behind it. She laid it on top of the storage island. She felt under the top shelf of the island until she found the key that was covered by tape and removed it. She took the key and the box and sat cross-legged on the floor. She opened the box and an instant rush swept over her. She looked at the little reminders of her past, paperwork and photos. She held the picture of her and her parents that was taken on her father's birthday.

"You two said I would never amount to anything. I wish there was a way to show you just how wrong you were. If you at least treated me like a human being, I'd have you set up in a nice house. But no, you treated me like shit. And look where you are still and where I am. I hope you both rot in hell." Olivia closed her eyes and breathed in deeply. "I've still won. Regardless of anything else, I've won."

Chapter 38

Olivia was growing restless. Gino had decided they should take the girls to the new attraction at Knott's Berry Farm, Camp Snoopy, on the same afternoon Anton wanted to see her. There was no plausible reason she could give Gino as to why she couldn't come, so her hands were tied. All she could do was hope the girls would tire out as soon as possible. It had been weeks since she last saw Anton. She hated how he had total control of when they were together. Sometimes it would be months until they saw each other and he would pick up the phone and summon her. There were times her pride wanted to turn him down but that wasn't an option for two reasons; one he had information about her that she didn't want him to reveal, and two, she wanted to see him. She craved him. Despite him taking her on an emotional rollercoaster for nearly three years as he vacillated between warmth and coldness toward her, she still needed, wanted him desperately.

In the beginning, Olivia thought she would at least be able to see Anton when he visited his brother. However, he hadn't been to the house since the night of the wedding celebration. She knew Anton and Gino weren't close but she soon realized the only tie binding them was the business their father started. There was no stopping by the house, not even to see his nieces. He would send gifts on their birthdays and at Christmas but that was it. He only lived a half hour away but he might as well have been in another country. Seeing him so infrequently was torture to her.

If he wanted to marry her, she would leave Gino in a second. But he wasn't the least bit interested in marriage so she stayed where she was. Sure she was guaranteed three million dollars if she divorced her husband, but she wasn't willing to let go of the prestige and honor that went with being Mrs. Valente. She loved the way people treated her upon knowing who her husband was.

The shops and boutiques she frequented would practically roll out a red carpet upon her entrance. And not once did she ever inquire on the price of anything. If she liked it, she bought it. There was no such thing as her waiting for a table at a restaurant or not gaining entry into a club. She was afraid, excluding having money, some of the other privileges she enjoyed being married to a wealthy and well-respected man would greatly diminish if she were to become the ex-wife.

She lightly drummed her fingers on the table as Gino and the girls finished their meal at Mrs. Knott's Chicken Dinner Restaurant.

"Father, I'm so glad I saw Snoopy!" exclaimed an excited Sofia as she held a biscuit in one hand. "He's my favorite character!"

Gino beamed at his daughter. He was tickled at how she tried to say "character" but it came out as "carrotuh" and "father" always came out as "fodder". Though she didn't necessarily pronounce certain words correctly, her speaking abilities and vocabulary was more befitting a five-year-old than a two-year-old. He didn't want to have a favorite child and he loved all his daughters, but Sofia was special. She had already developed a feisty and sparkling personality that reminded him so much of his beloved mother Gina.

Lourdes was becoming more and more like her mother—a spoiled princess who felt her hands should receive whatever her eyes saw. Isabella was very quiet, always observing everything and everyone around her. She didn't speak as much but he could tell she was a smart one as well. He hoped she would get more of Sofia's spark because she had a tendency to fade in the background, becoming overshadowed by the stronger personalities of Sofia and Lourdes.

"And you know who else I liked?"

"Who was that, sweetheart?"

"Charlie Brown! Lourdes was scared of him but I wasn't. I gave him a big, big hug!"

"You sure did."

Sofia turned her attention to her mother. "Mother, you not hungry?"

"No, I'm not. And you don't need any more biscuits." She didn't like that Sofia seemed to be retaining her baby fat. She tried implementing a diet for her but that tattler, Mrs. Petrova, went to Gino about it. He came to her screaming about her trying to do such a thing to a two-year-old. Olivia didn't understand why he didn't go along with her considering he worked out and watched what he ate most of the time. At that moment she didn't even have to look at him; she could sense his eyes were burning right into her.

"Eat your biscuit, sweetheart," Gino instructed Sofia without taking his eyes off Olivia.

As Sofia enjoyed the rest of her biscuit, Olivia looked away from her so as to not show her detestation. *Go ahead and become a fatty then like that no good mother of mine. When you do, you'll have your father to thank.* She turned her attention to Lourdes as she reached over and stroked her hair. *My Lourdes isn't going to turn out that way, that's for sure. Every day she reminds me more of her aunt. My sweet little princess will be a heartbreaker; I can see that already.*

Gino was mildly irritated with Olivia. Lately he saw she constantly harped on Sofia about what she ate. He didn't want Sofia having junk all the time, but he sure wasn't going to deprive his daughter of food. If his wife had her way, she'd be eating nothing but celery sticks and lettuce. Olivia had gotten better at mothering, at least as far as Lourdes was concerned. She spent more time with her but not as much with the twins. He was told she would often take Lourdes out with her but would leave Sofia and Isabella at home. He talked to her about it many times but she continued doing it, which is why he decided to take some time from the office to try and spend quality time with all the girls.

One thing he was going to put a stop to all the unnecessary toys Olivia bought Lourdes. She now had her own room and it was filled with so many toys she couldn't possibly play with them all if she wanted to. She would tell Olivia—not ask what toy she wanted and she had it the next day. The only request Olivia wouldn't give in to was the one for a puppy. He was bewildered at how she stood her ground on that issue. Later when he questioned her about it she said she was allergic to pet hair. He should've reined Olivia's spending in a long time ago and that was about to happen. He had to put a stop to Lourdes's ever-growing spoiled behavior and make sure it didn't spread to the other two. As if on cue, began Lourdes pulling at Sofia's stuffed animal.

"Give it!"

"No!" Sofia shrieked.

"Lourdes, let go!" Gino admonished.

Lourdes held firmly onto the stuffed animal and looked at her mother for help.

"Sofia, let her have it," said Olivia. "You can have hers."

"No, she can't," interjected Gino. "All the girls picked out just which stuffed animal they wanted. We're not going to make Sofia give up her toy just because Lourdes decides she now wants it."

Gino took the stuffed animal from the girls and placed it on the seat next to him.

"There you go, Sofia. It'll be right here, sweetie."

Sofia nodded while Lourdes burst into tears and then went into a full-blown tantrum on the floor.

"Take her out of here!" Gino demanded Olivia in a harsh whisper.

Olivia rolled her eyes at Sofia and Gino and proceeded to pick up Lourdes off the floor to carry her out of the restaurant.

Chapter 39

ino was doing some work in his study when the phone rang. He wasn't going to answer it, until he noticed it was his business line and not the house one.

"Gino Valente."

"Mr. Valente, Larshman here."

"It's a little early in the week to do your weekly check in isn't it?"

"This is not a check in, Mr. Valente. I have a new development on your wife."

Gino took off his reading glasses.

"I'm listening."

"Right after you and your family returned to your home and Mrs. Valente went back out, I trailed her."

"Where did she go?"

There was a moment of silence on the line.

"She went to Mr. Valente's house, sir."

"My brother's house?"

"Yes sir. When she first arrived at his residence at seventeen thirty hours, it appeared they got into some sort of argument and he slammed the door in her face. After a minute she started back to her vehicle when Mr. Valente re-opened the door and summoned her inside."

"She was gone for about three hours. Did she spend the whole time there?"

"Yes, she did sir. She didn't exit the residence until approximately nineteen forty-five hours. Luckily, the pile of newspapers on the stairs of the house next door indicated the neighbor was away, so I got a good vantage point in their backyard."

"What did you observe?"

Gino's body was knotted with tension and he sat perfectly still. He had to or else he would get up and punch a hole in every room of the house. His thoughts went back to what initially caused him to suspect his wife of having an affair. Over the last two years, though they slept in separate bedrooms, one would occasionally show up in the other's room for intimacy. About a month and a half before, after sharing almost two bottles of wine after dinner, they went upstairs to her room. He wanted to be adventurous and try making love in a different position. Before they'd only done it missionary-style and side-by-side when they were intimate during her pregnancy. That night he decided they should do it with her on her knees and him entering from behind. He had already slipped inside her when through his tipsiness, finally realized he was inside her anus and not her vagina. He hadn't heard any protest from Olivia so he continued.

Afterward, as she drifted off in a slightly drunken sleep, she muttered, "We shouldn't have done it that way. He would be so mad if he knew."

He couldn't get her words out of his head.

Who was *he*?

Supposedly other than the man who attacked her that one time, he was the only man she'd been with and they'd never had sex that way before. When they first had sex he had to enter her vagina with care, so he wondered why her anus was so easily accessed. And not only was she enjoying the act, she obviously was used to it. That's when it then became apparent that the only explanation was she having an affair.

The next day he called Larshman, who had done investigative work for Valente Construction in the past when they needed the histories of potential business partners or high level employees checked out. Larshman tailed Olivia for weeks without finding anything. Gino was just about to call it off when he received the phone call. A couple of days later Larshman brought over the developed photos that were now on his desk. The pictures were taken from the neighbor's yard and through Anton's bedroom window. They depicted sex acts between his brother and wife. One act in particular she'd never performed on him yet in the photos she was happily obliging his brother.

He pounded his fist on the desk.

Over the next few weeks Gino said nothing to Olivia or his brother about what he found out. With the assistance of his lawyers, he put into motion all he needed so that he could cut both Anton and Olivia out of his life.

Shelley Halima

Chapter 40

Olivia deliberated whether a particular outfit she was eyeing would look flattering on her. She took another sip of the complimentary champagne supplied by the boutique.

"Mom could we like hurry up?" whined a teenager nearby.

"Tammy, did I rush you when you were getting your things?" asked the girl's mother. "Now let me shop in peace."

"What about this outfit? It's totally bitchin'!"

"You know I don't like showing my arms. What do you think of this one?"

"Eww, like barf me with a spoon! It looks like something Gran would wear."

Olivia walked closer to the mother and daughter to get a glimpse. She peered with antipathy at their appearance, especially at the daughter's teased and glittered hairstyle and leg warmers. *No class whatsoever. I won't be coming back to this boutique anymore if people like that are going to be shopping here! They should be at the mall, not in this place. They don't look like they could afford a scarf from here, much less an outfit.*

The daughter turned her head and glimpsed the disdainful way Olivia was regarding them.

"What are you looking at?"

"Nothing much," Olivia sniffed.

"Excuse me, Mrs. Valente."

Olivia turned to the store clerk.

"Yes?"

"I'm sorry to ask you this but do you have another credit card? We've been trying to put this one through but it keeps getting declined."

"Declined? That's impossible. Try it again."

"We tried several times, Ma'am."

Annoyed, Olivia reached into her purse and produced another card. The clerk soon informed her it was declined as well. After going through other cards in her purse and finding they were all declined, a flustered and embarrassed Olivia informed the clerk that obviously there was a malfunction with the store's machine. She strode past the other customers, ignoring the smirk on the teenager's face, and out of the boutique.

Olivia walked to her vehicle to use the car phone and dialed Gino's number at the office. She was told he went home early so she called their home phone.

"The Valente residence. May I help you?"

"Mrs. Petrova, put my husband on the phone."

"Is this Mrs. Valente?"

"You're a quick one. Put my husband on the phone. Now!"

A moment later Gino was on the line.

"Yes?"

"Gino, what's going on with my credits cards? Have you paid the bills?"

"I've been calling around looking for you. You need to get home as soon as possible."

"Is everyone okay? It's not the children is it?"

"The children are fine. We have a visitor."

"Who?"

"Just get home as soon as you can." With that he hung up the phone.

"What is going on?" Olivia asked aloud.

As she pulled past the gate she noticed Anton's Lamborghini parked in front. *What in heaven's name is Anton doing here? Something has to have happened for him to come here. Maybe it's the business! What if Gino has lost his money and that's why all the credit cards were declined? This can't be happening!*

Olivia parked and rushed inside. She found Gino and Anton in the study. Anton was casually inspecting Gino's collection of classic car replicas near the window. Gino was going over some paperwork. He looked up and saw Olivia standing at the door.

"Olivia, come in and have a seat."

Anton glanced over his shoulder at her. She tried to read in his eyes an answer to what she feared. There was none. He took a seat next to her in front of Gino's desk.

"All right Gino. Are you ready to tell me what's going on and why you've called me here?"

Gino tossed his glasses on the desk and leaned back in the chair.

"I've called you here to let you know Valente Construction will soon be no more; at least in its present state."

"Oh God," Olivia moaned. Her worst fear had been realized. *What am I going to do now? I can't go back to being poor. I just can't!*

"What the hell are you talking about?" Anton barked.

"I'm dissolving our partnership."

"You can't do that!"

"Watch me," Gino replied in a measured tone.

"I've already got things in the works to begin a brand new company in Georgia. I'll be relocating there in the coming months."

"Georgia?" asked Olivia. "Gino, I don't want to move to Georgia of all places."

"And you won't have to. Because you see, I'm dissolving my partnership with you as well."

Olivia was too taken aback to even respond.

"I've already had papers drawn up to begin divorce proceedings."

For a minute or so no one said anything. Anton studied his brother and soon he had it all figured out.

"You know, don't you?" Anton asked.

Gino turned his gaze from Olivia to his brother.

"Yes, I know."

"Know what?" Olivia directed her question to Anton.

"About us," he stated matter-of-factly.

Gino removed some photographs from beneath the pile of paperwork and slid them across the desk toward Olivia. With trembling hands she took them. After quickly shuffling through them she let the photos fall to the floor and she covered her face with both hands.

"I can understand you wanting a divorce," began Anton. "But to leave the company our father worked so hard to build? You can't be serious."

"Oh but I am. I'm more than well aware of the fact that I'm leaving our father's company. The only reason I've even been able to co-exist with you all these years is because I know it's what our parents would have wanted. But there is no way in hell I'd come to work and look into your face knowing you've been screwing my wife!"

"Do you know what your leaving will do?"

"Not my problem."

"You selfish son of a bitch!"

Gino leaped from his chair. "You have the nerve to call me selfish?! You weren't thinking about this company or me when you had your cock up my wife's ass!"

Now it was Anton's turn to leap from his chair.

"And that's all she was to me—a piece of ass! She's certainly not worth throwing away our family's legacy! I wonder what our parents would think about their favored son now!"

"You're lucky I don't take you out right now."

"You don't have the balls, big brother."

Gino, with the dexterity of a man half his age, leaped up and across the desk, grabbed Anton by the lapels. They fell backward on the floor and Gino began pummeling his brother. Olivia got out of her chair and tried to pull Gino off of Anton.

Gino reached around with one hand and, with a mighty push, Olivia fell back toward the desk where she slid to the floor. While Gino was distracted with Olivia, Anton managed to land a blow to Gino's jaw. Gino in turn rained even more ferocious hits on his brother. He stopped only when he heard a tiny voice calling him from the doorway.

He saw it was Sofia.

"Father, why you hitting that man?"

Gino wiped his hand that was smeared with blood from Anton's nose, on his slacks. He went over to Sofia and picked her up.

"It's okay, honey. We were just wrestling."

At that moment Mrs. Hopkins arrived. She looked at Olivia sitting dazed on the floor and then at the gentleman laid out and bloodied opposite her.

"Mr. Valente. I'm so sorry. Lourdes put paint all over the wall of the playroom and when I was cleaning it, Sofia slipped away."

He planted a kiss on Sofia's cheek and handed her to Mrs. Hopkins. "Just please get her out of here."

"Yes, sir."

After Mrs. Hopkins left with Sofia, Gino went over to his brother.

"For as long as I can remember you've whined about how Mom and Dad loved me more. You really need to put this stupid, petty, sibling rivalry bullshit to rest. But I tell you one thing. If our parents did love me more than they did you, it's because you've never in all your miserable life thought of anyone else but yourself. So now I hope you feel you've exerted your spiteful revenge on me for being the so-called favored son by sleeping with my wife. As far as I'm concerned, you may as well be buried with our parents. Now get out of my house!"

Anton strained to get himself up and when he did stumbled to the doorway and out of the room. Gino went to the credenza and poured a glass of sherry. He drank it in one gulp and poured another glass.

"Gino…"

"I don't want to hear anything you have to say. You're a deceitful bitch and I can't wait until you're out of my life, too. I should've listened to Betty. By the way, I'm getting custody of the kids."

Those words brought her out of her stupor. She sprung to her feet to face Gino whose back was still to her.

"You're going to take my kids from me? You can't do that!"

"I'm so weary of you and my brother saying what I can't do. It's already done. I've already compiled my arsenal in case you want to fight me. I have statements from the hospital staff about how you showed no interest in our babies. I have evidence of you leaving them a mere two weeks after their births to unwind in a Palm Springs resort. Of course my staff here will be more than willing to testify about how your stunts put you in contention for Worst Mother of the Year. On top of that you don't have the money or clout that I do. It's a battle you are in no shape to fight much less win."

"At least let me have Lourdes," she pleaded in a desperate whisper. "She's not even your flesh and blood, Gino. Please don't take her away from me. Please! I beg you!"

Gino turned around. Gone from his eyes was anger. Instead it was replaced by morose.

"Any other mother standing where you are would plead for all her children but you only want one. I've seen from the time they were born you didn't have the love for the twins like you did Lourdes. Still, somewhere inside I hoped I was wrong. You know, even if my parents did care little bit more for me than my brother, they would fight equally hard for both of us. But you...Never mind, I won't waste my breath. Despite everything that you've done and all that's transpired, it would be nice if you showed an iota of devotion for the children you had with me."

Chapter 41

As Olivia drove to Anton's, she thought over the events of the past twenty-four hours. She was certain Gino would give her custody of Lourdes. He didn't outright say it but she felt assured he'd do the right thing. One conclusion she came to was that Gino's investigation was aimed only at finding out about her affair. He didn't mention anything about knowing her identity was false so she felt safe knowing that was still under wraps. There was no reason for Anton to tell Gino anything at this point. When she arrived at Anton's she hoped it would show him she still wanted to be with him and she wasn't only seeing him because of what he knew about her. She also needed to make him see she would be a good partner for him—a good wife. Anton always said he wasn't interested in settling down but she would work to convince him marry her. There was not a chance that Gino would ever reconcile with her and if she couldn't be Mrs. Gino Valente, she needed to become Mrs. Anton Valente. She didn't want to lose the status that being attached to that name brought.

Olivia exited the car and walked to Anton's door and knocked. A minute later he opened the door. Most of his face was covered with bruises.

"What are you doing here?"

"I'm here to see you, obviously."

He walked away from the door and sat down on the couch. Olivia entered, closing the door behind her. She took a place beside him. She reached out brush aside a stray hair from above his brow. He jerked away from her touch.

"Would you like for me to prepare something to eat for you?"

"What could you possibly prepare? You only know how to be waited on hand and foot."

"I could make you a sandwich. Would you like that?"

"No."

"Why are you being so cold?"

"Better question—what are you doing here?"

"You've already asked me that. I wanted to be with you. Now that everything is out in the open, we don't have to hide our relationship anymore."

He looked at her and a slow smile spread across his face. She returned his smile. He took her hand in his, brought it to his lips to kiss it. She found the sweet gesture touching.

"Take off your clothes."

She found herself getting aroused at the sound of his words. She got up and stood before him. She stepped out of her heels and kicked them to the side. With slow seduction, she took off each piece of clothing and undergarment until she was naked. He took in her body from head to toe.

"You know what's so funny?"

Olivia giggled. "I hope nothing right now, silly."

"Oh yes there is. It's so funny that you came over here thinking I'd be interested in a continuing any kind of relationship with you."

All amusement quickly left her face.

"I thought I'd give you a great good-bye fuck, but I don't even want to do that. You have ten seconds to put back on your clothes and get out."

"What do you mean?" She shook her head. "I don't understand."

"You don't? Let me help make it clear for you."

He bent over and picked up her clothes and shoes. He then violently grabbed her by the arm and dragged her to the front door.

"Stop Anton! Don't do this! I can't lose you!"

Anton stopped pulling on her and glared at her.

"You stupid little bitch. You never had me."

He opened the door and tossed out her things onto the steps and lawn. In that formidable instant she knew what he planned to do next. As she tried to run to the safety of a nearby room, he grabbed her again and pulled her screaming outside. He shoved her onto the front lawn and went back into the house and slammed the door. Olivia began to cry hysterically as she fumbled for her clothes. She heard the door open only to see Anton toss out her purse before slamming the door closed again. She hurriedly put on her clothes and gathered her underwear and purse. As she stumbled to the car, she saw there was an open house for a home up for sale across the street. She saw the shocked faces of people there to look at the house. She turned her eyes away from the witnesses to her humiliation and got into the car and sped off, swerving down the street.

Part Two

Spring 2006

Chapter 42

Côte d'Azur, France

Olivia Valente-Castelli-Von Hausmann scrutinized her naked body in the full-length mirror. Her breasts, though not sagging, were no longer as perfectly pert as they once were. She was quite pleased with the rest of her body though. She had been diligent about regular exercise for years—something she picked up from Gino during their brief marriage, and it had paid off. Her nearly forty-five year old body could rival most women half her age.

Her frame was lean and sinewy courtesy of yoga, Pilates, and cardiovascular workouts. She stepped closer to the mirror for an inspection of her face. Olivia still thought of herself as a beauty but there were a couple of things that needed a tune up. She didn't like the extra skin in the folds of her eyelids and the crow's feet that deepened every year despite the expensive caviar-based cream she used religiously. That would have to be taken care of. Plus, the collagen in her lips had been absorbed and needed a retouch.

Olivia put on some Chanel No. 5, slipped on her robe and went to look for Lourdes. She padded through the villa, which she received as a gift from a wealthy suitor a few years before. She finally found her daughter sunbathing topless on the rooftop. Olivia took a seat in a nearby lounge chair and opened up an umbrella she kept handy.

"You are going to get skin cancer if you don't stop this sunbathing. Or should I say sun baking?"

"Mother, I don't want to hear it. I don't have the natural hint of a tan like you and my sisters. I have to work on mine."

"Why don't you try that suntan concoction that you get sprayed on? Isn't that what your friend Noèmi uses?"

"Yes, and she looks like an Oompa Loompa. The mere sight of her makes me crave chocolate."

Olivia let out a light laugh.

"You're too much, Lourdes." She leaned back and swung her legs up on the chair to her side. "I think it's time we head back to the States and visit your sisters."

Lourdes opened her eyes and looked at her mother.

"I can't leave now. You know I'm dating Christophe and plan on marrying him."

"Darling, I hate to tell you this, but that's a lost cause."

"And why do you say that?"

"I had a long talk last night with Ètienne D'Aubigne. He said Christophe has wasted most of his inheritance on bad investments and gambling. On the trip to Monaco last week to visit his uncle, he lost half a million at Le Grand."

"Half a million?!"

Olivia nodded.

"Do you know what he could have bought *me* with half a million?"

"He doesn't have all the money he appears to. So for him to waste that amount indicates he's foolish and what's to stop him from losing the rest of his money?"

"But when we go out he only takes me to the very best clubs and restaurants."

"From what I understand, due to his family name, those places pick up the tab just for the privilege of having him patronize their business."

"Now that I think about it, all the times we've been out together I've never seen him pull out his wallet to pay for anything."

"And that gravy train will come to a stop once the word gets out, family name or not. Learn from my mistakes. Don't go after a man who you think has money but rather one you know has money. I found out the hard way with Günter. When he died after that accident, I got the surprise of my life when I found out he didn't have very much at all. I don't want that to happen to you."

Lourdes waved her hand and closed her eyes again.

"Christophe wasn't that great in the sack anyway. I've had sneezes that lasted longer than him. So why do you want to go visit my sisters?"

"Do you know their birthday is coming up soon?"

"So? We could send them a card."

"Their *25th* birthday," Olivia said pointedly.

Lourdes's eyes flew open again.

"Their 25th birthday?"

"Yes, and they'll be coming into the first portion of the money bequeathed to them; twenty million dollars—each. How in heaven's name could you forget that?"

Lourdes pursed her lips to a pout.

"That's so unfair. Both of them will receive a portion of their money on their 25th birthday and the rest when they turn thirty. Why did Father put in his will that I can't get anything but a stupid monthly allowance until I'm thirty?"

"I know it's not fair. He believed Sofia and Isabella to be more responsible, which is ludicrous."

"That man may have given me his name but his actions show he didn't really think of me as his daughter. Until I'm thirty I'll have to live off a paltry twenty-one thousand a month."

"How do you think I feel? At least you will get a great deal of money eventually. He got rid of me for the home in LA, a year old Bentley and a lousy three million and child support for you. I could just kick myself! I was so young and naïve and he took full advantage of that. I thought three million was the world back then, but I went through it like that!" She snapped her fingers for emphasis. "That wasn't nearly enough to keep up the lifestyle I became used to for long. I knew he was rich but I had no idea just how rich he was. His portfolio alone was worth a vast fortune with all the property and stocks he owned and investments. He knew he was cheating me out my fair share by having me sign those papers. Your sisters think he could no wrong but they have no idea how conniving he was."

"Those two don't even know what to do with all that money anyway. We would really make good use of it. But they are just like Father."

"You're right. We need to go and get our hands on some of that money."

"Mother, you know it's always been us and them. I doubt if they would suddenly want to be generous and share the wealth."

"Perhaps not Sofia, however, Isabella is a different story. Besides, I was reading one of those business journals from back home. An interesting new prospect is going to be setting up headquarters in Chicago sometime within the next few months. We can cool our heels in Atlanta in the meantime."

"Who? Is he for me or you?"

"He's for me. His name is Jameson Fauntleroy. He's so old he probably urinates dust. But having one foot in the grave can only work in my best interest."

"Why can't I be his Anna Nicole?"

"Oh, very funny. I need you to be on your best behavior with your sisters, especially Isabella. No egging her on with snippy comments. I know how you like to needle her."

"It's such fun. She's such a mouse. It's so funny to watch her get all flustered and not be able to think of a comeback. At least Sofia can give as well as she gets."

"Lourdes..."

"Okay, okay. I'll be good."

Lourdes sighed.

"It's going to be pretty hard to leave the French Riviera for Geor-juh," she said with an affected Southern accent. "I guess it's good-bye *foie gras* and *Sauternes* and hello grits and biscuits. Instead of saying '*bon jour*' it'll be 'hey y'all'. The things we do for money."

Olivia chuckled.

Lourdes opened her eyes again and looked at her mother.

"I hate to bring this up, Mother but I actually do miss Günter sometimes. I liked him more than any of the others. He was a nice man."

"He was a broke man!" Olivia spat.

"Still, I liked him. If I'd found him at the bottom of the stairs like that, I would've lost it."

"Can we change the subject, please?!" Olivia snapped. "I don't need any reminders of how his sister Elizabeth accused me of having something to do with the accident. She tried her best to get the police to investigate it further. And they would have if the blood alcohol in his system didn't show it was no surprise he fell down those stairs. And all you can talk about is what a nice man he was."

"I'm sorry, Mother. I won't bring it up again."

Olivia stared off in the distance as she recalled watching Günter tumble down the long, winding staircase and seeing his horribly twisted body at the bottom. Günter death didn't make her cry but the reading of his will certainly did. Most of the money that he had left had gone to various creditors. She sold off his prize purebred horses and had his art collection and antiques auctioned by Sotheby's. She received a tidy sum from the sales but it wasn't nearly what she thought she would get from her marriage to Günter. If she'd known he wasn't worth as much as she thought, she wouldn't have given him that little push when she saw him drunkenly trying to make his way down the long staircase. As a matter of fact, she wouldn't have even married him. Then to add insult to injury she found out Günter's sister had convinced him to take her off his insurance policy and made Elizabeth sole beneficiary. She thought she would get not only Günter's supposed fortune, but also an additional insurance payment. Neither of those happened.

She was sick of getting shafted by men. Gino pulled one over on her with the prenuptial agreement, locking her out of tens of millions. Then his brother Anton dumped her without a thought. Her second husband Bruno Castelli was a sneaky bastard who did a great job of playing cloak and dagger with most of his assets before divorcing her and running off with his best friend's wife. She didn't even want to think of the men in between her marriages. She had been so misused by them but she was determined it wouldn't happen again. She would do a better job of researching a man's financial status and make sure she had a firm, ironclad grip on his funds. No pre-nuptials and no hiding assets. When she traveled to Chicago to set her trap for Jameson Fauntleroy, she would be victorious.

She wasn't too hopeful about gaining entree into Sofia's funds. She was too much like her father. But Isabella...She had no doubt she could get some of Isabella's inheritance. She was always such a pushover. Olivia didn't make much effort to see Isabella or be a big part of her life. She would make up for that and lay the groundwork for part of the inheritance. If things worked out the way she planned with Jameson, she wouldn't necessarily need Isabella's money but she would take it anyway. Part of that money was owed to her and Gino cheated her out of it. Either way she would get what was rightfully hers.

Shelley Halima

Chapter 43

Alpharetta, GA

Sofia Valente whipped her silver Mercedes E500 sedan into the driveway, causing a squirrel to scamper across the yard and up a nearby tree and a small flock of birds gathered on the driveway to quickly take flight. Sofia was a skilled driver but a fast one as a few Fulton and DeKalb County police officers could easily attest. Although she had been pulled over a number of times, she charmed her way out of most of the tickets and only had two on her record. She got out of her car and retrieved two grocery bags from the trunk. As she was doing so, she caught the appreciative eye of a young man who was walking his dog. He slowed his walk at the end of the drive and took in her lush curves accentuated by her form fitting skirt and blouse.

"Hello!"

Sofia turned to the sound of the voice coming from the end of the drive.

"Hi! How are you?"

"Much better now."

She flashed him a smile and winked at him in response to his flirting and turned to go inside.

The home she shared with her sister Isabella was a beautifully constructed English manor estate surrounded by three and a half acres of woods with a stream running through the back of the property. It had been their home since her father Gino relocated to Georgia. She couldn't wait to soak in the tub and veg out in front of the television. She had a tiring day at Bonança Bay, the spa she ran with her best friend since high school, Grace Toussaint. Sofia came up with Bonança, which was Portuguese for tranquility, and Grace added the Bay part since she was from Montego Bay, Jamaica.

"Isabella!" she shouted as she went to put the groceries in the kitchen.

A few moments later, Isabella entered the kitchen carrying one of the cordless phones and looking forlorn.

"Hey you. Why so glum?" Sofia asked as she put away the food.

"Guess who's coming to town."

"Who?"

"Mom and Lourdes."

Sofia paused and rolled her eyes. "Great. I knew things in my life were going too well. When are they arriving?"

"Friday. Mom wants me to make reservations at The Dining Room. And she wants us get the house in Buckhead ready for them. I haven't seen Lourdes since last year and I could go at least another five years quite honestly."

"I could do very nicely without seeing either of them."

"I'm not talking about Mom, Sofia."

"Well, I am. And why do you still let Lourdes intimidate you so? If she starts ragging on you, just do what I do—tell her to fuck off!"

"I can't use language like that."

This time Sofia's eye roll was directed at Isabella.

"I can't, Sofia." She took a seat at the kitchen island.

"I figured those two would take some time from their cross continental prostituting and come here when it got close to our big birthday."

"Sofia! You shouldn't say that about our mother!"

Sofia turned away from the cabinet and to her sister. "Grow up! You know that's all they do—sell their privates to the highest bidder. If our mother and sister had a resume it would say under objective: to find rich men, bed them, and sponge off of them until either they get tired of us or we find bigger wallets."

"I know Lourdes is like that but Mom, that's another story. I think she keeps getting married because she's trying to find a replacement for Dad."

"Are you serious? She loved Father so much yet couldn't make it out in time for the memorial service but just in time for the reading of the will. You just insist on making up this nice little fantasy about our mother. *O pior cego é aquele que não quer ver.*"

"I didn't take up Portuguese like you did, Sofia."

"Essentially it means the worst blind is those who don't want to see."

"I think you're the one who doesn't see things as they really were. You blame her for her and Dad's divorce and you refuse to see there could be two sides to the story. You ever stop to think Dad wasn't so perfect and maybe he had a hand in their divorce?"

Sofia put her hands out in a stop gesture. "You know what? I am not going to get into this conversation with you again. Let's change the subject. What time did you make the reservations for?"

"Seven."

"Fine. I'll let Grace know I'm leaving the spa early. Are you feeling any better?"

"I still feel a little light-headed but better. I figured it was going to be my turn to catch that stomach flu that's been going around."

"Maybe it's not the stomach flu. Maybe you're pregnant."

"Ha-ha. Very funny."

"I'm going up to take my bath. I didn't feel like cooking and figured you didn't either so I stopped at that new gourmet shop and picked up some things."

"What did you get?"

"I bought Gazpacho, Panini sandwiches and arugula salad. Plus a few other items we needed."

"Sounds good. I'll try and eat some of it. Thanks."

"You're welcome."

Sofia adjusted her bath pillow and leaned back. Her tired muscles welcomed the warm, soothing bath water. The main thought running through her head was how she was not looking forward to the visit from her sister or mother. There could never be a doubt Lourdes was her mother's child. They were so alike it was frightening. As for Isabella, she knew she had a void from not having a mother around most of the time and admittedly there was a part inside her that was the same way. But seeing how Lourdes turned out, she had no doubt she and her sister were much better off being raised by their father. On top of that, Sofia would never have the self-acceptance she did had she been raised by her mother.

Every single time she had visitation with her mother, her weight was brought up. She was a chunky baby who grew into a chubby kid and teenager and settling into a curvaceous young woman. Her mother's nickname for her for years was "Chunk". It wasn't until she was around fifteen that she stood up to her mother and demanded she stopped calling her that. After a slip up or two her mother finally did. As a youngster, at mealtime everyone else would have a regular meal but her mother would only serve her something like a bowl of plain oatmeal for breakfast or a salad for lunch and dinner. Though she would come back from visits with her mother a pound or two smaller, she regained it right away because once home she would eat even more to compensate for her deprivation. Such an emphasis was put on her weight that Sofia knew she would get more praise calling to tell her mother about a lost pound than an excellent school grade or academic award.

When she was eight-years-old and visiting her mother, an incident occurred that resulted in a change in visitation. Still hungry from the light dinner she was given, she snuck downstairs to the kitchen to get something to eat. She saw the remaining portion of the cake from dinner that everyone was allowed to have a slice of except her. Just as she was leaving the kitchen with a slice of cake wrapped in a napkin, her mother came in. She made her hand over the napkin. Once she saw the contents, she told her to sit down at the table. Her mother then removed the cake and a container of milk from the refrigerator and placed them in front of her. Her mother sat down and told her to eat. When Sofia asked for a dish, utensils and glass, her mother said, "No, pigs don't use those things." She didn't know what to do and sat looking at the cake. Her mother hit the table hard with her hand and demanded she start eating.

"I've been trying to save you from being a fat pig but obviously that's exactly what you want to be so I'm going to let you! Now eat and eat with your hands!"

Tears began to trickle down her face and with trepidation she broke off a piece of the cake with her fingers and put it in her mouth.

"Oh no, fatty. You can do better than that. Now grab a nice chunk with your hand." When she hesitated, her mother shouted, "Do it!" She did as she was told. The cake was a bit dry and she opened the milk and swallowed some down. After eating about three handfuls, which paired with being frightened by her mother's demeanor, she began to feel ill.

She asked her mother if she could stop because she was feeling sick. She was told no and that she wasn't going to stop until all the cake was gone. After another mouthful she held more cake in her hand but couldn't muster up the will to eat it. Her mother demanded her to eat but she just couldn't. Her mother jumped from the chair and rushed over to her. She stood looking down on her with such hatred and disgust; it made her cry even more. Her mother raised her hand as if she were going to slap her. Her hand paused mid-air for a few seconds before she balled it to a fist and put it back to her side. Then she grabbed a handful of the cake herself and screamed for her to open her mouth.

Her mother proceeded to stuff the cake into her mouth—gagging her in the process. She grabbed another handful and smeared it all over her face. Another handful went into her hair. Her mother didn't stop until all the cake was gone and all over her. She couldn't hold it in any longer and she threw up. Vomit spewed onto the table, floor and her nightgown. Her mother said for her to stay put in the chair and proceeded to walk to the sink and wash her hands. She heard her mother leave the room. A few minutes later she returned with her sleepy-eyed sisters. They became wide-awake when they saw their sister. Her mother stood between them with her hands on their shoulders.

"See what a filthy, disgusting pig your sister is? Look at her and look at her good. You don't ever want to be like her. Do you?"

They didn't say anything at first.

"Do you?" Their mother prompted them again. Her sisters both shook their heads in response. "Isabella, go get Miss McCullough and tell her we have a mess that needs to be cleaned up in the kitchen. And you, Sofia, go upstairs and take a bath. Hurry up before I change my mind and make you stay like that!"

She quickly got up from the table and dashed from the room to upstairs. After she had cleaned up and changed her clothes and got into bed, she cried herself to sleep.

When she got home, her father knew something was wrong but she didn't tell him what. After a few days she finally broke down and told him what happened. He stared at her for a while not believing what he'd heard. He called Isabella into the room and asked if she knew what happened the night of the incident. She told him their mother woke up her and Lourdes and brought them down to the kitchen and Sofia was covered in cake and vomit. He asked what their mother said to them after she brought them down and she told him. He grabbed Sofia and brought her to his lap. He hugged her tight and kept saying he was sorry. She didn't understand why he was crying and apologizing for something her mother had done. Her father took her face in his hand and turned it to him. "I promise, nothing like that will ever happen to you again. Okay? Never." She gave him a long hug.

After that she and Isabella weren't allowed to see their mother for a while. However, Isabella begged their father and eventually he relented. He said they could no longer visit their mother out of state though. Visitation could only take place at the house in Buckhead he'd purchased for when Olivia and Lourdes came to town. And they could only visit under the supervision of Mrs. Hopkins who relocated from California with them.

Sofia turned on the hot water tap to warm up the cooled water. It was a lot more than the cake incident that caused the estrangement with her mother. Mrs. Hopkins being present during the visits didn't deter her mother from making a verbal jab at her size. But it was the overall sense of disapproval and lack of emotional warmth from her mother that caused their estrangement. Although Isabella understood why their father did what he did in regards to the visitation, Sofia always sensed her sister resented her for the restricted time with their mother.

Their mother never taunted or blatantly mistreated Isabella but she wasn't given much attention from her either. It was almost as if she wasn't there. Sofia saw how that lack of attention from their mother made Isabella seem to want it even more. To this day she was constantly trying to curry her favor by sending extravagant gifts. And always tried to appear as perfect as possible—not wanting to do or say anything her mother would disapprove of. One of the reasons Isabella disliked Lourdes so much was envy. She would do anything to have been the one who lived with their mother instead. She was so caught up in gaining their mother's approval and love, she couldn't truly appreciate that it was what their father lavished on them. All Sofia could do was hope one day her sister would finally realize that them not being raised by their mother was not a misfortune but an infinite blessing. Something told her however that this realization would come at a heavy price.

Chapter 44

Sofia entered Bonança Bay and punched in the alarm code for the security system. She then proceeded to go through the spa to prepare for the day's clients. The spa was she and Grace's pride and joy. It was something they had envisioned since they were teenagers. While most girls were out partying or chasing boys they were huddled together planning out their future business endeavor. She shared her ideas with her father and he as always, encouraged her. Grace was more adept at numbers and business plans while her forte was creative ideas such as the design layout and decoration as well as choosing products. She and Grace wore many other hats and obtained licenses in massage therapy and nail care and could step up in a pinch if needed.

They both were determined to not just be a couple of rich girls mooching off of their family's hard-earned money and they wanted to make their own marks in the world. Grace's father was a world renowned neurosurgeon and her mother ran four Jamaican restaurants located in Georgia. Mrs. Toussaint also came up with her own special organic jerk sauce that was sold nationwide in both chain and independent grocery stores. The two young women felt they had to live up to what their parents had achieved. Allowances they received from their parents went into a joint account they opened up specifically for their business. Even though it was their parents' money that helped fund their venture, they wanted their determination and business acumen to be what kept it afloat. Sofia could have held off opening Bonança Bay until she received her inheritance this year but she didn't want to. She didn't plan on touching that money any time soon unless it was necessary. Their long-range plan was to open spas across the U.S.

The spa turned out just as she and Grace envisioned. The décor consisted of tile, stone and woods and the colors throughout were calming neutrals. Wall water fountains were placed in many of the rooms. They served refreshments such as a variety of teas, cheeses, fruit, crackers and wines. Near the front of the spa was the shop area where clients could purchase hair and skin products and custom-made signature oils and lotions. Though the clientele was mainly comprised of women, they did have a separate area where women could bring in their boyfriends or husbands for pampering.

A few minutes later, one of the masseuses Zahira, entered the shop. She was about five-six and despite an appetite that could rival a Sumo wrestler, she was quite slender. She was a raven haired beauty of Chaldean descent who moved to Atlanta from Dearborn, Michigan a few years before.

"Good morning, Sofia!" she chimed.

"And how are you this beautiful over the hump day?"

"Just great! I finally got the okay to move into the condo." She made the thumbs up sign.

"That's wonderful! I know you've been going crazy waiting for that tenant to leave."

"After they paint, I'm in there."

"Oh, Grace had a doctor's appointment. She'll be in later."

"How's Isabella? I called her line last night but she didn't answer."

"She's still a bit under the weather. I told her she should take another day off before she goes back to work."

"Oh. Well, I hope she gets better. I feel so bad because I know she caught that bug from me."

"Not necessarily. Almost everyone I know has gotten it. By the way, we got a new shipment of Aveda products so get ready to put your employee discount to use."

Zahira clapped her hands.

"You know that stuff is like a drug for me."

By mid-morning a stream of clients had begun to come in. Most of the women who frequented the spa during weekdays were either housewives or executives who could take off from work mid-day.

Grace entered carrying a basket of fresh croissants from a nearby bakery. Grace stood two inches shy of six feet but there was nothing gawky or awkward about her. Her name suited her, for she embodied the grace of a gazelle. She didn't just walk into a room as much as glided into it. She began ballerina lessons at the age of four and was one of the top dancers in her class. Even though a growth spurt during the span of a summer prompted her teacher to inform her she no longer had a chance for prima ballerina status, she still to this day took classes for enjoyment. Her skin was dewy perfection the color of dark cinnamon, which was contrasted nicely by black micro-braids that cascaded down her back. Penetrating almond-shaped eyes, high cheekbones and sensual full lips that many women sat through collagen-filled needle shots to obtain accentuated her pretty face.

Although she'd lived in the United States since she was a pre-teen, she still had a bit of a Jamaican accent and her words were peppered with lingo from the island.

"Good morning, ladies!"

"Good morning!" Sofia, Zahira, and a couple of women waiting for treatments replied.

"How are you?" inquired Sofia.

"All fruits ripe," she responded as she set the basket on a cart. "And yourself?"

"I'm all right. I called last night to tell you about the samples I tried out from this new company but all I got was your voicemail."

"Girl, you know not to call me when Tapestry and Love Tales is on. By the time I checked my phone and called you back I got your voicemail."

"I guess last night was a bad night for people trying to get in touch with one another."

"How did you like those samples that came in?"

"I left some in the office for you to try out. I think they'll be a hit."

"I'll have to check them out. Sofia, I just learned some news. Mrs. O'Reilly is closing her shop next door. She wants to retire and move back to Massachusetts. She's already purchased a home on Martha's Vineyard so she's for real this time."

"Really? Is someone taking over her business?"

"She said no because she doesn't trust anyone to run it as she did. She plans to be gone in the next few months."

"I'm going to miss her!"

"I will miss her, too. But do you know what this means?"

"No."

"Remember how we were talking about how nice it would be to expand and add a separate area for a hair salon?"

"Yes! We could have it right next door instead of trying to build onto our place."

"Exactly! Maybe knock down that wall."

"I already got one hairdresser y'all can hire," said Josie, one of the nail techs sitting nearby.

"Do tell," said Grace.

"My cousin Odell is leaving Detroit and coming back here soon. Honey, that boy can do some hair! Grace, you know that actress from that show you're crazy about Tapestry—the one that plays Veronica?"

"Yes."

"He did her hair for her wedding."

"Get out of here! You never told me that! I saw those pictures in Essence. He did a beautiful job."

"I thought I told you, Grace."

"No, I would've definitely recalled something like that. So he knows Nikki Moreno?"

"He knows her and her cousin Rosie from before they moved to Hollywood. He's good friends with them."

"Well, once we get this off the ground tell him to come and talk to us."

"I sure will."

"Excuse me," interrupted Suzy, one of the employees who did waxing. "I'm sorry to interrupt." She took Sofia and Grace each by an elbow and guided them away from the ears of the customers. "We have a problem."

"What?" asked both Sofia and Grace.

"It's the new girl. She has Mrs. Thompson's eyebrows almost looking like Whoopi Goldberg's."

"But Whoopi doesn't have any eyebrows," replied Sofia. Then in an instant it hit her exactly what Suzy meant. "Oh!"

Sofia and Grace exchanged distressed looks.

"Let me take care of it," Grace volunteered.

Sofia gave her the crossed fingers sign and headed toward the office.

A short time later Grace entered the office she and Sofia shared. She closed the door, put her back to it and heaved a dramatic sigh. She walked to her desk fanning herself.

"Was Mrs. Thompson upset?" inquired Sofia.

"First of all, that Emily is going on pedicure duty for a while. I had to offer Mrs. Thompson some free services and show her how to fill in her brows with shadow until they grow back. Oh, I forgot to tell you something. No sooner than I receive a slice of cake from my cousin Monette's wedding, I get a call this morning from my other cousin Teja that she's now planning her wedding."

"To whom? Not that guy she just met!"

"Oh yes. When Monette announced her wedding plans last year, Teja tried her best to drag her ex down the aisle to race Monette to the altar and ended up running him off in the process. She's been on the hunt ever since and now she's got that ne'er-do-well to agree to marry her. And of course he would. He needs a roof over his head. Her red eye is going to be her undoing. Her parents are trying to talk sense into her but her ears hard."

"I'm having the same situation with someone whose ears hard. Isabella. My mother and sister are on their way here from the south of France."

"Uh-oh."

"Right. We're going to have dinner with them on Friday at seven so I'll be leaving a bit early to get ready."

"Hmm. They're coming to get an early seat at your big birthday, huh?"

"Thank you! I tried to tell my sister that's why they're coming back but do you think she listens?"

"Sweetums, stop telling. She'll learn. Time is longer than rope. Nuh, true?"

"I know. And quite frankly I'm tired of talking about it. I'll try and let it go."

"Don't just try. Do! For your own sanity if nothing else."
"You're right."
"But of course," Grace replied with a wink.

Chapter 45

Sofia and Isabella followed the hostess to the table where their mother and sister were waiting. Olivia stood to greet them and gave a discreet nudge to Lourdes to do the same but she remained seated.

"Hello, my darlings!" Olivia gave them each a warm embrace. "It's so good to see you."

Lourdes made a slight coughing noise and looked away.

"And how are you, Lourdes?" Sofia inquired as she took a seat.

"I'se just fine and y'all?"

Sofia and Isabella gave her cold stares.

"That is so old," remarked Sofia.

"What is?" Lourdes gave her an innocent glance.

"You know what. That stupid accent you put on whenever you come here. You've done that ever since you were a kid. The thing is you're an adult now so start acting like one."

Lourdes's pseudo-innocent look quickly faded into an irritated one.

"Girls please," Olivia implored. "You've barely been in each other's presence two minutes and you're already at one another's throats. Can we please have a nice, warm reunion over dinner?"

Lourdes took out the compact from her purse and checked her perfectly made up face. Olivia tapped Lourdes's foot with the toe of her shoe in a covert signal. Lourdes put her compact away.

"I'm sorry. I was only teasing and meant no harm."

Neither of her sisters acknowledged her apology.

"Sofia, I like that new hairstyle of yours. It's really cute."

"Thanks."

Lourdes looked at Isabella's flat locks. Not finding anything to positive to say she just flashed Isabella a smile.

Sofia decided she would try and make nice with her sister and give her a compliment as well.

"That's such a pretty halter dress you have on." She couldn't help but notice that she and her sister only had compliments about the other's appearance for pleasant conversation.

"This old thing? This is like the third time I've worn it. I'm about to toss it."

Sofia held her tongue but couldn't resist sneaking a tap on Isabella's leg.

"Well, regardless, it's very pretty. Where did you get it?"

"It's Armani. Oh, but they only go up to a size twelve. What are you an eighteen or twenty?"

Olivia silently cursed Lourdes. It was not that she cared about her making remarks about Sofia's size but just didn't want her to do it now.

Sofia took a deep breath and smiled at Lourdes.

"I wasn't asking because I intended to buy one like it. Though I could since I'm a size twelve I get in just under the gun. Anyway, the cornflower blue color is a perfect match for your blue eyes. Speaking of which, where did you get those? Are they from Armani as well?"

Lourdes smiled widely and spoke through her perfectly bleached and veneered teeth.

"No, sister dear. These are courtesy of Bausch and Lomb if you must know."

"With the blue contacts and newly blonde hair, you could be a clone of Paris Hilton. All you need is a little dog and the paparazzi following you," said Sofia.

"I love my new look and I think it suits me just fine."

"It does, you just look different from the last time I saw you. Thank goodness you still have the same smug look on your face or else I wouldn't have recognized you." Sofia returned her sister's false smile.

Olivia cleared her throat as she stared down at the menu. "I think I'll start off with the Cocoa Bean Soup. And for the main course the Seared Veal Loin with Wilted Spinach looks delish." She glanced up from the menu. "Come on, decide what you're going to get. Mother's starving."

"I need a drink," replied Sofia. "I think I'll have a glass of Pinot Blanc." Cutting her eyes to Lourdes, "I might have to move on to something harder after that."

"I'm in the mood for a nice *Èchezeaux*," announced Isabella.

Lourdes turned to Isabella.

"It's pronounced, *ay shay zo*, not *ek zo*. Father was quite the wine connoisseur so one would think you'd know that. Jesus, Bella Boop."

Isabella turned a beet red. She hated that her sister always made her feel so unsophisticated. Sofia was about to give Lourdes a verbal swipe on Isabella's behalf but decided not to. It was time her sister learned to speak up for herself.

Just as the women were starting dessert, Sofia happened to look up and see a familiar face walking toward their table. She turned to Isabella.

"You have company," she informed her dryly.

Isabella looked up and smiled at the young man. She stood and gave him a quick kiss.

"Mother, I hope you don't mind but I invited Jeremy to join us. I wanted you to meet him. Jeremy Walton this is my mother Olivia Von Hausmann."

Jeremy reached over and shook Olivia's hand.

"It's a pleasure to meet you, Mrs. Von Hausmann."

"Same here. And please, call me Olivia." She beamed at the young man. She could tell right away he had good breeding and the smell of old money practically oozed from his pores.

"Oh, and this is my sister Lourdes."

Jeremy shook her hand.

"It's nice to meet you."

Lourdes stared at Jeremy wondering what in God's name was he doing with Isabella. She assumed they were only friends. She couldn't imagine a man like him being romantically involved with her mousy sister.

The hostess brought a chair for Jeremy and he sat down between Sofia and Isabella.

"And how are you doing tonight?" he asked Sofia.

"I'm just fine, Jeremy." She went back to her dessert before she said what was on her mind. She was so disappointed with Isabella.

"Aren't you going to fill me in, Isabella?" asked Olivia. "Tell me about your friend. Or are you two more than that? Are you dating?"

Isabella and Jeremy exchanged smiles.

"Yes, we are dating," acknowledged Isabella. "We've been going out for about three months now."

"Why didn't you mention this to me last we talked?"

"Mom, I didn't want to jinx anything."

"What happened to your other little boyfriend, Bella Boop? What's his name—Ethan?"

"Lourdes," Olivia chastised. "Don't be impolite."

"I thought I told you I don't like that nickname." She looked away from Lourdes to her mother. "We decided to just be friends. Jeremy's family owns the Walton First Banks, Mom."

Olivia's eyes lit up. "Really? Those banks have been around since the before the turn of the century, correct?"

"Yes, ma'am. It goes back over five generations."

"And you two are dating?" asked a dumbstruck Lourdes. She still couldn't believe it.

"Yes!" Isabella answered testily. "I just said we were."

Jeremy put an arm around Isabella. "I'm quite taken with your sister."

Sofia smirked.

"I noticed the silver band on your finger," said Olivia. "Is that from you Jeremy?"

"Oh, uh, yes it is, Mom," Isabella said. "It's just a friendship ring though."

"I can't wait to see an engagement ring in its place, dear."

"Mom, we don't want to rush things."

"I'm sure you don't," snorted Lourdes.

"Who are you dating, Lourdes?" Isabella asked.

"I'm dating a dashing young man named Christophe. He's back in France and missing me terribly I'm sure."

"I'm sure," Sofia mocked softly.

"Excuse me?" Lourdes asked.

"Nothing."

"You know I saw the new video by James this morning. Or I guess JB as he's called now. Are you two still in touch?"

Sofia's cheeks burned with fury. She threw her napkin down and got up.

"I'm going to the ladies room."

She stalked out of the restaurant and to the lobby where she took a seat. She crossed her legs and furiously drummed her fingers on the arms of the chair. She wished she'd stayed home. Then she wouldn't have to put up with her fake mother, a bitchy sister and another sister with her pretend boyfriend that she's using to gain favor and approval from said fake mother. Jesus! And for Lourdes to bring up her ex-boyfriend James…At that moment Sofia noticed someone had taken a place in the chair next to hers. She looked over and saw one of the most handsome men she'd ever laid eyes on. He appeared to be of Latino descent, with a tanned complexion, short black wavy hair, and sexy brown bedroom eyes that were rimmed with long lashes. His jaw was strong and angular. He was wearing a well-tailored business suit, Italian loafers and there was a briefcase at his feet.

"Hello," he greeted her.

"Hi." Her voice sounded breathless to her ears.

"I was leaving a meeting and on my way out to my car when I saw you sitting here. I had to walk over and find out why a beautiful young woman would have such a frown on her face."

Sofia felt the warmth of embarrassment inflame her face.

"My name is Javier Torres." He reached out his hand to her.

Sofia's hand became lost inside his big one. "I'm Sofia Valente."

"Mrs. or Miss?"

"Miss."

"Miss Valente, may I ask what has you over here looking like you want to commit a capital offense against someone?" Reluctantly, he let go of her hand.

"Aren't you inquisitive?" she teased. "I'm here having dinner with my family and I had to get away for a minute before I, as you said, commit a capital offense against someone."

"No further explanation needed. I love my family dearly but I too have had those moments."

"You say you were here for a meeting. What kind of meeting?"

"I can tell I'm not the only inquisitive person in this lobby." He gave her another engaging smile. "I'm an attorney and I had a meeting here with one of my clients."

"What type of law do you practice?"

"Business Law. What about you?"

"Oh, I don't practice law."

"Very funny," he responded with a chuckle.

"Perhaps I should've warned you that I'm a bit of a smart aleck."

"No warning needed. I like that."

"I run a spa with my friend. It's called Bonança Bay. It's over in North Atlanta."

"Now how about that? Who knows, you may need my services one day."

"I guess we'll have to find out."

"I guess so. You know, you probably should get back to your dinner before they begin hunting for you."

"Are you trying to get rid of me already? After only a minute?"

"Definitely not."

"Better not."

Javier's interest in the young lady was even more piqued. He was drawn to women with strong personalities and a quick wit. He had to get to know her.

"May I call you sometime?"

"Yes, of course." Sofia was relieved. She hoped he would be interested enough to ask for her number. She looked down at her lap and then at her feet and realized she left her purse at the table. "I'm sorry. I don't have my purse with me and my cards are inside it."

He slid a card out from inside his jacket and handed it to her.

"You promise to call?"

"Yes."

As he rose from his seat, Sofia followed suit.

"I'm not going to have to look up Bonança Bay in the Yellow Pages and make an appointment just to see you again will I? Not that I'd want to be caught in a spa."

"Hey! Men come to our spa too."

"They do?"

"Absolutely. But no, you won't have to do that. I will call you."

"I look forward to hearing from you."

Sofia shook his hand again and walked back toward the restaurant. As she walked away, Javier's eyes wandered over her round posterior that swayed seductively with each step. He could not wait to find out more about Sofia Valente.

Sofia took her place back at the table and without a word to anyone, slipped Javier's card into her purse and finished up her *Sachertorte* dessert.

"What's up with you?" inquired Lourdes.

"Hmm?"

"You went off in a huff and now you're back with a cat that swallowed the canary look on your face."

"Oh, no reason."

Olivia turned to her. "Jeremy and Isabella are coming over to the house for dinner next week. You're more than welcome to join us."

"Who's going to cook?"

Olivia glanced over at Lourdes and chuckled.

"Certainly neither of us. An old friend of mine recommended a personal chef for us during our stay now that our old cook here has retired."

"Things are pretty busy at the spa. I'll let you know." She already knew full well she wasn't going to show.

"Speaking of your little spa," Lourdes interjected. "I'm going to stop by tomorrow around three for some treatments, if that's okay."

"Sure," Sofia replied with no enthusiasm. "Mother, are you going to stop by our 'little spa' also?"

"Some other time, dear, I have appointments tomorrow." She'd scheduled consultations with two plastic surgeons.

Sofia was glad Isabella had followed her to the restaurant in her own vehicle because she didn't have to put up with the awkwardness of the ride home together. Yet again Isabella was jeopardizing her relationship by flaunting to their mother a young man she knew would meet with her approval. Sofia liked Jeremy a lot but she wasn't pleased with him going along with the ruse. But he was just being a friend to Isabella.

Chapter 46

Sofia nestled comfortably under her covers and shut off the bedside lamp. Her mind then switched to Lourdes's comment about James.

James Brooks Marston had been her boyfriend for a year and half. They met when Sofia had just started to come to grips with her father's death and reenter the world. For almost six months after his passing from a brain aneurysm she practically became a hermit and rarely went out or communicated with anyone other than Isabella and Grace. Meeting James was just what she needed to help her further get back into the swing of things.

He was an aspiring singer in the blue-eyed soul vein. When they met he was still shopping for a record deal but had already garnered many fans on the urban club circuit. His mainly African-American audience never ceased to be amazed at the sight of the cute young White man with curly blonde hair and thin build get up on the stage, open his mouth and hear a voice reminiscent of soul singer Teddy Pendergrass come out. Sofia was the recipient of many soulful serenades that helped propel her even more into love.

James not having an actual record deal didn't stop him from having groupies. At first it was difficult for Sofia to deal with, particularly when many of the women would look right past her and boldly make moves on him. She never quite got over that discomfort but James went out of his way to let her know he only had eyes for her. When women would come on to him in front of her, he'd make a point of introducing her as his girlfriend. A few times that did nothing to deter his most ardent admirers and he would have to tell them point blank that he didn't appreciate them disrespecting his girlfriend. That helped build Sofia's trust in him.

Things were great between them until he got a new manager, George Mackey. George could see James's potential to be a star and wasn't going to let anyone—especially Sofia, stand in the way of that happening.

He didn't think it was fitting for a burgeoning heartthrob to be tied to a steady girlfriend. One of the first things George did was to change James's name. He christened him with the more hip moniker J.B. Mars. He also invested in James a new wardrobe to pep up his image. James's curly locks were shorn and replaced with a sleek, straight style and he was paired with a fitness instructor to help him add muscles to his slim frame. He found a couple of talented local producers to work with James and redo his demo.

George's effort paid off because he acquired a major record deal for James within months of becoming his manager. The record honchos were not only impressed with James's voice but also that he was already aesthetically packaged and ready to present to the image-conscious public. A short time later James put out a single that introduced him to radio as he worked on his album. The single went straight to the top of the R&B charts and crossed over to the Pop charts. James, who struggled for seven years to make it, was pegged as an "overnight sensation".

In the beginning James resisted George's suggestion that he not have a girlfriend. But after seeing the results George got for him, Sofia noticed he began taking heed. He stopped holding her hand in public and practically ignored her backstage after shows, and focused only on his fans and his musicians. As hurt as Sofia was by his actions, she clung to the relationship and James's word that he was only downplaying their relationship publicly for career reasons. When she would complain about his treatment of her in public, he countered that she was trying to sabotage what he was trying to build, so she voiced her hurt and concerns less and less.

She didn't even say anything when he gave an interview proclaiming he was too busy for a relationship and was single. Grace tried talking to Sofia about how James was treating her but she wouldn't listen. When they were alone, everything was different. It was as if she were all that mattered to him. She clung to those times and put out of her head the way he was outside that.

However, James finally humiliated her to where she could not make excuses. It happened on Grammy night. She knew James was in Los Angeles recording his album with new producers, but when she asked him if he was going to the Grammys, he said he wasn't. She watched the show every year and that year was no exception. She invited Grace and a few other girlfriends over to watch the telecast. They were all crowded in the theater room looking at the pre-show as all the celebrities arrived on the red carpet. They were doing their own critiques of the fashion victors and victims when one of the hosts pulled pop singer Amanda Bynton and her date in front of the camera.

Amanda's date was James. After the host asked them the requisite "who are you wearing?" she inquired about the status of their relationship. As they stood there holding hands and giggling like teenagers, Amanda admitted they were dating but coyly added that was all she was willing to say.

There he was, the man Sofia was in love with, on television with another woman. Not only another woman but the exact kind of woman he always said he had no interest in. He proclaimed to hate superficial women with boob jobs, overly bleached hair and that were high maintenance—all of which described Amanda. Sofia wondered what happened to his maintaining a single image. She supposed as long as he was attached to someone who was more famous in the industry than him, he and his manager decided to make an exception.

After a few moments, she ran to seek refuge in her bedroom. Grace followed her and comforted her as she cried for almost an hour. Sofia couldn't help but feel embarrassed at crying on the shoulder of the friend who tried to warn her about her boyfriend. But Grace never once said "I told you so". She simply wasn't the sort anyway. She did however hold her hand while Sofia called James and left a wrath-filled voice mail message. She also poured her feelings into an email.

She never got a response from James and the stubborn pride of hers that lay dormant during the time James was mistreating her, came back with a vengeance and wouldn't allow her to call him ever again. For a long time she was hurt and bitter and lot of that was directed toward herself for allowing the situation with James to go on as long as it did. She thought she not only let herself down but her father also. He raised his daughters to be women who would not allow any man to behave towards them in a way he didn't. He said he never raised a hand to them, berated or treated them in any way that wasn't respectful or loving; therefore they shouldn't expect any less from any man they became involved with. Sofia made a promise to herself that while James was the first man who didn't live up to that, he would definitely be the last.

Still, it took her a while to completely get over him. It didn't help that his CD took off and he was on nearly every music video and entertainment news show. His affair with Amanda Bynton fizzled but he was linked with several other women. All of whom were celebrities. When she finally was able to sit through a full interview with him, she didn't even recognize him as the man she once loved. The words coming out of his mouth didn't sound like things he would say. She noticed him sporting a colored string on his wrist, showing his affiliation with a religion popular with many in Hollywood. This was the same Methodist raised young man who mocked the religion when the subject was brought up once by saying it was for kooks. Lately he'd been making the news for getting into fights with the club patrons and photographers. There were also drug rumors surrounding him.

All things happen for a reason. She'd heard that saying for the longest but it wasn't until she was finally over James that she truly understood. There was no way she would want to be around him now. So, even though she was hurt by him, she was glad things ended between them. She was still annoyed with how Lourdes gleefully threw him up in her face. It wasn't as if they were close sisters by any means yet she would not have expected Lourdes to so blithely bring up the name of the man who broke her heart. Lourdes knew the whole story because Isabella told their mother everything.

Sofia had dated a few men since James but no one quite kept her interest once they caught it. Not until tonight anyway. She had a strong sense that Javier was going to be an exception. There was something so magnetic about him. One thing that impressed her was how he introduced himself. As much as she loved Atlanta, there was a high level of superficiality and emphasis on titles by many. What people did oftentimes came before who they were so she liked the fact that he didn't introduce himself as "Attorney Javier Torres" but

"Javier Torres". He put the man before the title. That was a seemingly small thing that left a favorable impression as to what kind of person he was.

She glanced over at his business card that she placed on her nightstand. For a few minutes she wrestled with whether or not to call him right then. She finally decided didn't want to appear overeager and to wait until the next day. Just thinking of his dark, soulful eyes made a shiver travel through her. She couldn't wait to talk to him again. She closed her eyes and tried to recall the woodsy scent of his cologne.

Chapter 47

Javier stared blankly at his date as she went on and on about things he had no interest in. He didn't care what store she finally found the outfit she'd been looking for or that she'd dyed her hair ten times in the last year before settling on the current color or how she was thinking of suing her former hair stylist because she thought dye was left on too long and that's what caused her hair to break. He ventured to guess it didn't cross her mind that perhaps the fact that she'd dyed her hair ten times within the past year could have possibly had something to do with her hair loss.

Javier simply nodded every few seconds to appear as if he were listening intently. He was going to call his friend Lorenzo as soon as he got home and let Lorenzo know he was not pleased in his choice for a blind date. Ten years ago he wouldn't have had many complaints. Back then all the mattered was that the woman looked good. But now at thirty-three years old he was older and far wiser and it took a lot more than that for him to be drawn to a woman.

His mind traveled to the young woman he'd met earlier. Just from the extremely brief conversation with Sofia, he felt a certain spark. He wished he'd been late for this date instead of rushing to end the conversation with her so that he could make it on time. He'd only spoken to her for a few moments but was certain she would never bore him with details on dye jobs. Those hazel eyes, the nibble-on-them-all-night-long lips and curves out of this world. *Man, I can only imagine what it would be like to…* His thoughts were interrupted by the waiter bringing their food. He hadn't eaten anything since lunch and his stomach was grumbling. He said a quick grace over his food and began to eat. In the middle of one of the bites he noticed his date was eyeing him with a look of disapproval. On closer inspection he pegged the look as more of one of aversion.

"Something wrong?"

"You're a meat eater. I thought perhaps you were a vegan like your friend."

"I'm not. Sorry."

He went back to his stuffed chicken and wished that she would get back to her spinach salad and let him eat in peace.

"That's chicken, isn't it?"

Javier let out a sigh and tried to control his growing irritability. "Yes, it's chicken."

"Are you aware of the conditions that chickens are forced to exist under in those factories? It's inhumane! You should really consider giving that up as well as all other meat. We weren't meant to feast on the flesh of God's creatures."

"Oh God," Javier said under his breath.

"I'm sorry?"

"I didn't say anything." He began eating the Parmesan Polenta and red cabbage.

"Next time I see you I'm going to bring some literature. Do you know you alone can save around eighty animals a year if you became a vegan? Jesus was a vegan by the way."

He found it humorous not only at her thinking there would be a next time but her surety of what went into the belly of Jesus. They fell into silence and Javier's thoughts went once again to Sofia.

"Javier!" said the blonde waving her hand at him. "You look like you're in another world."

"I was just thinking about all the work I have waiting at the office on Monday."

"Come now. You have the whole weekend to enjoy and I can enjoy it with you. What are you doing tomorrow?"

"Actually, I don't think all the work I need to do is going to wait until Monday. I'm going to go into the office and work this weekend."

"Oh phoo! I was hoping we could get together tomorrow or Sunday."

"I'll be stuck in a pile of paperwork. As a matter of fact, I'm really exhausted. Would you mind if I got the check as soon as you're done with your salad?"

She poked out her bottom lip.

God, let me hurry up and get away from this woman. He could almost overlook her saying "phoo" but the little girl pout was too much.

"If you insist. But only if you tell me something."

"What's that?"

"That you'll at least take the time to pick up the phone and call me."

"I'll call." *But it won't be to you. If I don't hear from Sofia by tomorrow I'll be looking up Bonança Bay in the phone directory. That's the woman I'll be calling.*

Chapter 48

Lourdes arrived at the spa before Isabella. Isabella found out from one of the girls that Zahira was in the bathroom. Isabella found her at a mirror applying lip-gloss. Isabella walked behind her and slid her arms around her waist. She pulled her hair off her neck and planted a kiss on it.

"Hello, beautiful."

Zahira's eyes met hers in the mirror.

"Get away from me, Isabella," she responded with a chill in her voice.

"Why? What's wrong?"

Isabella let go of her and turned sideways, looking at Zahira.

"You know very well what's wrong. Why didn't you tell me your mother was back in town? Grace told me Sofia left early to have dinner with you, your mother and sister. Is that why you made our phone conversation so brief yesterday morning? I'm supposed to be your girlfriend but someone else has to tell me what you should have. Did you know your sister was coming to the spa today?"

"Yes, I knew."

"You just let your sister walk up in here and you still had not told me anything."

"I'm sorry. She said she was going to come in later today and I figured I'd tell you before then. But you know my sister—she just does what she wants to do and doesn't pay any mind to schedules and times."

Zahira faced Isabella, folding her arms.

"This is not about your sister coming to the spa earlier than she was supposed to. That's so beyond the point. Just tell me this. Which merkin did you use to present to your mother this time? Ethan again?"

Isabella looked down and was silent.

"Answer me, Bella! Who?"

"Jeremy," Isabella replied.

Isabella could feel Zahira's dark eyes boring into her.

"I can't do this anymore, Bella. I refuse to continue becoming non-existent whenever your mother deems to show her face simply because you're not woman enough to tell her about you. About us! It's not fair to me to act in the role of 'just a friend' whenever she or Lourdes is around." She wiped a tear from her cheek and let out a half-laugh. "What's so funny is you're so scared your mother won't accept you when in fact, seeing that you're getting the first portion of your inheritance soon, she wouldn't care if you admitting to liking Billy goats."

"I see you've been listening to Sofia."

"No. It's just that I see what everyone else sees except you. But I'm done and for real this time. And don't for a minute think this will be like before when your mother left town where you can just show up at my place with flowers, whisper sweet nothings in my ear and make love to me and that will hold me over until the next time you want to shove me back in the closet. Unless you come clean about the woman you claim to want to spend the rest of your life with, I don't want to see you again."

"Zahira, please! Just hang in there a little while longer!"

"You've been saying that to me since we've been together. And I'm tired of hearing it."

"You don't understand how hard it is for me!"

"I don't understand?" Zahira asked, incredulous. "How dare you say *I* of all people don't understand?! I'm an outcast from my family who've severed all ties with me because of who I am. Have you forgotten that? I only have one aunt who will even talk to me. Bella, they kill people like us in my family's country and it's sanctioned! But still I couldn't live a lie anymore. I tell you all the time, hiding who you really are is a self-imposed prison. I found that out and now you need to do the same."

She removed from her finger the matching platinum band they exchanged a few months prior. She handed it to Isabella who refused to accept it. Zahira laid it on the sink and left out of the bathroom.

Isabella backed up against a wall and slid down to the floor. She pulled her knees to her chest and sat in quiet for a few moments before she began to sob.

Zahira went over to Grace who was standing at the reception desk flipping through a catalog.

"Grace, is it okay if I cut out of here early?"

"Oh no, you're the only other masseuse freed up for the *boopsie*. You're not sticking her with me." She turned from the catalog and saw Zahira's tear streaked face and red eyes. "What's wrong, honey?"

She grabbed her by the hand and guided her to the chairs near the counter where they sat down.

Zahira looked upwards, blinking away more tears.

"You're going to find out anyway. I just broke it off with Isabella."

"Why?"

"Grace, I can't take it anymore. I'm done with the whole situation. It took me a long time to rid myself of the shame of who I am but Bella stirs up all those feelings again by hiding our relationship. She has nothing to lose by telling her mother about us. Her mother will go along with it if only because of her greed."

Grace squeezed Zahira's hand.

"You've got that right. But I'm hoping she'll realize what she's losing."

"When she does it'll be too late. It's already too late."

"It's never that. You just feel that way because you're upset. It will all work out. I believe that. But you get out of here. Go home and get some rest."

They stood and Grace gave Zahira a quick hug.

"I'll let Sofia know."

As Grace was going to the room to begin work on Lourdes's massage, she saw Isabella coming out of the bathroom and her eyes were just as puffy as Zahira's.

Chapter 49

Lourdes lightly moaned as Grace kneaded her flesh.

"Grace, honey child, you're sure do work wonders with them hands. You go, girl."

Grace slowed her handwork to a near stop and did a quick mental weigh-in on whether she should ignore the condescending manner in which Lourdes was using the "sister-girl" talk or slap her clean off the table and back to France quicker than she could say "croissant". After realizing the repercussions of assaulting a client, she decided to ignore Lourdes and continue with the massage.

"Just be careful of this spot." Lourdes reached her hand back and pointed to the area right above her waist on the right side. "Somehow, when I was on the plane I fell asleep on my water bottle. I didn't even notice it until I woke up and it felt tender."

"Sure."

Lourdes fell silent for a while then to Grace's dismay began to speak again.

"You know what I don't get?"

"A lot I imagine," murmured Grace.

"Excuse me?"

"I said I can't imagine."

"If you and Sofia wanted to have this business of yours, why not just open it and let other people run it? Why are you both here doing massages and nails? Why not let the employees do everything? After all, that's what you pay them for."

"We like to help out," Grace replied dryly. She was in no mood to try and explain what a clue was to someone who didn't have one.

"Honestly, I don't understand why you want to work at all when you both already have money. I've never worked a day in my life and don't plan on it. Work is for people who have to do it."

Grace sighed. "*Fire deh a mus mus tail, him tink a cool breeze.*"

"What?"

"I was just thinking of something my mother says."

"Speaking of your mother, she runs what, a chicken place or something, right?"

Grace glided her hands to the spot Lourdes informed her was tender and pressed deep into the area.

"Ow!"

"Oh, I'm sorry. Did I go too deep?"

"Yes, you did! That hurt! I told you to watch out for that spot."

"Sorry about that. And by the way, my mother runs and owns four Jamaican restaurants and makes her a product she sells to stores all across the

United States. I told you that before. You're done." Grace walked over to the sink to wash her hands.

"Already?" Lourdes asked as she sat up.

"Yes. I'll let Emily know you're ready for your pedicure." She dried her hands and left a petulant Lourdes sitting on the table.

As she walked down the hall she almost ran smack into Sofia.

"Oh, now you're back from your errands. It's a good thing your mother didn't come." She pointed back toward the room Lourdes was in. "Because two of that I couldn't take in one day. Instead of giving her a massage I wanted to wring her puny neck."

"I thought Zahira was going to take care of her."

"She asked to leave early. Your sister has really messed up things up this time and Zahira broke up with her."

"Oh, no. I was afraid that would happen."

One of the other masseuses, Joanne, came down the hall practically running and smiling from ear to ear. She walked up to them and squeezed Sofia's arm.

"Oh-my-God! You won't believe who I just gave a massage to."

"Who?"

She covered her mouth and bounced up and down like an excited schoolgirl.

"Ease up woman and tell us who it is," said Grace.

"It's Tyler Harrison of the Atlanta Falcons! I almost died. His body is so beautiful. He's so gorgeous! My goodness—those dimples!"

"Really? Are you sure it's him?"

"Sofia, that man is the only reason I watch football. Of course I'm sure. He and some woman are in there getting the couples treatment. That woman he's with is Elaine Montoya of Fox News. She is not so cute in person by the way."

"Tyler Harrison! This is so exciting, isn't it Grace?"

"Oh yeah. Exciting." She did a half-hearted 'raise the roof' gesture. "Woo hoo."

"I'm going to go back there and see if I can help out with his other treatments. I just had to come and let that out." Joanne went back down the hall as quickly as she came.

"What's up?" Sofia had noticed Grace's less than enthusiastic response to them having such a celebrity in the place.

"Please, we get celebrities in here all the time. Miss Montoya is pretty well known, too."

"Yeah, but Tyler Harrison?! He's been getting plenty of endorsements and I heard he's even going to make a cameo in some film soon."

"That's nice."

Sofia grabbed Grace's hand and led her to their office where she shut the door. She turned to her friend and shook her finger.

"I've known you too long. Something is up. Now tell me what it is."

Grace placed her hands on her hips and gave Sofia a mischievous grin. Sofia had a feeling she knew what was coming and burst into giggles.

"Quit your tittering. Okay, I'll tell you, nosy girl. We had a little fling."

"And you never told me? Grace! Who is your best friend?"

"You are, nutty girl."

"Nosy girl, nutty girl. Quit it with name-calling. And if I'm your best friend then how come you never said anything about a fling with the Tyler!"

"This happened when Tyler was first signed to the Falcons. And it was also during the time you were recovering from your father's death and I didn't want to fill your ears about my lusty nights with Tyler. And later I didn't mention it because I didn't want to remember it after it became one of those things I wanted to forget."

"Tell me what happened. Especially the lusty nights parts."

"Look, we don't have time to *laba-laba*. We have too many clients here. And it figures you'd want to know more about that."

"We are not leaving this office until you tell me."

"Oh, all right. To sum it up quickly, I fell in lust and thought it was love. He was nothing but a ram goat who took full advantage of all the female adulation thrown his way though he told me he wasn't. Anyway, I found out the truth when we were getting dirty on the floor and I saw some panties under his bed that weren't mine. I didn't say anything but later that night I asked if he could go to the store and get me something and while he was gone I tore that place up looking for more evidence. And boy did I find it. Rollers, lipstick, and other feminine things either accidentally left behind or on purpose by girls marking their territory. I went home before he got back and that was that. It was a short fling that left a long burn."

Sofia reached out and stroked her arm.

"You should've told me, Gracie. I could've been there for you."

"No, no. Like I said you were going through your heartache and grief and I wasn't going to bother you with that foolishness. I think I was more hurt by the loss of what I thought it could be than what it actually was. But what's done is done."

Neither of them said anything for a few moments.

Grace gave Sofia's shoulder a nudge. "I suppose you want to know about the dirty part now."

"You know I do."

"Let's just say he received an overall grade of A despite barely passing the oral exam."

Sofia began to laugh.

"I'm serious. I kept pointing and guiding but the boy never did put the tongue in the right spot. I almost stopped to draw him a map." She held out her hand and with other pointed to the bottom of it. "I wanted to say 'you are here and you should be here'." She pointed to the tip of her index finger. "He had some serious tongue action too. I kept thinking, 'oh if only he was hitting the target he'd be pulling me down from the ceiling'. Instead I just tapped him on the head and said, 'I'm good'."

Sofia fell back against the door. "You are insane!"

"You're calling me insane?" Grace took Sofia's hand and shook it. "Nice to meet you, Pot. I'm Kettle."

"Whatever! I may have some stories for you soon."

"Really? Do tell!"

"Grace, I met one of the most handsome men I've ever laid eyes on last night. It was at dinner. As usual, Lourdes said something that pissed me off--"

Grace's hands flew to her chest. "No! You must be kidding! Not Lourdes!"

"Ha-ha. So anyway, I left out of the restaurant to cool off in the lobby and that's where I met him. His name is Javier, he's an attorney, and did I mention he was handsome?"

"Um, I believe you may have."

"You know how you just meet someone and you have that spark?"

"Girl, yes." She closed her eyes momentarily as if she were reminiscing.

"That's how it was. We talked for maybe two minutes but just that quickly something happened between us."

"Did you give him your number?"

"No, I left my purse with my cards in it at the table."

"Um, I don't suppose you thought to write it down on something."

"No, I didn't. I could barely think straight. But he gave me his business card. It has his cell phone number on it and I wanted to call him last night but you know I had to play it cool."

Grace looked at her watch.

"It's one-thirty and you still haven't called? Such restraint."

"You're just full of jokes today, lady. I'm going to call him in a few minutes. I can't contain myself any longer. I want you to meet him. Not only so you can see what I'm talking about but also, you know you and your intuition. You can always pick up on things about people. I don't want to be blindsided again. Unlike with James, I'll listen this time. No matter how much I like this guy already."

"I would love to meet him. Does he have a brother?"

"I don't know but I'll be sure to find out," she said with a chuckle.

"Ah *dawta*. If only this intuition of mine worked on myself then maybe I wouldn't have gotten caught up in Mr. Harrison's love trap."

"That was a while ago. He may have changed."

"It wouldn't matter if he had. I wouldn't give that *sanfi* another chance so I wouldn't know if he'd changed or not. What does that look mean?"

"You are not fooling me. I don't think you're quite as over Tyler as you claim."

"Instead of trying to read my feelings you need to be on that phone calling this Javier and finding out if he has an equally fine sibling for me."

"You're right."

Sofia went over to the desk. She slid the card from her pocket and picked up the phone. She paused for a minute, and then began to dial.

"I'll give you some privacy and go check on things," said Grace as she opened the door. She held up two crossed fingers and left.

Just when it looked like the call would go into Javier's voice mail he picked up.

"Hello?"

"Javier?"

"Yes."

"It's Sofia."

Javier's face immediately lit up. He sat down on his weight bench.

"Sofia? I know you from?"

Sofia was mortified. Obviously he didn't feel the electricity she did if he'd forgotten about her in a matter of hours.

"We met last night."

"Let's see, I met a few Sofias last night. Were you the lovely Sofia wearing the silk purple blouse, black skirt, with the long reddish-brown hair? That Sofia?"

Sofia beamed once she knew he was teasing her.

"Yes, that Sofia. You scared me for a minute. I was about to hang up."

"I'm glad you didn't. I've been waiting for your call."

"Sure you were."

"I'm serious. I'm about to work out and I brought my cell phone with me, which I never do cause I don't want anything to break my concentration. But I didn't want to take a chance and miss your call."

"Are you at the gym?"

"I'm at my place but I set up one of the rooms here as a home gym. So when can I see you?"

"When would you like to?"

"Now."

"I'm at the spa right now and I hate to cut out so early again but I'll do so a little later. How about we get together around six?"

"My place?"

Sofia didn't answer right away.

"You'll be safe. I know you only met me last night but I promise you I'm not a rapist nor do I have dead bodies in my backyard."

"That's good to know."

"When I give you my address, let someone know and give it to them as a precaution. I just bought this great new Weber grill that I've been dying to finally light up. We'll chill out on the deck and talk. Or if you're still not comfortable with that, you can pick out a restaurant."

"No. Your place sounds good."

"Let me give you my address and home number."

Sofia grabbed a pen from the desk and scribbled his information. Her pulse was racing. Never in a million years would she have thought she could go over to a man's house that she'd only shared a few minutes of conversation with. Yet, that was exactly what she was doing.

Chapter 50

As Grace was walking down one hallway, Tyler was walking down the hallway that crossed it. He and Grace spotted each other at the same time and stopped in their tracks.

"Grace?"

"Tyler? What are you doing here?" She asked, pretending she was unaware of his presence in the spa.

"I came here for a massage and was on my way to the sauna. Now what are you doing here?" He walked toward her.

"Working. I run this place with my friend Sofia."

"Really? Man! You told me you were going to do that and I'll be damned if you didn't, girl."

His deep, sexy voice with its slight southern drawl still made her pulse quicken. Grace tried to keep her eyes away from his handsome face, especially those now famous dimples and cleft in his chin—those were always her weakness. She glanced at his hair. When they were together his hair was braided in twists that were about two inches long. His hair had now grown into long dreadlocks that fell below his shoulders. They were neatly done and tied back in a ponytail. Unlike some men with long hair, his didn't detract from his masculinity in the least. In fact it gave him a certain edginess. She trained her eyes on his white robe. Then she began to think about the well-sculptured body underneath that gave her so many hours of pleasure so she averted her eyes elsewhere.

"Why are you looking everywhere but in my face?"

"Uh, what?"

"You're looking at my slippers, the wall, and the plant against the wall..." He reached out and lifted and turned her chin with his index finger. "That's better. It's good to see you again."

"It's nice to see you."

"What a coincidence that I've never in my life been to a spa and the first time I go to one it's the one you co-own. It must be fate."

"I don't know if your lady friend would think so."

"My lady friend? The one I came here with?"

"Yes, that would be the one."

He began to chuckle. "You were acting as if you were surprised I was here. So how do you know I came with a lady friend?"

Grace worked at suppressing a smile.

"So, you're playing it all cool with a brother, huh? You are looking so good, girl. I like your hair this." He took one of her micro-braids and caressed it with his thumb and forefinger.

Get it together, Grace. Do not let this man get to you. Don't get sucked back in.

"For your information, the woman I'm here with is just a friend."

"Yes, I remember you having quite a few of those. And I'm sure with all your endorsements you have even more."

"Those aren't the kind of friends I want anymore."

"What's changed?"

"I have."

"Really?"

"You don't sound as if you believe me."

"Why should I? Just because you say so?"

"It would be nice if you'd let me show you."

"Look, I have to get back to my office. I have some paperwork to do. It was nice seeing you." She stepped to the side to walk past him.

Tyler blocked her by placing a hand over her hip. "Don't go."

Damn you, Tyler. Be strong. Remember how he hurt you.

"I really have missed you. Me and my boys were talking not too long ago about that special woman that we let get away and you were the woman I named."

"That's interesting."

"Can we talk sometime? Maybe have dinner or something?" He gently stroked Grace's hip.

Grace could do nothing but stare into his eyes as if mesmerized.

"Tyler!"

They both looked to the sound of the voice. It was Elaine Montoya. She was standing nearby and Grace could almost feel the optical daggers being thrown at her.

"I thought you were on your way to the sauna."

"I am, Elaine." He turned back to Grace. "But then I saw a very special person that I haven't seen a long time."

"I'm on my way there now. We can walk together."

"You can go. I'm talking to Grace right now."

Elaine stood there for a moment. Her mouth was tight, pressed into a thin line. She gave Grace a long, hard look before finally walking away.

"Yikes. Don't be surprised if you don't get any tonight."

"I told you she's just a friend. It won't be possible to even be that soon."

"A friend that you came here with for the 'couple's treatment'?"

"It's what she wanted to celebrate her new contract with the station. She convinced me I needed some relaxation too. I know she wants to be more than friends but that's not happening. She's way too clingy as a friend. I don't even want to imagine how she would be as a girlfriend."

"It was nice seeing you, Tyler. Now if you'll excuse me, I have to get back to work."

He reached out his hand to stop her again but this time she moved it out of the way.

"I remember all of your friends from when we were together and I don't even want to deal with that anymore. Now, goodbye."

She walked down the hall and disappeared into one of the rooms. Tyler looked in the direction she went.

"Now that I've found you again, you're not going to get rid of me that easily."

Chapter 51

Isabella sat in her car in the parking lot outside Bonança Bay. She'd knew she had lost Zahira and for good this time. All she wanted was for her to understand her situation and realize she needed more time. The first time she laid eyes on Zahira it was instant lust. She was deeply attracted to her dark, sultry looks, the way she moved—everything about her. For a while she kept her feelings for Zahira to herself. But even Sofia noticed how Isabella stopped into the spa more frequently. She finally figured out it was because of Zahira. One day Isabella got up the courage to ask Zahira out to lunch. She didn't expect anything to come of it other than the opportunity to spend some time with her.

Over the course of the lunch, Zahira mentioned she'd just gotten out of a relationship. Then she said her ex's name–Judy. At first Isabella thought she misunderstood and Zahira had said "Jude". But as she continued to speak she definitely said "Judy" and used "she" and "her". She knew she'd heard right but just to be sure she came out and asked her if she were gay. Zahira informed that yes she was and asked if she were bothered by that. Isabella told her she wasn't because she herself was gay. She and Zahira continued meeting for lunch and dinner and catching a movie together.

Isabella wasn't the type that opened up easily to people but with Zahira, she did so quickly. There were things she didn't feel comfortable sharing with her sister that she had no problem talking to Zahira about. She'd never been around someone that she felt so completely free around. She adored how Zahira could make her laugh. Sofia always accused her of being a fuddy duddy, yet Zahira had a knack for bringing out her silly side. Though she had an immediate attraction to Zahira it was weeks before she made any move.

One night when Isabella was over to her house, they were on the couch watching television when Zahira dozed off. Isabella glanced over at her and by the glow of the television, gazed at Zahira's beauty as she'd done so many times. Her head was tilted to the right, exposing the left side of her lovely, slender neck. Sofia couldn't resist any longer. She leaned over and planted a gentle kiss on her neck and then let her lips graze across it, enjoying the softness. She slid the tips of her fingers across her collarbone. At that moment Zahira opened her eyes. Isabella didn't move. She waited for what Zahira's reaction would be. Zahira placed her hand over Isabella's and with her fingers made a soft, sensual trail up her arm, to her shoulders. Zahira leaned in until their faces were about an inch apart. They looked deeply into each other's eyes. Zahira opened her mouth and with her tongue traced Isabella's lips. She flicked her tongue in the corners of Isabella's mouth causing tingling sensations to course through her. Her tongue then slid into Isabella's mouth. Isabella was almost faint with longing. They made out for the rest of the night as well spent a lot of time talking.

Soon after that night, Isabella informed Sofia that she and Zahira were a couple. Sofia was accepting if not enthusiastic about their relationship. She was still getting used to the fact her sister was gay. It was only a short time before Isabella met Zahira that Sofia found out she was a lesbian. One morning Sofia came home to retrieve some paperwork she left behind. She had seen Isabella's car out front and wondered why she was home. When she peeked into Isabella's room she found her sister and a woman having sex. Isabella didn't even know until later that night when Sofia confronted her with what she'd seen.

Isabella admitted that she was indeed a lesbian and had known since she was a teenager. Sofia asked if she were sure and Isabella let her know she was. Sofia's response wasn't overwhelmingly approving but more like she was resigned to who her sister was. Isabella always wondered if somehow Sofia knew all along but just never said anything. Isabella was never very close to her sister but she appreciated that she encouraged her to come out with her sexuality to everyone. She was just not ready quite yet especially when it came to revealing her sexuality to their mother.

She felt a closer bond with her mother was always just outside her reach. She didn't want to risk anything turning her mother away before they had the chance to have a true mother and daughter relationship. Isabella wanted to come out in her own time and was frustrated that her sister and Zahira didn't understand that. Growing up seeing their mother only a few times a year didn't seem to bother Sofia but it hurt her deeply. She longed for a mother to be around all the time. She sensed that now was the opportunity to have a deeper closeness with her mother and she wasn't going to let Zahira, her sister or anyone else stop that from happening.

Chapter 52

Javier gave such precise directions to his subdivision; Sofia had no problem finding his home. It was in the Smoke Rise section of Stone Mountain. Sofia checked her makeup one last time in the rearview mirror before getting out of the car.

He opened the front door before she could ring the doorbell. Javier was wearing a white sleeveless t-shirt, more commonly known in urban circles as a "wife beater". He was also wearing black jogging sweats. Sofia took in what was covered by a suit the night before–rippling muscles. His arms and shoulders were perfectly chiseled. She could see the firm outline of a muscular chest and stomach through the fabric of the t-shirt. She realized she was gawking and finally opened her mouth.

"Hi! As you can see I found you okay."

"Welcome!" He waved her inside. "And as you can see, I like to dress down when I'm at home."

"I don't blame you one bit. You have such a fantastic—um, place," she said as she looked around.

"Thank you. Come with me. I'm prepping dinner in the kitchen."

She followed behind him as they passed through the living room and dining room. She admired how he had his home decorated. It was done in a typical "men are from mars" style with big furniture, dark leathers, woods and fabrics. The kitchen was substantial and opened out onto the great room. From the huge bay windows where the kitchen nook was located, there was a view of the deck and swimming pool. A sound system was pumping saxophone-driven jazz music throughout the house.

"I take it you aren't suffering for clients."

"I guess I'm doing okay."

"So, what's on the menu for tonight?"

"Grilled vegetables and filet mignon. You're not a vegan are you?"

"No, I'm not."

"I'm only asking because of my experience last night. First, I have a confession to make. The reason I had to cut our conversation so short last night was because I had a blind date waiting for me down the street at Sambuca's. I swear that's my last one. I've had people closest to me, who know me up and down and in circles, set me up on those things and not once has it worked out."

"Same here. I've never been on a good blind date. My best friend Grace couldn't even pick the right one. What went wrong with this one?"

"She was a vegan. Now, I don't have anything against vegans. My best friend Lorenzo is one and my younger sister and her husband are also. But they respect the fact that I'm not and don't try and convert me. I'm sitting there enjoying the heck out some of the best stuffed chicken I've ever had and this lady is looking at me like I'm eating a baby."

Sofia let out a laugh.

"It wasn't very funny last night. I was hungry and I couldn't even enjoy my meal. I came home and ate two sandwiches. Tell me about your last blind date."

"It was last year," she began as she washed her hands and started to help slice the vegetables. "You know the rapper Eminem?"

"Of course! You went out with him?"

"No, I went out with the guy who's trying his best to be Eminem. Shawty Dawg."

Javier burst into gales of laughter.

"You're kidding me, right? You went out with that clown? How did that happen?"

"I used to date J.B. Mars and--"

"You dated J.B. Mars?"

"Yes. A mutual friend of ours who is a stylist for a lot of people in music convinced me to go out with Shawty. She said he was a nice guy and he is but he is just such a poseur. He spoke perfectly proper English when we were alone but when one of his fans came around he started saying things like, 'what's up, yo?' and 'gimme some love'."

"I knew he wasn't hood. What a joke."

"And what would you know about what's hood?" she teased.

"Don't let the law degree fool you. I grew up living a completely different life than the one I have now." He picked up a platter of vegetables. "Can you grab the filets from the fridge? They're on the top shelf."

"Sure." She retrieved them and followed him outside to the deck.

Sofia and Javier sat down at the outdoor table after they prepared their plates.

"So your life growing up wasn't like it is now?"

Javier took a swig of beer.

"No, not at all."

"Are you originally from here?"

He shook his head.

"I'm a Chi-town Rican. I grew up in a neighborhood called Bucktown. My father took off when I was six, leaving my mother to raise five kids on her own."

"That's terrible."

"My mother held our family together. She worked two and sometimes three jobs. When she was out working though, I was out getting into trouble.

I began running with a gang and doing things I'm not so proud of. My mother tried to talk sense into me but I was too bull-headed. I thought she was foolish for going out and working all those jobs. Sometimes I could bring home more money from the streets in one day than she made in two weeks. I tried to give her money but she would never accept it and told me not to bring dirty money into the house. She came close to kicking me out a few times but could never go through with it."

"How did you get on the right track and become a lawyer?"

Javier paused for a few moments before going on.

"My boy Joaquin literally dying in my arms is what did it."

Sofia opened her mouth to say something but couldn't find the words.

"We were tight from kindergarten. Everyone referred to us as JJ, like we were one person because you didn't see one of us without the other. One night we called ourselves going to settle a score with members of another gang for a fight one of our boys got hurt real bad in. They were ready for us. Before we even got to the house where they hung out our car was hit, seemingly from all directions. There were four of us in the car and by some miracle we all didn't die that night. I was the only one who didn't get a bullet. This dude we called Zorro was driving and he ended up with three gunshot wounds. Somehow he managed to speed off. If he didn't I know I wouldn't be here today. He got us to the hospital but on the way there Joaquin died. The other guy with us, Pete, he was shot in the arm and shoulder. That night changed me forever. It didn't change the other two though. As we were walking away from the cemetery after having watched Joaquin get put into the ground, Zorro who was on crutches and Pete, who had his arm in a sling, started talking about retaliation. I finally saw how foolish all of it was. We were going to keep retaliating until we were all dead or in jail. That's exactly what happened, too. I heard Zorro was killed and Pete got sent up and was let back out only to do the same stuff all over again. Now he's up in Stateville. I say I heard about it because my mother sent me here to live with my Uncle Roberto. I didn't argue with her because I wanted to get away."

"Thank goodness you did. Who knows how your life could have turned out?"

"That's true. I'm sure eventually I would've gotten sucked back into that life either by pride or misplaced honor. I missed my family but it was for the best that I moved out here. My uncle didn't take any mess and was stricter than my mother. I kind of resisted at first and we butted heads a lot but it was just what I needed though. I buckled down in high school and graduated. I obtained an athletic scholarship to U of NC at Chapel Hill, came back to here to Emory where I received my JD, flunked the bar the first time out then passed the second time, and here I am."

"That is quite simply, amazing."

"I don't ever remember being referred to as amazing before," he responded with a grin.

"There's a first time for everything. How did you become interested in business law?"

"My uncle wanted to quit his job at the plant go into business for himself and open up an electrical repair shop. I would go to the library and look up a bunch of stuff on what he needed to know on the business end and that was it. It surprised me how searching through these books and trying to interpret it into layman's terms, really caught my interest. I even put together his business plan for him to use to get a loan by going on a model of one I found. Now enough about me, I would like to find out more about you."

"Ah, let's see. Me and my twin Isabella were born in California."

"Wait," Javier interrupted. "You have a twin?"

"Yes. We're fraternal twins. I have a sister named Lourdes who is our mother's first and may I add favorite child. We have different fathers. My parents divorced when Isabella and I were about two-years-old. Our father got custody of me and my twin while our mother retained custody of Lourdes."

"How did your father get custody? Most of the time the judge rules in favor of the mother."

"If you knew my mother you would know how easy it was. Just because a woman gives birth doesn't make her a mother."

Javier let out a light whistle. "That's deep. I take it you and your mother are not very close then?"

"To say the least. I was always closest to my father and as I said; Lourdes received all of our mother's love and attention. Isabella wasn't as close to our father as she could've been. She spent most of her time pining away for a mother that didn't want much to do with us. By us being twins you would think we're very close but we're not. We get along most of the time but there's something missing. It's like there's this wall between us."

"What about your other sister?"

"What about her? She is a carbon copy of our mother—selfish, vain, shallow, manipulative, untrustworthy...I can't completely blame her for how she is. After all she was brought up under our mother's influence. She was raised to think life is about nothing but shopping, rich men and more shopping. Don't get me wrong, I like nice things too and I've been known to wear the magnetic strip off the back of a credit card from time to time. But to me it's just a small part of life. For them, it is their life. It's like their voids are shopping bags and they have to fill them constantly. Both she and our mother are in town right now. I guess the picture is a little clearer on why I had to take a breather in the lobby last night."

"Yes it is. It's too bad that you don't seem to be very close to your family."

"The person I feel most connected to isn't even related to me. My friend Grace is more like a sister to me than either of my blood ones."

"Grace, she's the one who runs the spa with you?"

"Um-hmm. She and I have the type of relationship I wish I could have with my sisters. Maybe it's in the blood. My father didn't have good relationship with his brother."

"What about your mother?"

"She doesn't have any siblings. Her parents died before I was born. So all I have from her side of the family is our heritage."

"Tell me how the spa came about. That's pretty impressive that you're a co-business owner at your age. What are you, twenty-three, twenty-four?"

"You're very good. I'll be twenty-five the thirtieth of next month. From the time we were teen-agers Grace and I were determined to do this. We planned and saved and saved and planned. My father was supportive but I know he really wanted me to work at his property management company. Isabella ended up being the one to work with him. He passed away five years ago of a brain aneurysm."

"My condolences to you."

"Thanks. It was very hard. I honestly don't know how I made it through that. I'm a true blue Daddy's Girl and not ashamed to admit it. But somehow I found the strength to find my way on the other side of grief. I concentrated on finishing up my courses and preparing to finally open the spa. What's the matter? You look like you're thinking about something."

"That's because I am. You said your father's business was a property management company?"

"Yes. He was in business with his brother but he severed their partnership, moved here and began another business."

"Your father was Gino Valente wasn't he? The company with his brother was Valente Construction and he came here and started up Valente Property Management?"

"How did you know all of that?"

"I know all the big names in business. I've read up on all the major players in finance and business and he was one of them. So he's your father, huh? It didn't even cross my mind that you were related. Are you serious about this running a spa or is just something to do?"

"What do you mean am I serious? Of course I am!"

"Sofia, I don't mean to be rude--"

"That's exactly what you're being! What if I were to ask if being a lawyer was something you were serious about or if it was just something to do?!"

"Look, your father was loaded and I'm sure left a bunch of money to you so I'm wondering if your spa is an avenue to do something with all that money."

Sofia stared at him for a moment, her eyes flashing fire. She scooted her chair back and stood up. She walked back into the house, picked up her purse from the counter and headed toward the front door. Just as she put her hand on the knob she heard Javier come up behind her and felt him tug at her arm. She snatched her arm away.

"Let go!" She turned to face him and placed a hand on her hip. "You don't know me! Understand? I thought that's what we were doing out there—getting to know each other. I'm opening up to you, telling you things I don't tell to just anyone and you jump up and make all kinds of assumptions about me. For your flipping information I've worked since I was ten-years-old. My father had both my sister and me doing odd jobs to earn money. Just because our father was rich doesn't mean we had everything our little hearts desired. He did not spoil us like that! Yes, our father was wealthy and yes he left us well provided for but neither of us are the type to live off of Daddy's money! I put blood, sweat and tears into that place! This is my dream come true and I refuse to let a jerk like you minimize it to just being something like a hobby to pass the time!" She jabbed her finger at his chest. "You owe me an apology! And I want it right now!"

Javier tried his best to not smile. In that moment she'd won his respect. He couldn't help but give it to someone who demanded it. He saw he was completely off base in his assumptions. She wasn't like the spoiled little rich girls he'd run into before. She looked even more pretty and enticing with her hazel eyes wild with anger and her sensuous mouth set so tight.

"Well? I'm waiting! Don't just stand there!"

"I apologize, Sofia." He put his hand over hers and pressed it to his chest. "I mean it from the heart. I'm sorry. I was wrong for saying that."

She tried to move her hand but he held it firm.

"I thought you were this great guy. I even did something that I never do which is come to the home of a man I met for a minute and a half. Everything is going fine and you open your mouth and spill out that crap!"

"I am a great guy. But I'm a guy who says the first thing that comes to his head. I'm blunt to a fault sometimes. And you know some of my clients have these little princess daughters who want to open boutiques and salons. They have no concept of what it takes to run a business, they just think it will 'be like so cool' as one young lady said to me. My experience with the rich kids back in school didn't help my perception either. Quite a few of them were sliding by with subpar grades but because they had a parent who was an alumnus that gave big monetary gifts to the school they got away not putting forth much effort. I was there on my own merit and working my tail off. Yet some of these same kids would look at me like, 'what is your Puerto Rican ass doing here?' But I shouldn't have instantly lumped you into that category with spoiled little rich girls. Again, I apologize. Can we please go back outside, warm up the food since I'm sure it's cold as ice, and continue to get to know one another?"

"No more assumptions about me."

"No more. I promise."

He pulled her to him for an embrace. She put her arms around his waist and her head to his shoulder.

He feels so good, Sofia thought. He feels too good. He smells like cologne mixed with mesquite from the smoker and even that's turning me on.

When Sofia felt the evidence of him being turned on too, she knew they'd better get back to the deck before there was no turning back. She lifted her head and looked at him.

"Let's go warm up that food."

Chapter 53

Isabella and Olivia sat down on the patio of Milan restaurant and waited for their order. Olivia could tell something was bothering Isabella. She didn't really care but thought it best to act as if she were interested. She reached over and stroked her arm.

"What's the matter, sugar plum? Didn't you have a good time today shopping with Mommy?"

A slight smile came to Isabella's mouth. "Yes, I did. It was fun. I don't go shopping nearly enough."

I can tell. Sofia's wardrobe could still be brought up a notch but still; she was a better dresser than Isabella. Thank God, Lourdes inherited my sense of style.

"I wouldn't think you did. You look so glum. Is it boyfriend problems? You and Jeremy have a fight?"

"Yes, um, something like that."

"Don't let it trouble you. You'll get over it. If I could make it through all the heartache men have caused me, you certainly can get over an argument."

"Mom, did you want to divorce Dad?"

"No, I most certainly didn't!" *As if I'd want to voluntarily get off that gravy train.* "I wanted to keep my family together. But it took more than me wanting that. Your father had to want it, and he didn't. More than anything, I want to try and make up for some of the lost time. Once Gino restricted my visits to seeing you only in Georgia, it kind of drove a wedge between us I think. I know Sofia never wanted a relationship with me because she believed everything your father told her, but I never knew if you really wanted one with me."

"Why would you think that? I've always wanted a stronger relationship with you!"

"You did?"

"Yes!"

"Maybe I thought you didn't out of my own guilt for not fighting Gino hard enough. He had so much power and money it really was like David going up against Goliath. Only I didn't believe I could conquer Goliath. I would love nothing more than to be closer to you."

She knew Isabella was jealous of the relationship she and Lourdes shared and decided to play on it. "If I tell you something, do you swear not to tell either of your sisters?"

"Sure, I swear."

"You may think Lourdes is my so-called favorite but that's just because she was with me all the time. I know if you were allowed to live with me, you and I would be the closest. I really believe that."

Seeing the emotion in Isabella's eyes let Olivia know she struck just the nerve she was looking for.

"Do you mean that, Mom?"

"I truly do."

"But it seemed like a lot of the time you didn't even know I was there."

"You're right. I didn't give you much attention and it was because I was so scared of getting closer to you and having your father turn you against me like he did Sofia. I couldn't bear opening up those floodgates and having you..." She paused as if she were overcome with emotion. "I'm sorry. All I know is I want to make up for lost time with my daughter. And I don't want us to let anyone interfere with that. Not Lourdes and not Sofia. Agreed?"

"Agreed."

Isabella had been feeling down about the breakup with Zahira and the tension between her and Sofia. Yet, hearing her mother say this, made everything else fade away. No matter what Sofia or anyone else said, her mother loved her.

Olivia took out her compact mirror and put a little powder on her nose and chin. She frowned as she looked in the mirror.

"What's wrong, Mom?"

"These darned crow's feet. I've tried everything I could to get rid of them. It's so depressing sometimes. I would love to get married again and get it right this time. Yet, I'm out here competing with perfect little twenty-year-olds. I've been looking into some plastic surgeons but the really good ones with excellent reputations are out of my price range right now."

"Don't worry about that. I think you're beautiful and wouldn't change anything. But if you're unhappy, why don't you go ahead and schedule an appointment with the doctor of your choice. I'll cover all the expenses."

"Oh sugar plum, I couldn't ask you to do that. The doctors I checked into are so expensive."

"It's fine, really. I want to do this for you."

"The thing is I wanted to get...this is so embarrassing."

"What is it?"

"I want to go up a cup size. As you can see you and Sofia didn't get your bust size from me. I'm looking to get some implants. You know have everything done at once. I'm not trying to look like Pamela Anderson or anything, just to be a bit bigger."

"Mom, I'll take care of all it."

"You will? It's not too much?"

"Of course not. So it's a done deal."

Olivia grabbed Isabella's hand. "Thank you! You're such a sweet daughter."

"You're welcome."

She was pleased do something that would make her mother happy.

Blinding Mirror

Olivia grinned at Isabella. There was so much more she intended for her daughter to pay for. Picking up the tab for her plastic surgery was only the beginning.

Chapter 54

"Grace, are you sure you don't mind me leaving early yet again?" asked Sofia.

Grace cut her eyes from the clipboard she was writing on.

"If you ask me that one more time, I'm going to smack you. I can handle things for a couple of hours 'til lights out. Now where are you two headed off to?"

"We're going to dinner and then he wants to drive to Sweetwater Lake."

"How romantic!"

"Is it? I've never been there."

"I went there a couple of times with the *sanfi* Tyler. It's very nice and peaceful."

"I'm glad you're finally going to meet him."

"Me too. I've got to see the man who has you all a twitter," chuckled Grace.

"A twitter?"

"Hush. If he's picking you up, what are you doing with your car?"

"Isabella is going to have Jeremy pick her up and drop her off and she'll drive it home."

"How is Isabella?"

"Don't ask. Mother put a pod under her bed and it took. She came home yesterday in an outfit that looked straight out of Lourdes's closet. I'm kind of ticked with Isabella because she opened her big mouth to Mother about Javier."

"Uh oh."

"Of course Mother called, questioning me about him. I don't know why she's so nosy when she couldn't care less about me. First thing she wants to know is what he does. Then she asks me about his name."

"What about his name?"

"She had the nerve to ask, 'He isn't Mexican is he?'"

"Why am I not surprised? She acts as if it causes her indigestion to even speak to me."

"I know. It's not as if she's some snow queen or something."

"Truth be told, she looks a lot like some of my fair-skinned relatives in Jamaica."

"I recall you showing me pictures and you're right. If I can help it, Javier isn't going anywhere near Mother or sister dear any time soon."

They were interrupted by a knock on the office door.

"Come in!" Grace responded.

Zahira opened the door with a mischievous grin on her face. "Sofia, your visitor is here."

"He is? He's a little early." She ran her fingers through her hair.

"You look great," said Grace.

"Can you please show him in?" Sofia ran her fingers through her hair once more.

"Sure thing." Zahira left to get Javier.

Sofia got her purse out of the drawer and laid it on top of the desk. She crossed her legs and clasped her hands, trying her best to appear calm and collected. Grace let out a giggle and covered her mouth.

"Shh, over there. I'm trying to look cool."

"But you're looking like you're about to give the State of the Union Address. Relax, *dawta*, relax."

Javier peeked his head in and then entered.

"Hi ladies."

"Hey you." Sofia got up and walked to him. He gave her a quick kiss on the cheek.

"Javier, this is my very best friend Grace Toussaint. Grace this is Javier Torres."

Grace stood up from behind her desk and extended her hand. Javier leaned toward her to shake it.

"Very nice to meet you, Mr. Torres."

"Same here Ms. Toussaint."

They both laughed at their formalities. Sofia couldn't help but smile with relief. They looked as if they were hitting it off already.

"I've heard a lot of great things about you."

"Oh really?" Javier looked at Sofia. "You left out that bad part I hope."

"No, but she understood."

"I didn't lose points?" Javier asked Grace.

"Not really. But you do have a slight probationary period for making such snarky remarks."

"How can I make up for that?"

Grace waved her hand. "The office is filled to the gills with roses so you're on your way. So how do you like our spa that we are so serious about?"

"I'm never going to live that down."

Grace and Sofia exchanged smiles. Javier glanced at them both.

"You two are enjoying making me squirm aren't you?"

"Yes we are!" answered Grace. "We're just teasing you."

"I think you both did a bang up job with this place. As soon as you walk through the door an instant calmness comes over you. It's very serene. I like that."

"Think we should let him off probation for that compliment?" Grace asked Sofia.

"I believe so. He sounded awfully sincere. I think he meant it."

"Yes, so do I. My full assessment of his aura isn't complete but I think he might pass the muster."

Javier let out a sigh of relief. "Thank God. I know how hard it is to pass muster with, as you ladies say, the BFF."

"So I hear you have brothers but they're back in Chicago and they're married."

"Yep. Did Sofia tell you about my friend Lorenzo?"

"Just that he's on the market."

"He does graphic design work and shares custody of his little girl named Skye who just turned five. Lorenzo's a good guy who works hard. Maybe the four of us can get together one night and hang out."

Grace folded her arms and nodded. "As long as he's a decent man and hard worker it's a go. Beyond that I'm not *fenky-fenky*."

Javier looked puzzled.

"That means picky."

"Oh, I see."

"I look forward to meeting your friend."

"I'll call him tomorrow and get the ball rolling."

"Sounds terrific. All right you two. Get on and enjoy yourselves. It was a pleasure to make your acquaintance, Javier."

"Same here." He shook her hand again. "Are you ready?" he asked Sofia.

"Indeed I am. I'll see you later, girl." Sofia gave her a wink.

As soon as Sofia and Javier left, Grace plopped down in her chair and fanned herself.

"Good heavens he is something! Sofia—you lucky girl!"

Chapter 55

"Are you comfortable?" Javier asked.

"Very."

They were snuggled together on a bench and looking out on Sweetwater Lake.

"I'm glad you told me to bring a sweater."

"Me, Lorenzo and another friend of ours come out here to fish once in a while and I know how chilly it be at night this time of year on the water."

"This is so nice."

"It is isn't it?"

"Is this where you bring all your ladies?"

"Nope, I've only been out here with the fellas." He chuckled and quickly added, "To fish like I said. Don't get any funny ideas."

"I didn't say a word," Sofia said, amused.

Javier brushed his lips across the top of her head, feeling the silkiness of her hair. He moved his mouth to her forehead and to the tip of her nose.

"Hey, let's go down to the edge of the dock," Sofia said, standing up.

"Sure," he responded, slightly bewildered.

Sofia took his hand and led him down to the dock. When they got there, she stood facing the water and he wrapped his arms around her from behind. They marveled at the beauty of moon shining down on the lake, its light dancing on the ripples of the water. Sofia eyed the trees that lined the water's edge.

"Although we're not too far from downtown Atlanta," Sofia began, "we might as well be a million miles away. There's no booming music from cars, honking horns from impatient drivers—just peace and quiet."

"I know. Beautiful isn't it? Just like you."

"Thank you."

For a few minutes they fell into a comfortable silence.

"*Amo-o para fora aqui. Deixe-nos fazê-lo nosso lugar especial.*"

"What did you just say?"

"I said I love it out here. Let's make it our special place. I don't think I told you but my mother is Portuguese. She doesn't know the language but I took a class to learn some of it."

"I didn't know you were mixed with Portuguese. That's what you meant when you said all you had from your mother's side of the family was your heritage."

"Yep. Do you speak Spanish?"

"Not really. I know a little bit. I plan on learning more. I'll probably get those language audiotapes. I've always felt funny about not knowing Spanish. Especially the times when I run up on another Latino who speaks the language and they instantly start speaking it, assuming that I do as well. It's kind of messed up when I have to stop them and tell them I don't speak Spanish. It's the look I get, you know?"

"I understand. My father was three parts Maltese and I tried picking up that language too but just couldn't really get a handle on it. And my father only spoke a little so I didn't get much help from him. I think it would be great if you learned Spanish. I've always wanted to learn Spanish so maybe we can learn together."

"I'd like that. You're quite an interesting combination—Maltese and Portuguese."

"And with some Scottish thrown in."

Javier brushed his lips on her neck and planted light kisses on it.

"Sofia?"

"Hmm?"

"Do I need a breath mint?"

She let out a raucous laugh. "No! Why would you ask me that?"

"I've counted about three times where we've come close to kissing–twice the night at my place and just a few minutes ago at the bench–and you turn away. So, I was wondering if I needed to pop a tic tac in my mouth or something."

"Absolutely not, silly. It's just that...I don't know."

"Go on."

She turned around to face him. "I'm going to be perfectly blunt. I've always been able to wait a good amount of time before going all the way with a man. But with you, there's such an attraction, a deep attraction, I'm scared if I even get things going I won't be able to stop myself."

"Let me tell you a story. There was this guy named Jack who was really feeling this new girl he met. She was feeling him, too. She didn't want Jack to think she was a bad girl or fast so she put off being intimate with him. Well, as it turns out Jack ended up in a fatal accident."

"Oh no! What happened?"

"He took a tumble down this hill and broke his neck in the process. The girl was left filled with remorse because she would never know what it was like to be with him in that special way. Poor Jill, she was never the same."

Sofia pushed Javier in the chest.

"Jack. Jill. Hill. You totally made that up!" She laughed.

"What? I said it was a story. I didn't say it was a true story. But somewhere in the world I'm sure something like that happened. Maybe their names weren't Jack and Jill..." He chuckled as he drew Sofia into an embrace.

"This is the deal. I'd much rather you're real with me and go with your feelings. If you wanted to go at it on my deck that first night I wouldn't have thought bad of you."

"Really?" Sofia sounded skeptical.

"I want a woman that goes for what she wants when she wants it and not put it off to the so-called appropriate time. Maybe there's still some of the rebel left in me but I hate rules like that. I don't want us to be caught up in the moment and have it shut down because the calendar says it hasn't been long enough. You know what I mean?"

"Yes, I do."

She wrapped her arms around him and tilted her head up closer to his. He put his mouth on hers and at first just let their lips touch. Slowly, their lips moved into a soft kiss. Their kiss quickly became ardent and they didn't break it until they both became aware of a commotion going on behind them.

Javier looked over his shoulder and then back to her.

"Looks like the park is closing. They have lousy timing."

Sofia's head and desires were undergoing an internal battle. Her head was telling her she and Javier should make plans for another date and then have him drop her off at home. But her desires were pulling her in a different direction. And it was a direction she'd never been and never thought she would be. When it came to men she always played it by the book and now here she was in the arms of a man who made her want to toss that book into the beautiful lake before them.

"I guess we'd better go. Do you want to go back to my place?"

"Javier, take me home."

He could barely hide his disappointment. "Okay, if that's what you want, babe."

"I want you to take me home so that I can pick up a few things. Then we can go to your place."

Javier drew her in for a brief but deep kiss.

"You won't regret this."

"I hope not."

Shelley Halima

Chapter 56

Are you really about to do this? Sofia asked herself as she dried her hair. *It's not too late to have him take you back home. You've always advised your friends to make a man wait and don't give it up too soon. Yet here you are in his bathroom about to go meet him in his bedroom. Are you sure you want to do this?*

Sofia looked into the mirror. "Yes."

She slipped on her short silk robe over her bra and panties and left out of the bathroom. She found Javier sitting on the edge of his bed flipping through some CDs. He was wearing only a pair of briefs. He leaned over and put in a CD and the room became filled with the sound of soft jazz music. He then became aware of her presence. He turned his head and when he saw her, a slow grin made its way across his face.

"I thought I'd put on some mood music."

He got up and went to the edge of the bed to sit. He reached his hand out to her and as she took it, she used her other hand to close her robe. Seeing his impeccably muscular body with not an ounce of fat on it, made her feel a modicum of insecurity about her voluptuous frame.

He pulled her towards him until she was positioned between his legs. He moved her hand away from holding her robe. He reached up and slipped her robe off her shoulders and to the floor. He placed his hands on her hips and planted gentle kisses on her round belly. For some reason him doing that put her more at ease. She ran her hands over his head, caressing the wavy texture of his hair. Javier leaned back on the bed, pulling her on top of him. His hands traveled over her backside to her buttocks. As he squeezed it he pressed his hips towards hers. She followed his lead and began to move her hips also. She bent her head down to kiss him. She then sat up in the straddle position to unhook and remove her bra. Javier felt himself grow even more erect as he saw her full breasts released from her bra. He pulled her back down and guided her upward till her breasts fell in his face. With a sensual languor he tongued her tiny, yet hardened pink buds eliciting a soft moan from her. He then shifted their positions so that he was on top of her.

He looked down at her flushed face. "You're so beautiful. Do you know that?"

Sofia merely smiled in response. He began his descent down her body and gingerly removed her panties. With one hand he parted her vaginal lips and with her clitoris exposed, began gently stroking it with the index finger of his other hand. He glanced at Sofia. Her head was turned slightly to the side and she was nibbling on her bottom lip. He was so aroused by her. He stopped touching her long enough to quickly take off his briefs. He moved up until his face was close to hers. He nibbled and tongued her earlobe as his hand went back to stroking her clitoris. His hardness rubbing against her thigh turned her on. She reached and took it in her hand. She was excited yet slightly frightened by the size of it. She'd never been with a man as large as he was. Her thumb slid across the wet tip of it.

"Turn over," he softly commanded.

Sofia did as he asked. He stroked her generous bottom.

"God, I love this ass," he whispered. He moved down and planted soft kisses all over it. He then got on top of her and ground slowly on her backside. He bent down to her ear.

"You ready, baby?"

"Yes."

He reached over and retrieved a condom he placed on top of one of the pillows. As he rose up on his knees to put it on, Sofia turned over and maneuvered her legs until they were on either side of him. Javier made a mental note that he would indulge in more foreplay the next time. He hadn't been with anyone in three months and was eager to make love. No more than a couple of minutes after he entered her, he let out a loud groan as he had an orgasm. Sofia was disheartened but tried her best not to show it.

"I'm sorry, Sofia," Javier panted. "It's been a while and I got too excited."

"That's okay."

Javier cursed himself. *I knew I should've let her jack me off first. Damn it! I feel like a high school kid getting his first lay.*

Sofia grabbed handfuls of the sheets and was on the verge of tears. She felt such sexual rapture to the point she almost couldn't stand it. Javier was more than making up for the first time out. He had her legs flung over his shoulders and he was balancing himself on his hands as he thrust passionately inside her. A short time later he pulled out and Sofia whimpered in protest. Javier rolled off of her and onto his back. He slid an arm under her waist.

"Come here, baby." He guided her to lie on top of him. "Straddle me."

Sofia did as he said.

"Now turn and face away from me."

"Away from you?" Sofia asked, not sure she'd heard correctly.

"Yes."

Again, she did as he requested. She rose up so that she could guide him inside her. It was her first time on top and she quickly began to enjoy it. And Javier enjoyed the view of her voluptuous bottom as it bounced up and down and gyrated. His hands roamed across it and he worked to maintain control. He spread her cheeks so that he could better see her sex. Soon he put his hands on Sofia's hips to stop her movements as a signal that he needed to cool down. When he was ready he began moving again and so did Sofia. She threw her head back as she relished the feeling of Javier hitting a spot inside her that had never been hit before. She'd heard all about the so-called G-Spot and chalked it up as some erotic myth until now. She was certain that it is what caused her such pleasure. She reached down and fingered her clitoris. A few minutes later she cried out as she reached her peak. It took a minute for her to gather her senses. Then she realized how wet she was, so wet for a second she wondered if she'd had an accident but knew she hadn't. Javier gently pulled her back toward him and they switched positions with him on top of her again. He got between her legs and she wrapped them around his waist. She grabbed him by the back of the head and they shared a steamy kiss. When he came again his moans filled her mouth. He collapsed on top of her and she stroked his perspiration soaked back. They held each other, both exhausted from their lovemaking.

Chapter 57

Sofia entered the spa a minute after Grace. Grace turned around and the look on Sofia's face spoke volumes.

"You bad girl!" Grace chastised her in jest. She went over to the smiling Sofia and they exchanged double high fives and squealed with laughter. "After two dates? This is a Sofia Valente record! Especially considering you made your last boyfriend wait almost eight months!"

"Grace I can't believe it. It's as if I just finished watching a movie and someone was playing me. You would not have recognized the wild woman I was last night. I'm talking unleashed!"

"Tell, tell."

"Being with Javier last night showed me what I have been missing. With James it was pleasant, you know? Not great but I enjoyed the actual closeness of the act more than the act itself. It was the same way with Ben. Neither of them brought me to orgasm."

"But Mr. Torres did, nuh?"

"Did he ever. Even if things don't work out with us for some reason, I never want to be with another man who can't make me feel the way Javier did last night. That kind of passion—I don't know what to say. I feel sorry for any woman who has never felt that. Grace, right now every nerve in my body is alive. Still." She stopped and shook her head. "I have all these thoughts and things I want to say and can't find the words."

"Boy, he really put it on you."

"And how. After I left his house on Saturday, I had it in my head how I wanted there to be this long romantic buildup before 'it' happened. Yet at the same time I knew that wasn't going to be the case. The chemistry between us is too electric."

At that moment Joanne and Zahira entered the spa and they all exchanged greetings. Sofia and Grace went to their office to continue the conversation.

"After work we're all meeting up over at Javier's place. You can follow me over there. His friend Lorenzo will be joining us."

"Gee, thanks for the notice. I hope his friend is half as hot as Javier and hopefully this Lorenzo has torn some pages out of Javier's lovemaking notebook."

"Gracie! Now look at who's being bad." Sofia leaned over and lightly pinched her friend's arm.

"Look woman, I have needs that haven't been met in a while. And quite frankly, you're stoking my competitive streak. I can't have you going around having all this fabulous sex and I go home to ride the silver bullet."

Sofia covered her mouth to suppress her laughter.

"I'm not playing. I'm even tempted to call up Tyler. Although I'm sure he doesn't have the same number."

"Um-hmm. And here you were trying to pretend your head wasn't the least bit turned by him stopping in the spa. It's strange that you still even have his number."

Grace made a face at her and arranged some paperwork on her desk.

"Graaace," Sofia said in a singsong manner.

"Yeees," Grace responded in a like tone.

"Guess what?"

"What?"

"I am considering doing that thing to Javier that I've never done to any other man."

Grace slowly looked up from her paperwork and over to Sofia, her mouth open.

"You mean that thing you were going to save for marriage?"

With a sly grin and a wiggle in her brow, Sofia nodded.

Grace laughed and slammed the desk with her palms.

"*Kiss me neck*! Who are you? And what have you done with my friend? Whatever that man has it needs to be bottled and sold out at the front counter! You vowed you'd never do that unless it was with your husband and he's got you to change your mind over the course of a weekend."

"That was years ago since I last said that. Gosh. Can't a girl change her mind?"

Grace grabbed her bottle of water, opened it and took a long swig.

"You are too much for me today."

"All right, enough about my exploits. Let's concentrate on you. I really hope things click with you and Lorenzo tonight."

"Me too. I need some clicking other than the button on my silver bullet."

Sofia let out a hoot. "Stop! Am I going to have do an intervention for you and that thing?"

"A man with what yours has is all the intervention I need, my dear. I'm very anxious to meet Lorenzo."

Blinding Mirror

Chapter 58

Sofia waited next to her car for Grace who was following not too far behind her. Grace pulled her car into the driveway and together they walked up to Javier's door. Before Sofia rang the bell, Grace faced her.

"Quick check. Makeup?"

"Flawless. Oh, wait a minute." Sofia reached in her purse and retrieved a tissue. She delicately wiped an eyeliner smudge on the outside corner of Grace's right eye.

Grace smiled wide to show her teeth.

"Nope. No lipstick on the teeth," Sofia informed her. "Now what about me?"

"Makeup is fine. Smile. Okay, no lipstick on yours either. Hair?"

"Good. Mine?"

"Good. All right, we're ready."

They gave each other the thumbs up sign and Sofia rang the bell. A moment later, Javier opened the door.

"Hello ladies." He stepped aside so they could enter. Grace went first and when Sofia walked in he grabbed and gave her quick kiss.

As they walked into the living area Grace saw the back of a man who was ending a call on his cell phone. All she could tell was he had a full head of almost bluish black hair curly hair that fell just below his neck. He laid his phone on the table, stood and turned to them. Grace gave him a huge grin as she tried her best to hide her disappointment. He was definitely no Javier. His complexion was an olive tone like Javier's but that's where the comparisons ended. He had large eyes, nose that was on the thick side and slightly thin lips. He wasn't exactly ugly but not very attractive either. He was very thin and when Grace went up to him to shake his hand she realized he was a good three inches shorter than she.

"Hello, I'm Grace."

"It's nice to meet you. I'm Lorenzo."

Grace saw that he had a great smile. He waved for her to sit down and he sat next to her. Javier and Sofia sat on the couch directly opposite of them.

"Lorenzo this is Sofia, the woman I've been raving about."

"It's nice to meet you, Sofia. This guy hasn't stopped talking about you."

Sofia grinned at Javier. He gave her a light kiss on the lips.

"It's nice to meet you, too, Lorenzo. Javier has told me wonderful things about you."

"I want to thank you for bringing over your friend," Lorenzo said as he looked over at Grace. "She's a beautiful sight for some very sore eyes. Some sore and tired eyes at that."

"Oh, thank you," replied Grace. "You do look kind of tired."

"I am. I just finished working on one particular project that was very complex and time consuming. I'm glad it's over."

"Javier said you're a graphic design artist."

"Yes. And not that I'm trying to scrounge up new business from you, but when Javier told me the name of your spa I looked it up online and saw you only have a one page website with a basic description. I think the more descriptive your site is, the more it will interest new customers. If you and Sofia would like, I can build it up for you. For instance, I could take some interior shots of the spa and add it to your website. I can even do a virtual tour if you'd like."

Grace looked over at Sofia.

"Uh-oh. Did I say something wrong?" asked Lorenzo.

"No, not at all. It's just funny because a few weeks ago I was telling Sofia that our website was kind of bland and it needed an overhaul. That would be great if you could jazz it up."

"Just let me know a good day to come by and take some photos and we'll get started."

"Sounds good to me. Thank you."

Javier leaned in to Sofia and whispered, "Let's give them some time alone." Sofia nodded in agreement.

"Hey, uh, me and Sofia are headed to kitchen to get things ready. We'll be right back."

After Sofia and Javier left the room Lorenzo chuckled.

"What's so funny?" asked Grace.

"They think they're slick. What could they possibly be getting ready in the kitchen when Javier said we're going to order in?"

As Sofia was going toward the sink, Javier guided her past it, to the laundry room adjoining it. He closed the folding door behind them. He grabbed Sofia into a passionate embrace.

"I've been thinking about you every since I dropped you off this morning. You really put it on me."

Sofia smiled as she thought about how that was the same thing Grace said he did to her.

"That sentiment is without a doubt mutual."

She put her hand on the back of his head drew it to her and they kissed with wild abandon. Their hands roamed furiously over each other. Javier lifted her up on the washing machine and unbuttoned her blouse.

"Javier, you want to—here?"

"Yes, here." He kissed the top portion of her breasts and rubbed his fingers over her nipples through the fabric of her bra.

Blinding Mirror

Sofia grabbed the bottom of her skirt, pulled it over her thighs and wiggled from side to side to maneuver it over her hips. Javier's hands traveled up her thighs and she again moved her hips so that he could remove her panties. He retrieved a condom from the back pocket of his slacks before sliding them along with his underwear down. He ripped open the condom packet with his teeth, tossed the wrapper in a nearby receptacle and put the condom on. Sofia moved closer to the edge of the washing machine and guided him inside her.

Grace bent over in a fit of laughter.
"You've got to be kidding me!"
"No, I'm not! It really happened!"
"Let me get this straight. An eighty-year-old grandmother of twelve had you put together a website of her in various nude shots. And she named the site--"
"Granny Gone Wild."
"Lorenzo, you are making this up!"
"You can't make that kind of stuff up. I did it though as well as a hundred Hail Mary's right afterward. You know what's crazy? Her site meter showed over twenty-five thousand hits within a couple of weeks. I don't know if there are people actually into seeing elderly women in the nude or it's due to some sick fascination people had with it. I put my money on sick fascination."

The last song playing on the stereo system ended. In the quiet a moan could be heard coming from around the kitchen area. There was the steady banging sound like a table being rocked back and forth on the floor. Then came another moan followed by a whimper. Grace and Lorenzo exchanged sheepish grins.

Lorenzo cleared his throat. "And here I was thinking they left out of the room so we could be alone."

"Um-hmm. So, I hear you have a daughter."

"Sure do. Skye, she's my pride and joy." He paused as the banging noise increased. He looked down at the carpet, trying to conceal his mirth before continuing. "She will enter kindergarten this year and she's so excited she had me buy some school clothes already. Hopefully she won't have some growth spurt over the summer. She has her little calendar counting down until August fourteenth."

"Aw, how precious. Do you have a picture of her?"

"Of course." He reached into his back pocket pulling out his wallet and pulled out of photo and handed it to Grace.

"What a cutie pie she is! Look at that head full of curls. She is adorable."

"Thanks. I know most parents think their kid is smartest but she truly is quick as a whip. She can already do little things on the computer." He stopped talking and began to laugh at the noises. Grace joined him.

"This would be a crack up situation on its own but if you knew Sofia the way I did, you'd really find it even more hilarious. This is so unlike her. I'm going to tease her about this until we're little old ladies."

Lorenzo said nothing. He was taking in Grace's beauty. She was exquisite. Her bone structure, skin tone, long and lean body, the full mouth...He knew he wanted to see her again but although she was certainly friendly he didn't get the feeling she was very interested in him the way he was in her. At that moment he made up his mind that he would somehow win her over. He wouldn't force the romantic angle but the friendship one.

"I love your accent. Jamaican, right?" Lorenzo asked.

"Yes. My family moved here to Georgia when I was just to begin high school. That was a heck of a transition. Entering high school was traumatic enough, it didn't help that I was also moving to a place where I knew no one. And though you may like my accent it made me stand out even more. But soon after that Sofia and I met and she helped me out a lot by taking me under her wing. She was very popular and that helped a lot as far as other kids accepting me. What about you? Where are you from?"

He tilted his head as if he were listening to something. "I guess they're done."

Grace let out a giggle. "I noticed that, too."

"Anyway, I was born in the Dominican Republic in Santo Domingo. When I was around my daughter's age my family moved to Puerto Rico. Soon after that we ended up in Florida. My parents are still down there in Clearwater. I moved here a few years ago to be with my daughter's mother. But that didn't work out and I ended up staying because it would be easier to share custody of Skye."

"I respect that so much." She smiled at seeing him blush. She liked his personality a lot.

At that moment, Sofia and Javier entered the room holding hands. They both were flushed and Sofia's blouse was buttoned wrong. The looks on the faces of Grace and Lorenzo let them know they were well aware of what they'd been doing.

"Is dinner ready?" teased Lorenzo. "Oh that's right we're ordering in. What was it again you two had to do in the kitchen?"

They all broke into laughter.

"Let me get the phonebook," said Javier.

"So what did you think about Lorenzo?" Sofia asked as she walked Grace to her car.

"He seems nice."

"Uh-oh. That doesn't sound like any clicking went on."

"I think he'll be a nice guy to hang out with. I'm just not attracted to him in that way."

"I thought you said you weren't *fenky-fenky*."

"I'm not but I still want to have that magnetic thing, like..."

"Like with Tyler?"

"Here we go." Grace got into her car, started the engine and rolled down the window. "I did have a great time though. I know you had an even better one, Miss Fassy."

"I don't know what you're talking about."

"Play innocent then. Kiss, kiss." She turned her cheek to Sofia who gave her a peck. "I'll see you tomorrow."

"Okay. Drive carefully."

Chapter 59

Much to Sofia and Lourdes's displeasure, Isabella and Olivia became inseparable. Under her mother's couture tutelage, Isabella's former normal attire of casual clothes and plain business suits became a thing of the past. Her wardrobe now touted designer names such as Marc Jacobs, Donna Karan, Dolce & Gabbana, and others. After her mother gave her some lessons, she was able to bear the strain of walking in high-heeled footwear by Christian Louboutin and Prada. Before, she rarely wore more than lip color and mascara, now she never left the house without being in full makeup.

On one hand, Sofia was pleased her sister was giving her appearance a much-needed boost. It was something she'd subtly hinted at for years. But on the other hand, this new Isabella was somewhat like a Stepford Daughter. It was as if she was turning into whatever she felt her mother wanted her to be. Sofia was confused as to why this type of behavior didn't take place during Isabella's teen years. It was odd that she would succumb to this "changing to please" as a grown woman.

Lourdes was unhappy because Isabella was monopolizing all of their mother's time. Even though Lourdes knew her mother's sudden expressions of maternal love were feigned and her mother was only buttering the bread for when Isabella received her inheritance it still annoyed her.

And she was none too happy with Isabella's makeover. One thing she could always lord over Isabella was that she was more stylish and put together. Now, thanks to their mother, she was competition in that arena. Though Lourdes hated admitting it, the right makeup, hairstyle and clothing brought out a beauty in Isabella that had been hidden.

Sofia was pretty but Lourdes felt she had an advantage over Sofia because of her size. However, Isabella was slender too and now with a new image going on, Lourdes didn't like it one bit. And to top it off she had a boyfriend whose family had the wealth she'd been seeking.

Something that caught Lourdes attention was how Isabella never mentioned Jeremy unless asked. From the beginning, she sensed Jeremy and Isabella's relationship wasn't all it appeared to be. It seemed so staged. She had felt the same way when Isabella introduced them to Ethan. She knew something was amiss and by happenstance she found out exactly what it was.

Olivia was going in for her plastic surgery the following Monday. She and Isabella went out to buy a few things for her stay at the after care facility. She had put off her surgery until the doctor she preferred was back in town from vacation. He was one of the top plastic surgeons in the country whose work had been featured on a popular makeover television show.

Lourdes stayed behind as usual and decided to go online to do what she and her mother called "research" where they looked up as much information as possible on potential rich mates. Her laptop was having trouble and the screen kept freezing up. Finally, after rebooting a couple of times, she gave up. As she walked through the dining room, she noticed Isabella had left her laptop bag on one of the chairs. Lourdes took the laptop out, propped it on the table and turned it on. She couldn't help but look at Isabella's files on her desktop.

"Let's see here. Meeting notes, Landlord Percentages, Home Owner Association, blah, blah, blah. Wait. Zahira? Isn't that the Iraqi, Lebanese, Pekinese girl from the spa? Let's see what that's all about." She clicked on the document's icon and opened it.

Lourdes eyes widened as she read the letter.

Dear Zahira,

This letter can in no way express how much I'm missing you right now. As hard as I try to keep myself occupied with other things, I can't get you out of my mind or heart. I miss you. I miss your voice, your touch, your scent, your taste…You probably think I don't give a damn about you when nothing could be further from the truth. All I want is for us to be together again. I want you to put my ring back on your finger and never, ever take it off again. I'm still wearing yours and I refuse to remove it because it symbolizes our love and commitment to one another.

Lourdes leaned back in the chair and folded her arms, chuckling to herself. *I'll be darned. My sister loves the ladies. I always knew there was something off about her and now I know what. The reason her boyfriends always seemed fake was because they were! I can't wait to tell Mother this. No, on second thought, I'll save this nugget of info for just the right time. This ammo is too good to fire off at any time other than the perfect time. The little lezzie has been hiding her true proclivities all this time. Oh my God!*

Lourdes sat up straight again. A smile lit up her face.

I don't have to tell Mother. But I can hold it over Isabella's head! Obviously our mother is the last person she wants to know about this. I can work this in my favor. Lourdes you're a fucking genius!

She found a wireless connection and clicked on the Internet icon. She went to her Gmail account, attached a copy of the letter and emailed it to herself. Just as she was about to turn off the computer, she got an idea. She opened up Outlook and went to addresses. She scrolled until she saw the name she was looking for and got up to get a pen and some paper to write down the contact information. She then decided to log back onto the Internet to make sure she received the email. Once she saw that she had she turned off the laptop and slipped it back into the bag.

"Oh, I think I'll get my list together of all the things I want my dear sister to buy me in exchange for my silence. Mother isn't going to be the only one enjoying pulling at her purse strings."

Chapter 60

Lourdes was lounging on the couch flipping through an issue of Vogue magazine when she heard her mother and sister enter the house. They came through the door laughing and carrying nearly a dozen bags between them.

"Hello, sweetie pie."

"Hi Mother. I see you two bought out the store again."

"They had some magnificent things that we couldn't pass up."

"Mom, I got a couple of my bags mixed with yours. Isabella took two of the bags and headed back outside.

"I'll be right back."

"All right, dear."

Olivia proceeded to take the rest of the bags to her room. A minute or two later Isabella came back into the house. She was about to go look for her mother when Lourdes stopped her.

"You two sure have done a lot of shopping."

"You were always so observant, Lourdes."

Lourdes noticed that with her new look, along the way Isabella somehow picked up some of Sofia's smart aleck ways.

"I need some things myself. Why just the other day I was at Lenox Mall and stopped in the Hermès store and quite a few things caught my eye. You could be a good sister and take me there and buy them for me couldn't you?"

"And why would I want to do that?"

"To keep my mouth shut to Mother about you being a lesbian." Lourdes batted her eyes in a look of innocence.

"What did you just say?"

"I think you heard me."

The sisters stared each other down.

"I don't know what kind of gossip you've picked up but I'm not a lesbian. I have a boyfriend."

"You mean the boyfriend you never mention unless someone brings him up? I know that he's just for show. Just like Ethan and just like the other boys before him."

"You don't know what you're talking about." Isabella started out of the living room.

"Dear Zahira. I miss your touch, taste, and scent," Lourdes recited in a melodramatic tone as she clasped her hands to together and looked upwards.

Isabella stopped dead in her tracks.

"I want you to put back on my ring and never, ever, ever take it off again." Lourdes glanced over at Isabella. "That's not verbatim but you get the gist."

Isabella looked to the dining room and her laptop bag in the chair. Right then she knew where and how Lourdes got her information.

"So, about that shopping trip, sis..."

Isabella turned around to Lourdes. "You're despicable, do you know that?"

"How about tomorrow? Let's say noonish."

"This is blackmail."

"On second thought let's make it around two. I'm going to hang out at East Andrews tonight and will probably close it down so I'll need to sleep in."

"It's your word against mine."

"You really don't give me enough credit. I didn't just peek at your letter; I emailed a copy to myself. All I have to do is show it to Mother. The file path will show where it came from and that'll be the end of that."

"You're such an evil bitch," Isabella responded in a tremulous whisper.

"Oh come on, Bella Boop. We'll buy shoes, clothes and other goodies. It'll be such fun. Oh, you know what? Come to think of it, I'm going to need something to tool around the city in since my cars are back in LA and over in France."

At that moment their mother walked through the dining room to the living room where they were.

"What are you two gabbing about?"

"We're talking about our plans tomorrow. Isabella is going to take me shopping for a change."

"Really?" asked Olivia with a raised eyebrow.

"I was just telling sis that we needed to spend some more time together and you know there's no better way to do that than in the stores."

Olivia was immediately suspicious. She knew her daughters could barely stand to be in the same room with one another much less spending time together.

"I was just telling Lourdes that I'm not sure if tomorrow is a good day or not. I have a lot to do."

"But then she said she's going to find a way anyhow. Isn't that sweet of her, Mother? I told her I wanted to go to the shop where she and Jeremy bought their friendship rings." She looked to Isabella. "Isn't that right?"

"Um, yeah."

"Two-thirty sound good?"

"Two-thirty is fine."

Lourdes smiled triumphantly while Olivia wondered what was really going on.

Chapter 61

Sofia stood in her mother's massive closet, amazed that one person could manage to accumulate so much clothing, shoes and accessories. Especially considering this wasn't even a location they visited frequently to have so much stored. Fortunately, her mother's outfits were color-coordinated which made it easier to find the one she wanted to leave the after-care facility in. She had forgotten to pack the outfit Isabella bought for her to come home in. Sofia found that silly since she was leaving to go straight home and not stopping by the Oscars. *And just how did I get stuck with this task anyway?* Sofia gathered the shoes, purse, and hat. As she was turning to leave out of the closet something caught her eye. The box. It was the little black velvet box she remembered seeing her mother store high in the closet on a couple of occasions.

Once, curiosity got the best of her, she got a chair and wrangled the box from behind other boxes. Much to her dismay it was locked. There was always such an air of mystery to the box and, as a child, she often fantasized about what secrets it held—everything from pirate's treasure to something magical like a golden key that unlocked a fairy tale kingdom. The last time she saw the box was during a visit to the California home when she was twelve. Her mother found her holding it and snatched it from her hand, screaming at her to never touch it again.

Sofia went to put the items on the bed then went back to retrieve the box from the shelf. She carried it to the vanity table where she sat down and pondered a few moments whether or not she should do what she was thinking. Her curiosity got the better of her and she took a bobby pin from her hair.

She manipulated the lock for ten frustrating minutes before the latch popped open. She lifted the lid and took out the contents; high school awards for excellence in various classes, tarnished mood ring, a faded autographed photo of Leif Garrett, a birth certificate, and an old Polaroid of three people. Upon closer inspection, Sofia recognized the young girl in the middle to be her mother. This was the first picture she'd ever seen of her as a young girl. On one side of her was an older man who looked to be Hispanic or Native American, and on the other side, what appeared to be a very light-complexioned black woman. At the bottom of the card were their names, Inès, Oliva, and Alphonso. Sofia thought whoever wrote her mother's name had made a slight misspelling. Then she went back to look at the certificates again. When she saw the name on the first one she furiously shuffled through the rest. They all said the same thing.

"Oliva Magdalena Delgado?!"

She stuffed the contents back in the box and fled the house with it, forgetting about the outfit she'd come to get for her mother.

Blinding Mirror

Chapter 62

Isabella sat listening to her sister as she looked through the papers from the box. Sofia was pacing back and forth, agitated.

"Her name isn't Olivia Machado! It's Oliva Magdalena Delgado! She wasn't born in Los Angeles, but Fresno. She's actually three years younger than what she says she is. Lord knows the reason she upped her age. I know that must've killed her as the years wore on considering how vain she is." She stopped pacing for a moment. "Did you look at the birth certificate yet?"

Isabella shuffled through the papers until she found it. After a minute she looked up at her sister.

"That's right." Sofia nodded and began to pace again. "Her parents are listed as Negro and White. I believe our grandfather was probably Mexican. I think that's just how they classified Mexicans back then. I can't believe this! She's never had anything good to say about Mexicans or Blacks and it looks like she's mixed with both. Self-hating shrew!"

"All this time Mother has lied to us about who she is?"

"No, Isabella. All this time she's lied about who she is as well as us!" Sofia finally stopped pacing and took a place next to her sister. "I feel like I just found out I was adopted or something. The other half of who I thought I was is not real. We're not part Portuguese."

"I don't even know what to say."

"Remember how when we visited her she used to only let us play outside for short periods of time and we figured out later it was so we wouldn't get dark?"

"Um-hmm."

"I guess she didn't like it because it was a reminder of our real ethnicity. One time we got so tanned she was furious and said we looked like little niggers. I'll never forget that and Father really laid it into her when I told him about it. We might have grandparents and other relatives we know nothing about. It's not likely they died in that plane crash like mother said they did."

"She wouldn't lie about them being dead, would she?"

"I wouldn't put anything past her. Let's get online and see if we can find out about our family and then we're booking a flight."

"Booking a flight? Where to?"

"To Fresno, of course."

Shelley Halima

Chapter 63

Lourdes smoothed out her trench coat before stepping off the elevator to Jeremy's penthouse apartment. He was standing in the hallway in front of his door. Lourdes put on a seductive smile as she slinked toward him. She kissed him on the cheek.

"I was surprised it was you waiting to be let in. How did you know where I lived? From Isabella?"

"Oh, I have my ways. Are you going to let me in or are we just going to talk out here?"

"I'm sorry. Of course, come in." Jeremy stepped aside so Lourdes could enter.

Lourdes sauntered in and was duly impressed with just the foyer alone and its marble flooring and painted mural. Jeremy walked ahead of her and waved her into the living area. The living room had floor to ceiling windows that offered a breathtaking view of the city skyline. Lourdes took a seat on the couch. As she did so, she pulled aside the bottom flap of her coat and crossed her legs, giving him a generous look at her slender gams. A slight smile touched her lips as she noticed her legs had caught his attention.

"Can I get you anything, something to drink perhaps? I was about to make myself a martini."

"A martini sounds good to me."

Jeremy walked over to the bar across the room and retrieved an ice bucket.

"I'll be right back."

"And I'll be right here."

Lourdes glanced around the room and did a mental tally of the cost of the artwork gracing the walls. *I've really struck pay dirt this time. Not that I had any doubt seeing who his family is and all. I think I sized him up pretty well at dinner and I know the direct approach as opposed to the coy, hard-to-get one is better. And he's not bad looking to boot.*

Jeremy reentered the room and went back over to the bar and proceeded to make the martinis. He brought them over to the couch and sat next to Lourdes. She took the drink he handed to her and sipped.

"Mmm, it's delicious," she said, not taking her eyes off him.

"So, did Isabella tell you where I lived?"

"We already covered that. I told you I have my ways."

"Are you sure she won't mind you coming over here?"

"Who cares if she does?"

"We are seeing each other."

"The jig is up on that, sweetie. I know you're just a convenient cover for my sister so that our mother doesn't suspect anything about her lifestyle."

"She told you?" he asked, flabbergasted.

"No, but I found out. I'm not going to tell our mother either. I'll let Isabella do that in her own time. Isabella and I don't really get along but I don't care about her being gay. I just want her to be happy."

I can see from the look on his face that I've scored some points for that little statement. Actually, I can't understand what thrill a woman gets from another woman. Isabella needs to spend some of that money on a good psychiatrist if you ask me.

"That's good to know. I've told Isabella over and over that she should just tell your mother but she won't. I don't know how I let her talk me into pretending to be her boyfriend. Your sister is quite persuasive."

Yeah, yeah, yada, yada. Let's get off this conversation train going nowhere.

"So, now that I know you're not dating my sister, are you interested in dating me, perhaps?" she asked flirtatiously.

"Y-you? See I'm kind of with someone…"

"You aren't married are you?"

"Well, no."

Not that I would let a little thing like marriage stop me.

"As soon as you came to the table that night, I was instantly drawn to you. But when I thought you and my sister were an item I figured there was no way I could get to know you in the way I wanted. But now that I know the real story…"

Lourdes leaned forward to place the drink on the table. She moved closer to Jeremy on the couch and slid an arm around his shoulders. With her other hand she took his drink from his hand and placed it on the table too. She caressed the side of his face.

"You are such a sexy man, you know that?"

Before he could reply she proceeded to give him a passionate kiss. She broke the kiss and stood up, leaving him panting.

"I'm surprised you didn't ask me why I'm wearing a trench coat this time of year. Let me show you."

Lourdes untied the belt and loosened the buttons. Slowly, she took off the coat and let it fall to her feet. She stood with her hands on her hips wearing only a thong. She then moved to straddle him. They began kissing wildly once more and Lourdes reached down and rubbed his now hardened penis through his slacks. The sound of their kissing and heavy breathing was broken by front door closing. Jeremy quickly moved his mouth from hers.

"It's Kelly!" He pushed Lourdes to the side. "Hurry and put on your coat!" He whispered sharply.

Lourdes took her time in reaching for her coat. *I think it's time that Kelly meets the future woman of the house.*

"Lourdes, please hurry! Please!"

She stood and stuck an arm in the coat when she looked up to see Kelly walk into the room. She was so disconcerted she almost dropped her coat.

Kelly was not a woman but a 6-foot tall, muscular man with an Army-type buzz cut.

"What the hell is going on here?!" Kelly bellowed.

"Kelly, this isn't what you think."

"I'm standing here looking at an almost naked woman in our living room and you're telling me it's not what I think?!"

"Baby, she just came over unannounced. I didn't know she would try and seduce me!"

Baby? Oh my God, what have I walked into? Jesus!

"Look, I was just leaving," said Lourdes, finally rushing to finish putting on her coat. She stomped past Kelly who was glowering at her. As she walked to the door she could hear Kelly's booming voice.

"I'm sick and tired of your cheating, Jeremy! Every time I turn around I find out about you with some man or woman!"

Lourdes slammed the door and went to the elevator.

Chapter 64

Lourdes climbed into the brand new midnight-black Jaguar Isabella leased for her. She and Isabella argued vehemently over the vehicle Lourdes truly wanted—an Audi Vanquish like the one she had back at her and her mother's home in California. Unfortunately Isabella said it was far too much and made her settle on the Jaguar. When she gave in about which vehicle she would take her and Isabella then argued over Isabella's insistence the car be leased. Lourdes wanted the car bought outright for her but again Isabella wouldn't budge. She wanted Isabella to hold off on telling their mother about her being gay for as long as possible because once she did, that would be the end of the blackmail gifts.

She hoped Jeremy would remain quiet and not reveal what happened tonight to Isabella. Her mother was counting on her to land the big fish but so far it had eluded her. She had managed to receive cars, money, jewelry and clothes from men but they were from boyfriends and occasional lovers. She and her mother wanted to land super wealthy husbands who would keep them in a continuously fabulous lifestyle.

She was glad her mother didn't give her hell for the Christophe fiasco that was waiting to happen. Perhaps her mind was focused on the upcoming birthday of the twins. Her mother had been really riding her about being more careful in choosing prospects, especially after she didn't receive nearly what she thought she would after Günter's death. It was so much pressure. All she wanted was to bring home the one and make her mother proud.

If I'd let her in on my intentions to snag Jeremy and tell her about tonight she would insist that I still pursue him and I'm so not interested in doing that at all. I don't want to be bothered with any queers. When I do get the brass ring, it's going to be on my terms and not hers. Never again will it be on her terms.

Chapter 65

As Isabella and Sofia drove in the rental car looking for the address of Inès and Alphonso Delgado, they both noticed the quality of the homes go from relatively nice and well-kept to poor condition and neglected. When they were in Atlanta, Sofia called the number listed in an online directory. A woman answered and Sofia asked if it was the Delgado residence. The woman said it was and before she could ask who was calling Sofia hung up the phone. Assured the information online was current; they took the first flight out the next morning. Isabella took another look at the map they printed from the computer. She leaned forward and squinted to see the street name ahead.

"Turn right at this next light."

Sofia turned down the street and slowed her speed. There were numerous children playing about and some were haphazardly darting into the street with their bikes and scooters. A group of teen-aged boys who were all gathered on the porch and lawn of one of the houses stopped their horseplay and chatter to eye the unknown vehicle entering their territory.

"Go down a little more. It's in the 6100 block."

Sofia drove down the street a little further.

"Stop! This is it."

Once parked, they stared at the dilapidated home. It was a small one-story bungalow with a wood exterior. The yellow paint and brown trim had almost completely faded away. The foot high grass and weeds looked to be in a fight for their place on the lawn. The shrubbery was just as unkempt with branches jutting out in various uneven directions.

Isabella turned to her sister. "I can't even fathom our mother having lived there. Do you think the home is still occupied?"

"I told you someone answered the phone and the telephone number was listed with this address." Sofia glanced about the neighborhood before unbuckling her seatbelt and exiting the car. Isabella reluctantly followed suit. Suddenly, every story she'd ever read or heard pertaining to car-jackings or robberies ran through her head. She would've jumped a mile from her skin if someone said so much as "hello" at that moment.

They walked up on the porch that was a cracked concrete slab with two old lawn chairs on it. Where there should've been a doorbell was loose wiring hanging out. Sofia rapped on the metal portion of the screen door. After a minute she repeated the knock.

Isabella continued to look about nervously. "I guess no one is here." She turned to start back to the car. At that moment the door creaked open. A small woman with chin-length gray hair, wearing an ill-fitting blue jean dress peeked out warily through the small opening of the door.

"Yes? What do you want?" she asked with a strong voice that belied her fragile appearance.

"Uh, we're looking for Inès and Alphonso Delgado," Sofia replied.

"What for? Who are you?"

Sofia glanced at her sister who she could tell was torn between staying and finding out more about their grandparents and fleeing the dangerous looking neighborhood to go back to the hotel.

"We're their granddaughters."

The way the woman stared at them they may as well have said they were Martians. The woman opened the door all the way.

"Are you Oliva's children or David's?"

"David?" asked Sofia. "No, we're the children of Olivia, I mean Oliva," Sofia answered, still not used to the slight variation that was her mother's real name.

She unhooked the latch and let them inside. As soon as they walked in they were hit with a plethora of smells; rotten garbage, cigarette smoke and urine. They were guided to a nearby well-worn sofa.

"Are you Inès?" Sofia asked.

"Oh no, I'm an old friend of the family. My name is Maribel. What are your names?"

"I'm Sofia and this is Isabella."

"We all wondered what happened to Oliva." She took in how well dressed and groomed the girls were. If they were any indication, Oliva hadn't done badly for herself.

"Are our grandparents here?" Isabella finally spoke.

"Your grandfather is in the back room. He's bedridden and has been for a while. He's getting some sleep now. I come here and check in on him whenever the nurse isn't here. I've been doing that for different people in the neighborhood for years. I'm like Florence Nightingale around here." She paused as if she were waiting for praise of some sort. When none was forthcoming, she continued. "As for your grandmother, she's living in San Diego with her niece."

"San Diego?" asked Sofia.

"She left about fifteen years ago after I found out she and my husband had had an affair." Maribel responded tersely. She never hesitated to take her place in the victim spotlight—even if it meant sharing intimate details of her life with complete strangers.

"Like they say, the wife is always the last to know. His uncle needed him to help out with his cattle ranch out in Texas. I refused to leave here. The house I live in is the one I've lived in all my life. That's when I found out what had been going on under me and Alphonso's noses. I overheard Carlos asking her to go with him. I confronted them and that's when it all came out." Her face became hardened at the memory. "Alphonso kicked Inès out and she went to live with an aunt and later moved in with the niece." She heaved a burdened sigh. "It was bad enough for me but your poor grandfather...He's had to endure neither his wife nor daughter being around for him. After a year had passed following the confrontation, he got the number to where Inès was and asked her to come back but she refused. At least she calls once in a blue moon unlike that Oliva who left and never so much as glanced back. Do you know Oliva left the night he was rushed to the hospital with a heart attack?"

Both girls shook their heads.

"Oh yeah. Your grandmother went off in the ambulance that night and when we got back here that morning, a suitcase was gone and so was she." Her hands flew up. "Just up and left without a bit of concern for her father! She was vindictive. I'm sorry. I know that's your mother but I have to be honest. I can't sugarcoat the bitter truth. No one heard from her again. Inès had to take care of him—with help from me of course. Your grandfather recovered but last year fell ill again."

"When we first arrived you asked us if we were David's children," began Sofia. "Does our mother have a brother?"

"He's her half-brother. I should've known you were Oliva's children since you said you were the granddaughters of Inès as well as Alphonso. I doubt if Oliva even knew about him. What was his last name? I've gotten so bad at remembering names lately. Oh, it was Stevens. Your grandfather got a White woman pregnant over in San Benito a little after Oliva was born. A couple of years after Oliva left, the young man came around here looking for Alphonso. Seems he finally found out the man who'd raised him wasn't his biological father. Anyway, he and Alphonso had a big blow up and he never came back around after that. It's funny because Alphonso always whined about not having a son but then he ran that boy off in no time. I don't know what Alphonso said but whatever it was I bet he wish he could take it back because I hear that David is doing very well for himself back East. Why he even bought his mother a huge fancy home."

Sofia turned to her sister. "We have an uncle that even our mother doesn't know about."

"Do you have our grandmother's number?" inquired Isabella.

With a crimp in her lip Maribel got up and left the room. She came back with a number written on a torn off piece of paper and handed to Sofia.

"Thank you."

"Can you tell us more about our mother?" asked Isabella. "We're curious as to how she was when she was younger."

"Why don't you know? Is Oliva still alive?"

"Yes, she is. But for some reason she's kept her past from us and we want to know more about it."

Blinding Mirror

"That's strange. I hate to say it but no one really liked Oliva. She was very cold and standoffish. She would walk into the house, see a living room full of people and not say a word. She never had any friends. Well, actually she did have one special friend." She paused to think of whether or not she should tell the young women everything she knew. She quickly decided they had a right to know everything about their mother. Everything. "In the months before she left she became very, very close to a young woman who had recently moved here. I always wondered why Oliva never had any boyfriends and that, uh, relationship let me know why. They were practically inseparable. Oh, the way they carried on." She paused for a moment. "It became the talk of the neighborhood," she embellished.

Isabella and Sofia looked at one another as the realization of what Maribel was implying sank in. A self-satisfied smirk settled on Maribel's face as she saw reaction of the women.

Isabella looked back at Maribel.

"Are you trying to say there was something more than friendship going on between our mother and this woman?"

"I know it's shocking to hear but I saw it for myself."

"Saw it how?"

"I was on my way home one night and I passed the woman's house. What was her name? Penny? Peola? Pilar! That's it. Her name was Pilar. Anyway, the curtains in the living room were wide open and I saw them embracing and kissing. It was disgusting, really, seeing them carry on like that. It's just unnatural."

"I'm a lesbian," Isabella stated firmly. "Forgive me if I don't agree with your 'disgusting' and 'unnatural' assessment."

Both Sofia and Maribel were shocked. Sofia was surprised because Isabella was admitting to someone she'd just met what she'd yet to admit to her own mother.

"I-uh-didn't mean," stuttered Maribel.

"I know exactly what you meant," Isabella replied. "But please go on. You're sure our mother was involved with this woman?"

"Yes, I'm sure. I think your mother was just going through a phase because the next thing I knew Inès was telling me Oliva was pregnant by Pilar's brother. Who knows what was going on? It was all very kinky if you ask me—bouncing between the sister and the brother. Supposedly he was some big shot in New York. Her parents figured she ran away to be with him."

Isabella and Sofia again exchanged confused looks.

"Not too long after Oliva ran away, there was a big commotion at that Pilar's house with police cars and an ambulance. Seems some man broke into her house and attacked her. Sliced her up something awful. She survived but within the next day the movers packed up her stuff and we never saw her again. It was probably the same sicko that attacked me when I was going into my own home. So, which one of you is the one Oliva was pregnant with at that time?"

"Neither of us," answered Sofia. "That's our half-sister and she's back home."

It seemed like each answer they received opened the door to new questions. They'd been told that Lourdes' father died in an accident before their mother even knew she was pregnant. And that he was from California—not New York and had no siblings or relatives. The story had always sounded strange but they never questioned it.

"I know you said our grandfather is resting, but is it possible that Isabella and I see him for a minute or two?"

"I guess it shouldn't be any harm in that. Where are you girls from anyway? I hear a hint of a southern accent."

"Georgia," Isabella answered. "We were born here in California but moved to Georgia when we were kids."

"Is that where Oliva lives too?"

"No, she just visits. She lives between LA and France," responded Sofia.

France? Humph! I guess Oliva is doing quite well, thought Maribel. She walked ahead of them as they went toward the back of the house.

With every step, their nostrils were increasingly assaulted by the smell of urine. When they got to the bedroom Sofia and Isabella immediately spotted the source of the fetidness. Next to the bed was a portable commode chair. Either the waste bowl hadn't been emptied recently or it needed a good washing out.

Sofia wished her allergies would make a sudden appearance. A stuffed nose would be a welcome respite from the putrid odor. Sunlight poured into the room through a naked window. The other window was covered with a sheet, used as a makeshift curtain. Sofia knew her allergy wish would soon be granted when she saw all the dust dancing in the sunrays. She and Isabella walked to the bed and got their first look at their grandfather. Through the sheet covering him, they could see his body was quite thin. His hair was mostly gray and wispy. Despite the ravages of ill health and time, his face still showed signs of a once good-looking man. Maribel went over to him and tapped him on the shoulder.

"Alphonso, wake up. You have visitors."

He opened his eyes, looked at her, then around to the strangers standing nearby. The sisters moved closer to him and Maribel stepped aside.

"Hello. My name is Sofia and this is my sister Isabella."

"Hi," said Isabella.

"Who are you?" he asked in raspy voice.

"We are Oliva's daughters. We flew out here because we wanted to meet you." Sofia reached out to hold his hand.

"Oliva? She still alive?"

"Yes, sir. You also have another granddaughter named Lourdes. She's back in Georgia."

"I always wondered what happened to Oliva. She's got three kids, huh? Where is she?"

"She's resting in a post-surgery facility."

"What's wrong with her?"

"She just had, uh, a light procedure done. It's nothing serious."

"Is she coming here?"

"I'm sorry but I don't think so."

"That's too bad. Can you give her a message for me?"

"Sure, what is it?"

He tugged at her hand to pull her a little closer. Sofia then felt warm, tobacco-scented spit hit her face. She jerked back, stumbling into her sister. She hurriedly wiped away the saliva with the back of her hand.

"As far as I'm concerned I don't have a daughter!" He paused to let out a cough rattled by phlegm. "I don't want to have nothing to do with Oliva or her bastards!"

Sofia stood frozen. She didn't know what startled her more, that her newly found grandfather spat in her face or seeing the rancor now emanating from him.

Isabella tugged at her sister's arm. "Let's get out of here."

They both quickly left the room with Maribel close on their heels.

"You'll have to forgive Alphonso. He gets crankier every day."

Sofia turned to her. "He's a hell of lot more than just cranky! I have never had anyone do that to me before! We came here with the best of intentions. We just wanted to know more about our family. After that," she pointed toward the bedroom, "I don't even care anymore. I'm starting to see why my mother left here and never looked back. After two minutes with that man I'm about to do the same thing!"

She and Isabella hurried out of the house and back to the car. They ignored Maribel when she called for them to come back. Disappointed, Maribel watched the car take off down the street. They left before she had the chance to ask for a little cash for helping out their grandfather.

Chapter 66

"Where have you two been?" demanded Olivia as Sofia and Isabella entered her room. "Neither of you have answered your phones. I've been trying for the last day to reach you. You know Lourdes is off gallivanting with God knows who. Sofia, where is the outfit I asked you to get for me?"

She looked on as her daughters took nearby seats and sat stone-faced.

"What is it? You look like you just left a funeral."

"You want to know where we've been?" asked Sofia.

"I just asked that didn't I?"

"We were in California."

"What were you doing in California?"

"Trying to find out more about a woman named Oliva Magdalena Delgado."

Olivia stiffened her body in an effort to quell the sudden involuntary trembles and she felt like fainting.

"What did you just say?" Her voice was shaking from emotion.

"You heard me, Mother. You have lied to us about everything our whole lives. I'm sitting here looking at you and it's like you're a stranger. You even lied to us about your name for God's sake! Your parents didn't perish in a plane crash. They're both alive. Your father is bedridden. Your mother is living in San Diego. Now do you want to fill in the blanks for us or do we have to continue to do our own investigating?"

"How did you find out?" Though the initial shock of her past making a reappearance hadn't worn off, her mind went into a whirlwind on how to get out of her predicament as unscathed as possible.

"That doesn't matter. Start talking."

"What do you want to know?"

"Everything, Mother! Everything! Why did you lie about your parents being dead?!"

"Because as far as I'm concerned they are dead! I'll finally tell you two what you want to know but I'm not going to apologize for what I've done!" After a few moments of silence, Olivia continued. "What was it like meeting my parents?"

"We only met your father and let's just say," began Sofia. "I got a little hint of what you may have put up with."

"What did he do?"

"He told me to come closer so he could give me a message to pass on to you. Then he spit in my face."

Olivia smirked and shook her head.

"I see time hasn't mellowed him. Not too long before I left home we had a falling out and he spat in my face. That's one of the worst things you can do to a person."

Blinding Mirror

"Yeah," said Sofia. "That and lie to them about the truth of who they are."

"If you had my history you'd do everything in your power to change it too." She leaned back into the pillows. "My parents never wanted me. My father longed for a boy and my mother only wanted pets. She had things in reverse. She treated her dogs like children and her child like a dog. The whole time I spent in that house I was beaten on a regular basis. Three or four times a week was the norm." She looked at her daughters. "I know you both think I'm the worst mother in the world but I've never beat you—ever!" Olivia paused for a few moments. "Here are just a couple of examples of what I went through. My hair was once so long it came to my waist. I used to wear it up in a ponytail all the time. Then I started wearing in down. I looked better than those girls in the shampoo commercials. I guess it brought me too much attention from men because my mother attacked me with scissors and cut off all my hair. When she was done I was practically bald. Another instance, I worked my butt off in a sweat shop one summer to buy myself new clothes and she and my father took them and burned them in a trash can in the back yard."

"*You* worked in a sweat shop?" Sofia asked with skepticism. Her mother was the sort who would pay someone to come over to change a light bulb.

"Yes, I did. I wanted to have nice things and that was the only way I'd get them. My parents certainly wouldn't provide them, even if they could. I wanted to die when I saw my clothes that I worked so hard for be destroyed. But that's just the kind of people they are."

"Do you remember Maribel?" inquired Isabella.

Olivia pressed her lips together to a tight line. "I remember that trouble maker. Why?"

"She said the same night your father was rushed to the hospital, you ran away. He sounds like a terrible man and we certainly got a glimpse of that, but wasn't there a little part of you that still cared for him as your father and as a human being? He could've died for all you knew."

"The reason I ran away that night..." She closed her eyes and worked on bringing the tears. "God help me. He beat me horribly. He was upset because I didn't finish my chores. I was sick of getting beaten for the least little thing. When he was attacking me, something in me snapped, and I decided to fight back. I guess struggling with me put too much strain on his heart. He began clutching his chest and fell to the floor. I shouted for my mother who was asleep in her bedroom. She finally came in and called for the ambulance. When they went to the hospital, I gathered my few things and left. And I never looked back. Believe it or not but I did feel guilty that I'd helped bring on the attack. If I'd just done all my chores he wouldn't have gotten so riled up." The tears began to leak through her closed eyelids. She opened her eyes to fully release them. Through her blurred vision she was pleased to see the dismayed looks of her daughters.

Olivia leaned over and retrieved tissues from the box on the night table to dab her nose but not her eyes.

"Mom, I'm so sorry you went through that. No one should endure that kind of abuse."

"Thank you, sweetheart."

"But why would you lie about our heritage, though?" asked Isabella. "Were you ashamed of it?"

"I just wanted to become a new person and live a new life. I didn't want any connections to the past. There was nothing in my old life to be proud of."

"Who we are isn't anything to be ashamed about," Sofia retorted.

"It wasn't like that for me. There was no sense of pride about our racial identity. My mother never even associated with her family much once she got married and I think it was because they reminded her of who she was. I remember overhearing her tell a friend of hers how the kids used to call her Memìn. That was a monkey-looking cartoon character back in Mexico. From what I gathered, most of the Mexican kids in her neighborhood made her life miserable because she was Black and the Black kids made fun of her family's Mexican heritage and the fact they spoke Spanish. And my father never talked much about his background. Another thing is, I was harassed constantly at school by the white kids. Every single day I went to school I was called a spic."

"But, when we went to your old neighborhood it looked to be all minorities," said Isabella.

"Well, back then the neighborhood was mostly white—poor whites. Even though we all were in the same boat, they still looked down on me."

"What made you choose Portuguese?" Isabella asked.

"Lourdes's father was Portuguese and before your father he was the only person that was good to me. I guess I latched on to his identity."

"You guess?" Sofia was finding it hard to contain her annoyance. "I don't think you understand exactly what you've done. I know you and Lourdes couldn't care less but Isabella and I have always felt strongly about celebrating our heritages. Now we've found out we've been celebrating one that's not even ours! My God, I even learned to speak Portuguese because I thought it was a part of our ancestry."

"I'm sorry! I know this is terrible news for you and I wish I could say you came from a better bloodline—"

Sofia held up her hand. "Whoa! Let's get on the same page here. I'm not angry with you because of who we really are. I'm angry with you for not telling us the truth! Unlike you, I'm not the least bit ashamed!"

Blinding Mirror

Olivia struggled to maintain her composure and not say what she really wanted to her daughter. In an instant she thought of a new twist to put on the story.

"I'm sorry but being ashamed was a seed that was planted in me from the time I was a child. And it was further reinforced by your father."

"Our father?" Sofia and Isabella inquired in unison.

Olivia hung her head. "It's the real reason your father left me. He found out about me."

Sofia furiously shook her head and pointed at her mother.

"No, no. You had an affair. Right before Father died, I asked him why you two divorced and he finally told me because he thought I was mature enough to handle it."

"I never cheated on your father, Sofia. He was the only man I ever loved, not including Lourdes's father. Even after he turned on me, I never stopped loving him. Someone who used to live in the old neighborhood moved to LA and began working at Valente Construction a few years after we were married. I went to visit Gino at the office and this person recognized me and told your father who I was. After he confronted me, I admitted the truth. He had his lawyers draw up the divorce papers. Next thing I knew, he moved out here with you with two. He had more money and power. There was no way I could fight him."

"If he had such a problem with your ethnicity why did he keep us?"

"Because Isabella, you were still a part of him."

"I don't believe that," said Sofia. "He was very open-hearted and open-minded. Mrs. Hopkins said back in California he actually turned his back on a business deal because the client didn't want the architect, who was African-American, to work on the project. His firm had the most minorities of any non-minority run company in the state."

Olivia gave her daughter the most sincere look she could muster.

"I promise you, I never cheated on your father. He left me because he found out the truth about me. And obviously he had an issue with it or else he would have told you two about your true background long before he died. But he didn't do that, did he?"

Neither of the girls responded.

"It was much easier to make up some non-existent affair than to tell you or the world who I really was. It's funny because right before I was going to tell him, he found out. And that's the honest truth. My conscience was getting the best of me and I decided to confess. I was just looking for the right time. But before I could do it...after seeing his reaction, I've never wanted to come clean again. I felt if the man I was going to spend the rest of my life with could treat me like that then I would continue the charade."

Sofia didn't believe a word that was coming from her mother's mouth.

"Mom, I have to ask this," began Isabella. "Maribel told us about your relationship with a young woman who lived down the street from you. She made it sound as if you two were—well, you know."

"Lovers? Is that it? Maribel was the biggest liar on the block. She was forever on the hunt for some dirt. Somehow, she saw my friend and me hugging and ran to my parents, blowing everything out of proportion. I received the worst beating ever because of her lies. The lady in question was a few years older than me and was my only friend. And we were never anything more than that. After all these years, Maribel should stop spreading dirt like that, especially to my children."

"You must've thought a great deal of her since Lourdes's middle name is the same as hers," said Isabella.

"Yes, I did think a great deal of her. She was my best and only friend."

"What about Lourdes's father?" asked Sofia. "Maribel said you became pregnant by Pilar's brother but you've always said Lourdes's father was an orphan like you claimed to be and he didn't have any siblings."

"No, her father was not Pilar's brother. That's another lie Maribel is spreading. She didn't even know Lourdes's father Ric. I may have lied about my life but what I said about Lourdes's father is the God's honest truth. He was Portuguese, an orphan and was killed in a motorcycle accident. By the way, how did you find out about everything?"

"Your little box in your closet," Sofia answered. "It's the same one I remember seeing when I was kid. I had no idea such a little box could contain something so huge."

Olivia began crying again.

"What's wrong?" asked Isabella.

"All the terrible memories are rushing back. I need to be alone for a while, okay?"

Sofia and Isabella both stood up. Isabella went to her mother and planted a kiss on her cheek.

"And I guess you should know we found out you have a half-brother," said Sofia. "His name is David Stevens and you may actually want to have something to do with him since we hear he's pretty well off." Sofia walked out the door, not bothering to say good-bye.

Olivia listened for the sound of the elevator bell, letting her know they had left her floor. As soon as she heard it she began pounding the bed with fists in a blind fury. Her anger was at such a peak she all but forgot about any pain from her surgery.

That bitch, Sofia! How dare she ramble through my things like that? I should have put all that stuff away in a safety deposit box. Damn it, on second thought I should've just burned it! Why did I keep that stuff for so long? After all these years it all comes out. Damn you, Sofia! Damn you to hell!

Isabella stared blankly at the road ahead as Sofia drove. She was still reeling from the confrontation with their mother. She looked over at Sofia's whose face was frowned up as it always did when she was deep in thought. Sofia glanced over at her as they were stopped at a light.

"I cannot believe you."

"What?"

"Why did you kiss her? You treated her as if everything she did was okay."

"I know it's not okay. But I feel sorry for her."

"Feel sorry for her? Why would you feel sorry for her when she's the one whose lied to us?! Colossal lies at that! You act as if she only lied about Santa Claus."

"Just put yourself in her shoes for a minute. Imagine being made fun of and put down by other people for your racial background. And let's not forget about Dad. He didn't help the situation."

"Oh no," Sofia retorted. "I don't believe it not for one solitary minute. After all, he isn't here to defend himself now is he? All we have is her word and that's not exactly worth its weight in gold. This is so typical of her, to get caught up in her own bull yet somehow makes herself the victim."

"I do wish there was some truth to what Maribel said about our mother and that woman. It would give me the courage to tell her about me."

"As I've already said, I don't believe anything she says. Therefore it's still possible that there was some truth to that as well. In any case you should want to tell her about you no matter what. And if Lourdes knew what was good for her she'd better check into what our mother has told her."

Chapter 67

Sofia waited for a response from Mrs. Hopkins to the story she just told her. She retired a few years back and lived in a condo Gino left to her in his will. She kept in touch with Sofia and Isabella, speaking to and seeing them often.

"Sofia, I don't know what to say."

"Say something. Please. What are your thoughts? And you know you can be perfectly blunt with me. I can take it."

Mrs. Hopkins took another sip of tea. After a few moments she continued.

"I hate to say this, I really do. I don't want your relationship with your mother to be any more strained, but she's not being truthful, at least about everything. I don't know about her life growing up, but I do know she's lying about your father."

Sofia sighed in relief. She was glad it wasn't just her who didn't buy her mother's story.

"I have a question for you and I want you to be as truthful as possible."

"Sure, honey. What is it?"

"What do you honestly think of my mother?"

"I don't think she's a completely evil woman. But I do believe she was and still is, wrestling with some demons. I don't know if she's capable of really loving people."

"She has no trouble loving Lourdes."

"That's not really love. It may seem as though it is, but it isn't. She replaces true motherly love with buying Lourdes anything she wants and indulging her in her every whim, and in the end, that's going to be to her detriment." She put her hand over Sofia's. "I don't believe your father knew about your mother's background. He would not have turned his back on her because of that. He would've been upset that she wasn't honest but I assure you that's not why he divorced her. You would think after all these years she would take some responsibility for her actions instead of trying to sully the memory of Mr. Valente."

"Was the person my mother had the affair with Uncle Anton?"

Mrs. Winters was nonplused. She was not expecting to hear that question.

"Um, I-I—Sofia, I don't think--"

"From your reaction I take it I'm right. It's something that's been nagging at me for the longest. Father never told me who the man was but I always suspected it was someone that he would never be able to forgive Mother for sleeping with. And when I really thought about it, the divorce and my father dissolving his partnership with Uncle Anton happened around the same time. Father tried to explain their estrangement on fights over how the business was run but I thought it went deeper than that."

"It's really not my place to talk about that. Besides, it's all in the past."

"I guess that answers my question. God help me for saying this but I don't feel like she's even my mother. She just gave birth to me, like a surrogate. You and Mrs. Toussaint have both been more like mothers to me. I don't hate her but I don't trust her nor do I want her in my life. I just wish Isabella would finally wake up. She can't see the reality of who our mother is because it's overshadowed by the fantasy she has of her."

Mrs. Hopkins patted Sofia's hand.

"You can't talk her out of that. I know you want to protect her but it's like you and I say all the time, there are things she will have to find out on her own. And she will. Just be there for her when she does."

Shelley Halima

Chapter 68

Olivia picked up the phone and dialed Lourdes again.

"Yes, Mother?"

"It's about time you answered your phone!"

"Mother, I'm on the other line with Lizzie. She's giving me the scoop on a big soiree taking place soon up in the Hamptons."

"Tell her you'll call her back. I need to talk to you."

"What's going on? Why do you sound so serious?"

"I'll wait while you clear the line."

Lourdes clicked back over. "I'm back. Now tell me what's going on."

"Your sisters just left here. They went out to California to find out about my family. I'm just going to cut to the chase. My parents did not die years ago as I said. They're alive."

"What?! I thought you said they died in a plane crash?!"

"Well, I lied!" Olivia snapped. "Trust me, you'd wish they were really dead. They're poor, shabby, classless people who you'd be ashamed to even walk on the same side of the street with. I've kept that part of my life hidden to protect you from it all but that fat bitch sister of yours went through some of my old papers and found out everything."

Lourdes was taken aback not only by finding out about her grandparents but she had never heard her mother speak about Sofia with such acerbity.

"Those people made my life a living hell. They abused me physically, verbally, mentally and ever other way you can imagine. And that Sofia comes in here all in an uproar because of her so-called heritage being lied about."

"Wait. Heritage? What do you mean?"

Olivia inhaled sharply. "I'm not Portuguese, all right?"

"W-well what are you?"

Olivia didn't respond right away.

"Mother? What are you?"

"I'm Mestiza!"

"What the hell is that?"

"It means mixed."

"Mixed with what? Will you just tell me already?"

"Both of my parents are from Mexico."

"Mexico?!"

"Yes. My father's people are Spanish and Indian and my mother's people are…"

"Are what?"

"Black."

Blinding Mirror

Lourdes was so dumbfounded by what her mother said, she didn't notice the light had turned red and drove through the intersection to the sound of horns blaring and tires squealing to a halt.

"Oh my God! Oh my God! OH MY GOD, NO! I can deal with the Spanish, maybe even the Indian but Mexican? And BLACK?! I can't be part Black, I just can't!"

"Lourdes will you get a hold of yourself? How do you think this makes me feel?!"

Lourdes pulled into a parking lot and cut off the engine. She turned the rearview mirror toward her and began to inspect her face to see if she noticed any black features that were previously overlooked.

"What about my father? Please tell me he was really Portuguese."

"He was. I promise you that."

Lourdes heaved a loud sigh of relief. "Oh thank goodness! And he was white, right? Not one of those dark Portuguese?"

"Yes, he was white."

Lourdes turned the mirror back to its original position, satisfied that her features didn't show any signs of her newly discovered ancestry. "Why would you lie to me, Mother? I can see everyone else but we tell each other everything." For an instant Jeremy flashed across her mind. "Pretty much."

"I did it all for you, Lourdes. Everything I've ever done, from hiding my background to marrying Gino and the others has been for you. From the time you were no more than the size of a tennis ball in my belly, I promised I'd give you the life I never had. You wouldn't believe it if I told you of the abject poverty I grew up in. There was no way in hell I was going to subject you to that. So when your father died, I went to LA and made sure I landed a rich husband so that I could give you anything you wanted. Do you honestly think we would have the life we do if Gino and the others knew who I really was?"

"No, I guess not. What if our friends find out?!"

"They won't. Don't be silly."

"What about those twins? I'm sure they'll flap their gums."

"It doesn't matter. We don't socialize in the same circles, so none of the people in our set have to know. You do understand why I did this, don't you darling?"

"Yes, I do. And to hell with those two if they don't. If you hadn't done what you did, Jesus, we'd probably be on welfare or something."

Olivia's heart swelled with love for her daughter. She knew she could always count on Lourdes.

"That's my precious. I think Isabella understands but you know the other one doesn't. Do you want to know what they found out when they went out to, Fresno?"

"Fresno?"

"Yes, that's where I was born."

"Fresno, Black, Mexican, poor—anything associated with that I don't want to know. Trust me, Mother. You won't hear anymore about this from me. Ignorance truly is bliss because the less I know about the past, the better."

"I'm glad to hear that. I'm going to work on getting a nice chunk of money from Isabella and after that we are out of here and we'll head out to Chicago. And, if they want to play Roots, and continue to research their family tree, it's on them but we're not having any part of it."

"Lizzie was telling me about this huge bash. She said the place would be swimming with tycoons. I say we go up there for a while until the party, then to Chicago. If things go well…"

"Between you and me we'll both have the money of tycoons at our disposal in no time," said Olivia.

Lourdes giggled. "Oh, I love the sound of that."

Chapter 69

Grace sat in silence as she took in what Sofia had just told her. "Sofia," Grace began. She paused and searched for the right words. "I know your mother is, well, is something else. But I don't understand why she would tell this humungous lie and keep it going for all this time."

"Neither do I."

"What do your sisters think?"

"Isabella is making excuses for our mother as usual. I called Lourdes and as soon as I brought up the subject she said she had to go and hung up. The thing with my mother is she has a habit of telling a little bit of the truth and throwing in a bunch of lies so you have to sift through the BS to get to what's real."

"Still, that's no reason for her to pull a Sarah Jane about her racial background."

A tiny smile touched Sofia's lips at the reference to the character from the movie Imitation of Life.

"You're so right," replied Sofia. "She could've separated herself from her parents without doing that. But what angers me more than anything was her trying to dirty my father's name by saying he knew and that's why he divorced her. He's dead and gone and you'd think she'd have the decency to not pull him into her deceit, but no. She's too low to be above that. If I'd gone to Portugal to research our so-called family like I've been meaning to do for the past few years I'm sure I would've found out sooner."

"What about your grandmother? Are you planning on getting in contact with her?"

"Soon. Just not right now. After the encounter with my wonderful sweet grandfather I'm going to need to recover a bit before I try and get in touch with her. In the meantime I'll try and find out as much as I can about the culture—my culture. I like to think that I'm very worldly and knowledgeable but I didn't even know there were Black people in Mexico."

Grace waved her hand. "Girl, we're practically everywhere. I don't know much about Mexico either but I do know there's a Caribbean community there."

"I was looking up different things last night. The only Mexican holiday I knew about was Cinco de Mayo. I found out about Posada, La Noche Buena, El Dia de Los Reyes, Dia de Los Muertos, and our Independence Day is September sixteenth. There is such rich history; I don't know why my mother thought it was something to shy away from."

Grace reached out and stroked her arm. "Let's face it, in this country Blacks and Mexicans are two of the most stigmatized groups. Unfortunately, many buy into that and they lose sight of the beauty and strength of their cultures and instead of embracing them they run away screaming and turn their backs on it. As for your mother, she's just a snobby witch—" Grace stopped herself.

"Hey, don't hold back on my account. What is that you always say? Tell the truth and shame the devil?"

"Yes, but that's still your mother. So out of respect for that I'll keep my mouth closed."

"I'm so angry with her." Sofia blinked back tears. "And I'm the only one. Isabella and Lourdes seem to think nothing of it."

"Listen. What is it I tell you? *Wha' noh poison, fatten.* You'll come out an even stronger and better woman through all of this. The most important thing is you're no longer living in the shadow of untruth. You know who you are now."

Sofia brushed away a tear as she nodded in agreement.

"And as for your sisters who continue to turn a blind eye and deaf ear to your mother—they'll find out. Trust me." She reached over and gave Sofia a big hug. "I'm going to get back over to the spa, okay? You just come in when you're ready."

"Thanks for everything, Grace. I'll walk you to the door."

Sofia opened the door just as Lourdes was about to ring the bell.

"What are you doing here?" inquired Sofia.

"I'm looking for Isabella. She was supposed to have met me over two hours ago! I called her cell phone and her office phone and kept getting her voice mail!"

"Where was she supposed to meet you?"

"Jimmy Choo at Phipps."

Sofia let out a sigh and rolled her eyes. "She's not here. As a matter a fact she said she had an important meeting in Doraville and I'm sure that's where she is so I don't why she told you she'd meet you."

Lourdes folded her arms like a petulant child.

"Girlfriend!" exclaimed Grace. "You're not going to say hi to me?"

Lourdes cut her eyes to Grace. "Hi," she replied in a dry tone.

"I heard the news! So, you're a sista, at least in part anyway. Isn't that something?"

Lourdes looked at her, aghast.

"Honey, you should come to the Juneteenth celebration with me on Friday."

"Juneteenth?"

"Yes! That's when we celebrate the day our people were released from slavery in America. My people were from Jamaica and yours from Mexico but we all started in the same place—Africa!"

Horrified, Lourdes quickly turned on her heels and rushed back to the car. Grace and Sofia burst into laughter.

Blinding Mirror

Chapter 70

"Mother, I'm back!" shouted Lourdes. She placed the bag on the table and dishes out from the cabinet.

"I'm famished," Olivia announced as she slowly entered the kitchen still a bit stiff from surgery. Her new breasts were healing nicely but the soreness hadn't completely left. She was about to attempt to open the kitchen window but thought better of it.

"Lourdes, can you open the window for me? I want some fresh air in here."

Lourdes went over and opened the window. They both sat down at the table.

"Mother, I got prosciutto wrapped melon, eggplant parmigiana, quiche Florentine, fruit and cheese. This should hold us over until the chef can come in later and whip something up."

"It all sounds delicious. I do believe I could eat it all."

"Careful, one Sofia is enough."

"Don't mention that sow's name."

"No problem there."

As Lourdes placed the food on her mother's plate, she paused when she noticed her mother staring at her.

"What's the matter?"

"Nothing," Olivia replied softly. "You just remind me so much of…of your father sometimes." She reached out and stroked Lourdes's locks.

"You really loved him, didn't you?"

"Yes, I did. I've never loved anyone else like I did him. One came close but still…"

"Tell me some things about him. What was he like? What were his interests? I know you told me before but I never tire of hearing of him."

"Hmm, let's see. He was the type of man that when he walked into the room or down the street, heads turned. He just had that spark that drew people to him. Oh, and he loved the arts—music, films, paintings. He was crazy about *fado* music. That's a form of music popular in Portugal. He loved that singer Amàlia Rodrigues. Of course you know you were named after his favorite artist Lourdes Castro. And he was so stylish! He looked and dressed like a movie star. You know how you always tease me for wearing Chanel No. 5?"

"Yes, I remember you wearing that even as a kid. No matter how many perfumes you get as a gift, you never give up that one."

"It's because it was his favorite fragrance and he loved for me wear it."

"Mother, you should see your face as you're talking about him."

"He was quite a man. He's the one who showed me that I could get out of the circumstances I was living in and have a much better life. I did and haven't looked back since. I don't have as much money as I want but I'm in no way hurting financially so I think I've done pretty well for myself and for you."

"And you will be doing even better after the twins' birthday that's coming up next week," Lourdes added.

"Yes indeed. Do you know I've convinced Isabella to give me five million dollars?"

Lourdes choked on a bite of eggplant parmigiana.

"Are you serious?!"

"Oh yes. I appealed to the businesswoman in her. I told her I was interested in starting my own upscale clothing line. I even had my friend Charles draw up a business plan to show her. Of course, after I've stalled enough without this clothing line coming into fruition, I'll say something like a big bad accountant ran off with the money to the Cayman Islands or something."

"So you may not even have to go to Chicago to stake out that old coot."

"Says who? I've had access to millions in my lifetime but now I'm aiming even higher."

Lourdes's eyes widened with excitement. "Billions!"

"Exactly!"

"I get chills just thinking about it. If things go as I hope we'll get up in that billion-dollar range. Please hurry and get that money from Isabella so we can get out of here," Lourdes pleaded.

"I don't want to up and leave right after she releases the money to me. That would be too obvious. I'll stick around for a few days. But after that, it's wide open. Spending some time in the Hamptons sounds like just what I need before heading to Chicago."

"I know it's been a chore for you to have to play the loving mother to her."

"It really has been draining," Olivia said with a sigh.

Lourdes and Olivia both jumped at a nearby sound. Startled, they looked up to see Isabella standing near the doorway of the kitchen. She'd tossed a Tiffany box onto the counter. Tears streaming down her face let Olivia know her daughter heard what had just transpired between her and Lourdes.

"Sofia and everyone were right about you!" Isabella screamed; her voice nearly choked with emotion. "They tried to tell me but I refused to listen! A drain, Mom?! Spending time with me and getting to know me was a drain?!"

"Isabella, I think you may have misunderstood what I meant by that."

"I didn't misunderstand anything! Did I misunderstand your saying you made up the whole business venture so you could get five million dollars out of me?"

Olivia was silent.

"Yes, I heard that too. I heard everything! As usual you and Lourdes were so caught up with each other that you didn't even know I was here. You won't ever again have to worry about me being a drain on you! I don't care if I never see either of you ever again!" She looked over at the Tiffany box she had thrown on the counter.

"You can keep that. It'll be the last thing you ever get from me."

Isabella stood there for a moment, wanting to say so much more but decided not to. She turned and walked out. Lourdes jumped from the table to follow her.

"Lourdes! What are you going to do?"

"I'll be right back."

As Isabella reached the front door Lourdes caught up to her.

"Isabella, wait!"

Isabella whipped around to her sister.

"What do you want?"

"Look, you're not going to take the Jag back are you?"

Isabella looked at her in disbelief. Her sister had to truly be one of the most selfish and heartless people she knew next to their mother. As far as she was concerned they deserved each other.

"Lourdes, just, just—fuck off!"

Olivia stared blankly into her plate. To her utter surprise she felt a tear make its way down her cheek. She quickly wiped it away when Lourdes came back into the room.

"I can't believe it, Mother. She actually cursed at me!"

"Of course. She was upset."

"You kept asking me why Isabella was buying me things all of a sudden. I think I might as well tell you now. She's a big lez. That's right, she's gay. I found out when I went on her laptop and saw a letter she wrote to this girl that works at Sofia's spa. She didn't want you to know, so I made her pay to keep my mouth shut." She folded her arms and waited for a reaction from her mother. Olivia remained quiet.

"Mother, did you hear me?"

"Yes I heard you, Lourdes."

"Aren't you shocked?"

"Not really."

"Why not?!"

"I've suspected as much."

"How? She had boyfriends and everything!"

"A mother knows these things. It's not a big deal these days, not like it was when I was coming up. Times have changed."

"Who cares about how it was when you were coming up?! I know you're not saying it's okay! I for one find it just despicable and I don't see how you can be so accepting of such deviant behavior." She picked up her fork and stabbed a piece of eggplant.

Olivia had lost her appetite. In truth, she had rather enjoyed Isabella's company. Until this most recent trip she didn't know how interesting her daughter actually was. Once she opened up she was a great conversationalist and had a quick wit. She said spending time with Isabella was draining because she knew Lourdes was jealous of the time they were spending together and didn't have the heart to tell her otherwise. Her intention had been to get her hands on some of the money Gino had left, but she didn't mean to hurt her daughter in the process.

Chapter 71

Just as Zahira was about to pull into the driveway of her condo she noticed Isabella's car parked in front. The car was empty but as she got in the driveway she saw Isabella sitting on her front steps. As she got out of the car she told herself to be strong and not get taken in by Isabella again. She vowed they were over and she wouldn't allow herself to weaken. As she got closer to the porch she saw the results of the makeover she heard Isabella had undergone. Her hair was a lighter shade of brown with blonde streaks and her clothes were more stylish. But her eye makeup was smudged and her eyes looked red and swollen as if she'd been crying.

"What do you want?"

"I need to speak with you."

"We have nothing to say."

Zahira walked past her and up the steps to her door.

"Please!"

Zahira paused with her key at the door. Isabella's plea sounded so wounded and plaintive. She put the key to the door and opened it. As she entered she glanced over her shoulder.

"I'll give you a few minutes."

She hung her purse on the coat rack and went to the kitchen. Zahira opened the refrigerator and got out a bottle of pear cactus apple juice and then two glasses from the cabinet. She put them on the table and took a seat as Isabella pulled up a chair.

"Your new place looks great. It looks a lot better than when I first came with you to see it. The old owner had horrible taste."

"I'm sure you didn't come over to talk about my decorating abilities," Zahira said as she poured the juice into the glasses. "What's on your mind?"

"Us."

"Bella, there is no more 'us'."

Zahira looked at Isabella and in her eyes she could see all the pain she'd heard in her voice a few moments before. Isabella's eyes filled with tears that cascaded down her face. Her mouth was open slightly as if she were trying to find the will or words to speak. Zahira didn't try to prompt her; she just waited patiently for Isabella to give voice to what she was feeling.

"I'm so sorry," she finally said. "I was wrong. I couldn't have been more wrong!" She lowered her head and began to sob uncontrollably.

Zahira moved aside her glass and grabbed Isabella's hands. Her own eyes became blurry from tears. Despite everything she still loved Isabella and it hurt to see her in such distress. She reached and got a napkin from the holder and when Isabella raised her head again she wiped away her tears.

"All these years I've hoped for the chance to have a real relationship with my mother. I thought everyone else was to blame for that not happening; my father for restricting visits with her, Sofia for being the reason the visits were restricted in the first place, and Lourdes because I thought she just wanted Mom all to herself. Everyone tried to tell me how my mother was but I didn't listen. I refused to. All I ever wanted was for her to love me like she does Lourdes. Hell, to just love me period!"

Isabella paused to take a sip of juice before going on.

"I remember I used to have a friend named Emma. We used to play together almost every day until one day when I beat her up. We had a little argument over a toy or doll or something and I pushed her. She pushed me back and after that I ripped into her. Even back then as a child I knew that fight had little to do with the toy; I secretly hated her because she had what I didn't which was a loving mother. You've never seen a more jealous kid than I was when I saw Emma and her mother together. The way they held hands, sometimes dressed alike, it killed me. Do you know I cannot recollect my mother ever letting me sit in her lap? I would try to do it and she always pushed me away. 'You'll wrinkle Mommy's clothes'. And then later I see Lourdes in her lap."

"Sweetheart, you've never told me any of this before."

"I know. Just as Sofia said, I made up this fantasy about my mother. Her main concern was always for herself and Lourdes. After the change in visitation, not once did she come here for Mother's Day. Not one single time. She was always on the other side of the world or caught up with a new rich husband or boyfriend. When our teachers had us do Mother's Day projects, Sofia and I would have to have our father mail it to her. I could sit here all day and talk about how she showed her lack of love for us and how I've pushed it out of my head." Tears began to fall again. "I just wanted her to love me. Is that so wrong?"

"No, there's nothing at all wrong with that. Bella, what happened to make you come to this realization?"

"I overheard her talking to Lourdes. She's only been trying to get close to me for my inheritance. No surprise to you I know."

"I would love nothing more than to have been wrong. I hope you realize that."

"My mother and I have one thing in common though."

"What could that be?"

"We both hid who we were from the other in order to get what we wanted—me, her love and her—my money."

"You were misguided in the way you chose to handle it but you had no ill intent. You can't say the same about your mother."

"At least it wasn't all a waste. I alienated Sofia, lost the love of my life, but hey, I got a great make-over."

"I don't care about this overhaul. It looks nice but the Bella I fell in love with was just as beautiful as the new one."

"Do you think you can fall in love with her again?"

"No." Zahira reached out and ran her hand through Isabella's hair. "I never fell out of love with her."

"You didn't?"

"No. Not even when I tried my best to."

"I love you," Isabella said softly. "If you give me just one more chance I promise--"

Zahira put her finger over Isabella's lips.

"No more words, okay? Prove it to me in your actions."

Isabella gazed into Zahira's eyes. She knew she would never risk losing Zahira again. She took her face in her hands. They both moved closer to each other and shared soft lingering kiss. Isabella stood and pulled Zahira up with her. Isabella's hands stroked Zahira's backside as she went back and forth planting kisses on her face and neck. Isabella stopped and unhooked her necklace. On it was the ring Zahira had given back to her. Isabella slid the ring off the necklace and held up to Zahira.

Zahira smiled and held her left hand up and Isabella slipped the ring on her finger. Isabella wrapped her arms around Zahira's waist and rested her forehead against hers.

"I love you so much."

"I love you too, Bella."

Zahira took Isabella by the hand and led her to the bedroom where they sat on the bed. Isabella moved her mouth to hers again. As they kissed, her hand went inside Zahira's blouse and found her hardened nipple. Isabella twirled it between her thumb and forefinger. Zahira wrapped one arm around her neck and with the other moved her hand to inside Isabella's dress slacks and her panties. Her finger glided over Isabella's wet clitoris. Isabella unzipped her slacks and slid her them along with her panties to her knees.

She opened her thighs and Zahira began her manipulations once more. This time she inserted a finger into Isabella's vagina, then two and finally three. As she licked Isabella's neck, she alternated between pumping her fingers in and out of her vagina and stroking her clitoris. After a few minutes Isabella moaned that she was about orgasm. Zahira trained her finger on her clitoris until Isabella cried out, her body jerking slightly.

A few moments later Zahira removed her hand and proceeded to fully remove Isabella's panties and slacks. She took off her blouse and bra. Isabella reached out to take off Zahira's clothes when she stopped her. She leaned over and turned the table lamp on. She got up from the bed, walked around and stood at the foot of it. She began moving as if to music, her hips swaying in a seduction dance. Slowly, she unbuttoned her blouse and eased it off her shoulders, exposing her bare breasts. She put her hands to her breasts and twirled her engorged nipples with the middle finger of each hand. Her hands lazily traveled down over her stomach to her twirling hips. Isabella watched as if hypnotized. Her hand went to her soaking wet vagina and she touched herself while watching Zahira's sexy dance.

Zahira unzipped the back of her long skirt and peeled it down her legs and off. As she danced with now just her panties on, she loosed the bun her hair was in and let her long, silky locks fall past her shoulders. She turned her back to Isabella as she glided her panties off her body. Her hands caressed her buttocks and hips. She spread her legs slightly and bent over, giving Isabella a view of her glistening womanhood. She reached between her legs and her middle finger slid up and down her pink slit. She then walked back around the bed to Isabella who was close to having another orgasm. Zahira straddled her and placed her hands underneath her breasts. At Zahira's invitation Isabella ravished her breasts with her mouth causing Zahira to whimper in delight. Zahira pushed Isabella down on the bed and bent down to lick and suck her breasts. She instructed Isabella to lie toward the top of the bed. She lay at the opposite end facing Isabella and slid between her legs. They grabbed on to the other's arm for support as they gyrated their sexes against one another. It was a favored position for Isabella as she found feeling Zahira's clitoris grinding against hers extremely pleasurable. Zahira was the first to orgasm soon followed by Isabella. Afterward, Zahira moved to where Isabella was. They kissed long and deep before finally falling asleep in each other's arms.

Blinding Mirror

Chapter 72

Sofia tapped on Isabella's bedroom door.

"Yes?"

"Isabella, can you meet me in the study when you get a moment?"

"Sure. I'll be right there."

Sofia went to the study and waited for her sister. She nervously turned the piece of paper in her hand. A minute later Isabella entered the room.

"What's going on?"

"Have a seat. We're about to make a phone call."

"To who?"

"I called our grandfather's house until I finally reached Maribel. She gave me the number again to reach our grandmother since I lost the piece of paper. Not after strongly hinting that she needed some financial help in order to take care of our grandfather. Personally, I wouldn't care if the old fart pickled himself in those urine stained sheets but I knew Maribel wasn't going to give up the number again unless I agreed to send a check."

Isabella took a seat on the other side of the desk where Sofia was sitting.

"After what happened in Fresno, I'm kind of leery, you know?"

"So am I," agreed Isabella. "This should be interesting."

"All right. Let's get it over with." Sofia hit the speaker button and dialed the number. After three rings there was a pick up on the line.

"Hello?" The voice answering was that of a child.

"Hi, is there an Inès Delgado there?"

"Inès? Yes, her here. Hold on. Tìa! Tele-phone!"

A moment later a woman's voice came on the line.

"Yes?"

Sofia glanced at Isabella and took a deep breath.

"Hello, Ma'am. My name is Sofia. I'm one of your granddaughters." Sofia braced herself, expecting to hear the sound of the phone being slammed to its receiver.

"My granddaughter?"

"Yes, Ma'am."

"Junior, go outside and play with your brother, okay? Excuse me. That was my niece's little boy. I'm so happy you called."

Both Sofia and Isabella were relieved.

"You are?" asked Isabella. "I'm your other granddaughter, Isabella."

"Hi. Yes, I've very happy to hear from you both. I heard from Maribel that I have three granddaughters. Is the other one there, too?"

"No, she's away right now," answered Sofia.

"I want to apologize for Alphonso's behavior. Maribel told me about that as well. What he did was uncalled for."

"What else did Maribel tell you about our visit?" inquired Isabella.

"Even though we're not friends anymore, Maribel never lets that stop her from gabbing. She told me you didn't know anything about us until recently and you wanted to find out more about your family."

"Right. It wasn't until I came across some items of our mother's that we found out about you. We saw her birth certificate and other papers. All these years we thought her name was Olivia Machado, she was Portuguese and her parents died in a plane crash." Sofia tried to hold back the bitterness from her tone.

There was silence on the line as Sofia and Isabella waited for a response from their grandmother.

"I guess it's true what they say about the apple not falling too far from the tree. I did almost the same thing."

"What do you mean?" asked Sofia.

"When I got married I left my family and had little contact with them. There were so many painful memories from my past that I wanted to separate myself from anything that reminded me of it, including my family. I was so fortunate that when I came back here I was welcomed with open arms. I shouldn't have taken out on my whole family what one person—my father—did to me. I'm not making excuses for your mother but I can't say I blame her for getting as far away from us as she could. I have a lot of regrets about my life but my biggest one is what a terrible mother I was to Oliva. Some people have no business with kids and that includes your grandfather and me. She took the brunt of all the anger and frustration we had. To this day I find it hard to sleep some nights when I think about the way we treated her. I talk to my priest and to God about it because it eats away at me. I know she doesn't want anything to do with me but I pray all the time that I see her just once before I leave this earth so I can tell her how sorry I am for the horrible things I did to her."

Sofia swallowed the knot tightening in her throat as she listened to the emotion in her grandmother's voice. The last thing she expected from this phone call was to feel even a modicum of sympathy for her conniving mother.

"I have a question," began Isabella. "What happened the night she ran away from home? Was she having an altercation with her father right before he was rushed to the hospital?"

"No, she was asleep in her room. He and I were having an argument as always when Al clutched his chest and stumbled into the hallway. Why do you ask whether or not they had an altercation that night?"

Sofia and Isabella shook their heads at each other at yet another one of their mother's lies.

"We have so many questions," said Isabella, brushing over her grandmother's question. "Is it possible for us to come there and visit you?"

"Visit me? I'd love to meet you! When can you come?"

"Um, next weekend?" Sofia addressed the question to Isabella who nodded in agreement. "Yes, next weekend if that's okay."

"That's great. You have a lot of family here from my side and some from your grandfather's. And don't worry; the ones I'm in contact with are nothing like him."

"That's good," said Sofia. "We really want to find out more about our family. I've found out some things online but I know there's so much that can't be found on a computer and only our family can tell us about."

"I'll tell you as much as you want to know when you get here. When I came back here I had to become reacquainted with my family and our traditions. I used to think that being progressive meant moving away from that."

"Grandmother, I can't wait to meet you," said Sofia.

There was silence on the line for a moment and Sofia thought perhaps she'd been a little presumptuous to call her grandmother.

"I'm glad you feel comfortable enough to call me that. You don't know how good it sounds."

"Isabella and I are twins and it will be our birthday when we arrive there. I can't think of a better way for us to celebrate it than with our family."

Isabella wrote down the address information before they wrapped the call. They told their grandmother they would call her after making firm travel arrangements.

"That went a lot better than I thought it would," Isabella said, after they ended the call.

"I know! I'm so relieved she didn't curse us out or something."

"She's sounds really articulate."

Sofia looked at her with a raised eyebrow. "I can't believe you said that."

"What? I didn't mean anything by it."

"I know you didn't but it sounds so patronizing. If she were white would her speaking articulately even get a mention?"

"You're right."

"Well, let's begin our preparations to meet our family."

Shelley Halima

Chapter 73

As Isabella drove down El Cajon Boulevard, Sofia pointed out their grandmother's street. Sofia spotted the address but there was nowhere to park in front of the house or in the driveway. Isabella drove down about three houses to a vacant spot. They gave each other reassuring looks before getting out of the car. Sofia's heart was racing. Isabella hadn't said anything, but Sofia was willing to wager she was equally nervous. The yard was full of children playing and adults standing about talking and laughing in front of the modest but well-kept Spanish Craftsman home. The bushes in front were decorated with streamers and balloons. Sofia and Isabella exchanged huge grins when they saw a huge homemade banner that read "Welcome Isabella and Sofia - Happy Birthday!" As they got to the walkway leading to the house, everyone turned to them. A little boy ran up to them.

"Are you Isabelle and Sofia?" he inquired excitedly.

"I'm Sofia and this is Isabella."

"Isabella. Hi! I'm Eber."

They took turns shaking his tiny hand.

An older woman who looked to be in her sixties came up to them.

"Look at what lovely young women you are! I'm your Aunt Adriana from your grandfather's side." She gave both of them a warm embrace.

Soon others gathered around and Aunt Adriana made introductions.

"This is Felix, you met little Eber, Thalia, Rafael, Karen, Benjo, Oscar, Heather, Suezette, Marycela, Tim, Javier."

"My boyfriend is named Javier. It must be a good name for handsome men." Sofia smiled as she saw the teenage boy blush.

Aunt Adriana continued introducing everyone who was outside. Sofia was amazed at the mixture of cousins, great aunts and uncles that were a variety of hues.

"Now let's go inside and so you can meet your grandmother."

As soon as they got to the front door, Sofia saw a woman standing inside the door who she was sure was their grandmother. Her short curly hair was mostly gray, and she appeared physically smaller than in the photograph. When they spoke on the phone again, she mentioned to Sofia that she'd contracted diabetes years before and had to change her diet. She was steadying herself with the use of a cane as she opened the door.

"Sofia and Isabella?"

"Yes, I'm Sofia and this is Isabella." They took turns giving their grandmother a warm embrace.

Blinding Mirror

"You both are so beautiful! Come in, come in. You've got more family here to meet."

They followed her into the kitchen where more introductions were made. There looked to be literally two dozen dishes made and placed in serving dishes on the long kitchen table.

"We can't tell you all how much we appreciate your going to all this trouble for us," announced Sofia.

"Don't even think about thanking us," chastised Aunt Adriana. "This is what we do for family. And that's what you are. Pepe, tell everyone to come inside, we're about to start with dinner."

There was not enough room at the dining table for everyone so many spilled into the kitchen and living room.

Inès stood from her place at the table and held up her glass.

"I want to give a quick toast." She paused as she gathered her thoughts. "I lost my daughter years ago but it is still in my prayers that I get to see her one day. One of the best days of my life was when I found out that I have granddaughters. I thank God for bringing them into our lives. Here's to Sofia and Isabella!"

The room was filled with "Salud!" and the clinking sound of glasses touching in cheers. Sofia decided to stand and say something as well.

"I just want to thank you all for giving us such a warm welcome. And I really look forward to getting to know all of you and about our family. This is my first time here but I feel as if I'm home." She sat back down as she was greeted with applause and cheers.

Sofia and Isabella were both curious about the names of the dishes being served. Their Aunt Adriana let them know they were, *pozole, enchiladas de mole, ceviche, nopalitos salad, carnitas, arroz a la poblana, chiles en nogada* and *frijoles a la poblano*. There were still more dishes in the kitchen. The girls tried to sample as many of the dishes as they could and barely had any room for the *tres leches* cake that was brought out for dessert.

After dinner everyone went back outside where some chairs had been set up in the yard. Sofia found out from her grandmother that the music playing from the huge portable radio was called *Norteño*.

"You know, I just realized I have no idea what the two of you do," said Inès to her granddaughters."

"Yes, what is it that you both do?" inquired Aunt Adriana.

"I own and run a spa with my friend Grace."

"A spa?" asked Inès.

"Yes and you both are invited to come to Georgia any time you want. I would love for you to have a day of pampering."

"That's so sweet of you," said Inès. "I would enjoy that very much. What about you, Isabella?"

"I run a property management company that our father started."

"That's great. Sofia, you mentioned your father passed away," said Ines, "I'm sorry to hear that."

"Thank you. He died from a brain aneurysm. It was very sudden," Sofia replied. "One day we were planning a trip to Europe and the next he was gone."

"That's terrible. What about my other granddaughter, Lourdes? What does she do?"

Sofia gave Isabella a quick glance.

"Um, she's between jobs."

"I wish she could've made it. I wanted to meet her, too."

Neither of the girls had the heart to tell their grandmother that it wasn't very likely to happen.

"I'm so proud of you. You are so young and yet successful businesswomen. Later on you'll meet your other cousins Lynette and Maria who have run their own businesses as well. You have another cousin named John who is planning to run for Senate in Corpus Christi. This generation in our family is doing things we only could dream of and you make us proud."

"Thank you," Isabella and Sofia said in unison.

"Do either of you happen to have a picture of my daughter?" Inès asked softly.

Sofia looked to Isabella.

"I still have one in my wallet. I'll go inside and get it."

Isabella said "still" because she had meant to take the photo out of her wallet. She went inside to retrieve the picture and was back a few minutes later.

"I'm sorry it took me a minute. I stopped to talk to Uncle Fredo. "Here it is."

Isabella handed over the picture to her grandmother.

"This is my Oliva?"

"Yes."

Inès began to cry. Sofia stroked her arm and shoulder to comfort her. Aunt Adriana leaned over to see the picture.

"Heavens, I haven't seen her since I came to visit when she was only around five-years-old."

"She was still just a teenager when I last saw her." Inès continued staring at the picture.

"You can have that if you'd like, grandmother," said Isabella.

"Thank you," Inès whispered. She became lost in her thoughts of past incidents and her regrets over them. There were so many things she would do differently if she could. She'd been back in San Diego a year when she fell into a diabetic coma. When she came back around she began to re-assess her life. She finally went to church with Adriana who had been begging her to go for months. After her niece, Karen convinced her to seek counseling, she eventually came to grips with the pain she'd been holding in about the abuse she suffered at the hands of her father and also how that pain was inflicted upon her child. She always told herself that besides a few incidents where she lost control with Oliva she wasn't nearly as bad as her father. Then she realized that withholding her love and affection was just as damaging, if not more so. There were times when she wished she had continued to hold everything in because the reality of her actions was almost too much to bear. What was most painful was she knew she would never have from her daughter what she wanted most–her forgiveness.

Sofia and Isabella decided to try and dance and they ended up laughing over Isabella's complete lack of rhythm. They decided to stand to the side and watch some of their relatives dance. Isabella put her arm around Sofia's shoulder. Sofia was surprised by the gesture.

And in that moment she realized how rare the moments of affection between them had been that her sister placing an arm around her shoulder could catch her off guard. She put an arm around Isabella's waist. As they looked at each other, they both understood that not only were they discovering a new family, but also each other.

Chapter 74

Olivia's head jolted up as she snapped awake. She was lounging on the patio outside the bedroom she was occupying during her stay in the Hamptons. The home was nothing short of spectacular and was located right off of Gardiner's Bay. The past few weeks had done wonders for her mentally and physically. Because she was a bit older, it took her longer to heal from her surgery than if she'd done it when she was in her twenties. But now she was back to normal and in her own estimation, looking even better than ever. She still felt a touch of sadness over what happened with Isabella, but there was nothing she could do about the situation.

Things were looking up for Lourdes. She'd met a man the night before at Lizzie's party. She called the house and had Charlotte relay a message to her that she wasn't coming home until today. She also told Charlotte to tell her mother "100 plus" which was their code word for a man whose net worth exceeded one hundred million. She couldn't be happier for her child. She hoped everything would work out to Lourdes's advantage. Of course, she would guide her the best way she could and make sure Lourdes didn't get duped by men the way she had been.

She had more than enough time to rest on her laurels. It was time for her to get back to work and stake her own claim on Mr. Fauntleroy. She would have her travel agent make reservations for Chicago and leave within the next day or so. She rose from the lounger and went inside to take a long soak.

Just as Olivia was drying off she heard a knock on the door. Before she could respond, Lourdes opened the door and peeped in.

"Mother, hurry and get dressed. I want you to come downstairs and meet who I hope will be your future son-in-law."

"And hello. How are you today?"

Lourdes let out a laugh. "I don't have time for formalities. Hurry! We'll be in the dining room. Charlotte has to go to a cocktail party but she's having her maid serve us up some lunch. Now come on!"

"Okay! Just let me get decent. I'll be down in ten minutes tops."

Lourdes gave her a wink and closed the door.

Olivia walked through the living room to the dining room. Lourdes and her new conquest were at the table laughing and talking.

Lourdes noticed her mother and waved her mother into the room. "Mother, I want you to meet a very special man."

He stood up from his chair and walked over to Olivia with his hand extended. There was something familiar about him but Olivia couldn't quite place him.

"Hello," she greeted him with a smile.

"It's a pleasure to meet you. I'm Tony. Tony Carvalho."

Blinding Mirror

Olivia drew her hand back as if it had touched a fire and stumbled back a step. Tony looked at Olivia, confused by her reaction. He turned to Lourdes who was equally perplexed.

"Mother, what's wrong?"

Olivia began to tremble uncontrollably. Like a blind woman, she felt her way to a nearby chair, never taking her eyes off of Tony as she sat down.

In an instant something clicked inside Tony. It had been a little over twenty-six years but he suddenly remembered the shabby but beautiful young woman. She now sat before him sophisticated and classy—older but still the same exotic beauty. She would've faded from his memory long ago had it not been for his sister who'd commissioned a painting to be done from a photograph of her. It was a picture that still hung in Pilar's living room above the fireplace. *It can't be.*

"Oliva? Is that you?"

Olivia didn't respond. Her lips quivered and pools of tears formed in her eyes.

Tony turned to Lourdes again. He remembered she told him her age the night before and he mentally did the calculations. A wave of nausea fell over him.

"Oliva, puh-please tell me she isn't my...I gave you money to..."

When Olivia bowed her head and sobbed, it was all the answer he needed.

"Oh, God!" He went to the living room where dropped down on one of the sofas.

"What is going on, Mother?! You and Tony know each other?" Lourdes went over to her.

There was something in the exchange between her mother and Tony that frightened her. What scared her more than anything was her mother. She'd never in her life seen her mother break down as she was doing at that moment. It was almost as if darkness had settled in the house. They obviously knew each other but something told her there was so much more to the story. She shook her mother's arm. "Tell me!"

"Lourdes, you know how much I love you." She covered her face with her hands and cried.

"Mother, tell me right now what's going on?!"

Olivia slowly removed her hands from her face. She knew what she was about to tell her daughter would destroy her but the cruelest of fates had removed the choice from her hands. There was no way out of it.

"He, he's your father."

Lourdes stepped backward until she was against the buffet table. She shook her head.

"No, that's not true. My father is dead. You told me that." She jabbed her finger in her mother's direction. "You told me he died. You told me. You told me..." Lourdes looked to the living room where Tony was now sitting with his head in his hands. The events of the last few hours swirled in her head. "Nooo!!!" Lourdes screamed. She grabbed the carving knife from the platter with the rack of lamb. She then lunged toward her mother, grabbing her by the neck of her blouse. With almost Herculean strength she lifted Olivia up with one hand and threw her to the floor. Lourdes pounced on top of her.

Olivia looked into the wild, enraged eyes of her daughter and winced as she felt the sharp point of the knife being held just beneath her chin.

"How could you do this to me?! I overlooked all of your lies, Mother! I made excuses for them! But this—I'll never forgive you! Do you hear me?! Don't you realize what I've done?!"

Olivia exhaled sharply as the tip of the knife punctured her skin slightly but she didn't try to fight. One of her biggest deceptions had been revealed and the effects were nothing short of horrendous. All she wanted at that very moment was for her daughter to sink in the knife because death would be welcome. Neither one of them would recover from the effects of her deceit nor did she believe she would be able to live with herself knowing she could have saved her daughter all this anguish if she'd just been truthful.

"Just do it," she whispered. "Please."

As her daughter drew back the knife, preparing to plunge it into her flesh, she closed her eyes and waited for an end so she would no longer have to bear witness to all the madness she caused.

Tony finally snapped out of his stupor and saw what was happening in the next room. He rushed in and managed to wrestle the knife from Lourdes's hand. Lourdes stared down at her mother. She got up and went into the living room and retrieved her purse. Without so much as a backward glance to her mother and Tony, she walked out the front door.

"How could you?!" Tony shouted. "You were supposed to have an abortion! Why didn't you tell her about me or me about her?!"

Olivia only stared up at the ceiling as she continued to lie on her back. Tony was standing right over her and screaming but he may as well have been miles away. She wished she had kept Lourdes over in France. Then none of this would have happened. Her true identity wouldn't have been revealed and Lourdes wouldn't have gone to that party last night. She would give her life if she could go back over the last few weeks and redo everything.

Blinding Mirror

Chapter 75

The incessant ringing of the doorbell awakened Sofia. She glanced at the clock and saw it was three a.m. She got up and grabbed her robe from the bottom of the bed and headed out the room. Isabella met her in the hallway.

"Who on earth could it be this time of night?"

"I have no idea." Sofia put on her robe and trekked down the stairs.

When she got to the door she peeped through the glass pane on the side of the door.

"Who is it?" asked Isabella.

"It's Lourdes."

"For goodness sake!" Isabella snorted. She turned and started back for the stairs just as Sofia opened the door.

"Oh my God, Lourdes, what happened?"

The concerned tone in her sister's voice caused Isabella to turn around, and she was thunderstruck at what she saw. Lourdes, who never left the house without being perfectly made up and coiffed, was a sight. Her hair was a disheveled mess. Her face was mostly bare from makeup but there was still some smudged around her eyes. She was wearing a pantsuit that was wrinkled and the silk shirt was sticking half out of her pants. But what was most shocking to her sisters was the dead and vacant look in her eyes. Gone was the cocky and arrogant Lourdes and in her place was a shell of someone whose spirit had been broken and soul shattered.

"I didn't know where else to go." Her voice was faint and quavering.

They all stood silent; none of them knowing what to say. They were snapped from their torpor by the horn from a cab in the driveway. Lourdes jumped from at the sound.

"I don't have any money to pay him."

Sofia turned to tell Isabella to get some money but she was already going up the steps to get her purse. Sofia pulled Lourdes in and leaned out the door and pointed her index finger upwards, signaling the driver to wait a minute. Isabella had soon returned with her purse and went out to the cab. Sofia had a hand on Lourdes's arm and felt her shaking. Despite their contentious relationship her heart went out to her. When Isabella came back into the house and closed the door, she exchanged perplexed glances with Sofia.

"Lourdes, do you want something to eat?" asked Isabella, not knowing what else to say.

Lourdes shook her head in response.

"A bath. I need a bath."

"I'll go and run some water for her, Sofia."

While Isabella went up the stairs, Sofia took Lourdes's hand to go upstairs as well.

Seeing the condition Lourdes was in, Sofia didn't want to leave her alone for too long. After a few minutes she went into the bathroom to check on her. She was just sitting in the tub staring down into the water. Sofia went over to the tub, walked up the stone steps and sat on the edge. She began to wash Lourdes's back, shoulders and arms. She then got the shower hose and shampoo from nearby and washed her hair. When she was done, she felt Lourdes's wet hand on her wrist. She looked at her sister.

"Thank you," Lourdes whispered.

"You're more than welcome," Sofia replied gently.

At that moment Isabella entered the bathroom and took a place on the edge of the tub opposite Sofia.

"Are you ready to get out?" asked Sofia.

"No, not yet. I know you both want to know what happened but I can't even bring myself to say it right now."

"Just tell us whenever you're ready," replied Isabella.

"All I want to say right now is that our mother is dead to me. I never want to see her again. She has ruined my life and I'll never, ever forgive her."

Sofia knew if Lourdes had turned against their mother she must have done something horrible.

"It's as if I'm finally coming out of a fog. I left New York with only my purse. I don't even remember what happened to it. I guess I left it on the plane or in the terminal. I don't know. All my life I thought I had the world's best mother. Somehow I thought she could do no wrong because everything she did was for me. Even when I was fourteen and she made me give up my virginity to a sixty-one year old man. She convinced me that because he was a duke and was so wealthy, that it was an honor for me to sleep with him. He paid her two million dollars for the privilege of deflowering me. I will just tell you this; my father is alive. He didn't die years ago as she claimed."

"What?!" Sofia exclaimed.

"He's alive?" asked Isabella.

Lourdes simply nodded. Both girls wanted to ask more questions but they knew it was best to let Lourdes tell them at her own pace.

"You met him?" questioned Sofia.

"Yes." Lourdes began to cry.

"Come on," began Sofia as she took Lourdes by the hand. "Let's get you into bed."

Blinding Mirror

As they all were walking down the hall to see Lourdes to one of the guest bedrooms, Lourdes paused in front of Gino's old room. She stood at the door for a few moments before turning the knob and entering. Her sisters followed her inside. Sofia flipped on the light switch as Lourdes walked over to his desk by the window and picked up one of the pictures of her.

"Did he love me?"

"Yes!" Sofia answered without hesitation. "He did. A few months before he died he told me he wished he'd fought to keep you but he thought he was doing the right thing at the time. He always worried about you."

"I never gave him a chance. I listened to her and because she had turned against him, so did I."

Gingerly, she put the photo back on the desk and went over to the bed. She pulled the covers back and lay down.

"I want to sleep in here if that's all right."

"Of course," responded Sofia as she pulled the covers over Lourdes.

Lourdes motioned for them to sit down.

"I'm going to tell you what happened. It's something that will shame me for the rest of my days but you need to know how our mother has destroyed my life. Then I don't ever want to speak of it again."

Sofia turned out the light and she and Isabella left the room, closing the door behind them. She and her sister could do nothing but look at one another in stunned silence.

"My dear God," Sofia finally said in a voice barely above a whisper. "How is she ever going to get over this?"

"I don't think she will, Sof. She shouldn't be alone."

"You're right. I'm going to stay with her. You go on and get some sleep."

"After what I just heard, I don't think I can but I'll try."

Isabella started for her room then turned and put her arms around her sister, clutching her tightly. She felt so foolish to have spent so many years envying Lourdes for the relationship she had with their mother and letting it cause a wedge between her, her father and sister. And she thanked God at that moment for being spared her mother's brand of love.

Lourdes turned on her back, staring up at the ceiling. Tears of shame, guilt and revulsion poured relentlessly down the sides of her face. *How could my mother do this me? I trusted her like no one else in the world! Why would she lie all this*

time about something as important as this? My life will never be the same. And it's all because of her. God, I hate her! I hate her! Somehow, some way, she needs to pay for what she's done!

Chapter 76

Olivia picked over her Peking duck salad, her eyes trained on the entrance to the restaurant for Jameson's arrival. She was lunching at the Shanghai Terrace inside the Peninsula Hotel in Chicago. She found out Jameson was staying at the hotel until renovations were complete on his North Astor Street home only a short distance away. She bribed one of the pages to find out Jameson's routine and learned he was a creature of habit. He ordered room service for breakfast daily. Mondays, Wednesdays and Fridays lunched at Shanghai. Tuesdays and Thursdays he lunched at The Lobby and every night he dined at Avenues. And he was normally alone which would be perfect. Except for the company of an old pal from his college days he was known for being a bit of a loner and that worked in her favor since the fewer friends and family around to influence or interfere with their relationship, the better.

She needed a couple of days at the hotel to recover from the incident in the Hamptons before embarking on her quest to land Jameson. *What did I ever do to deserve all that has happened to me over the last few weeks? First Sofia invades my privacy and brings the past I worked so hard to hide out into the light. And then the situation with Tony. Why of all the rich men in New York did Lourdes have to choose him? What a nasty twist of fate that was. I was so shocked to see him I didn't even get the chance to ask him about Pilar. I've missed her so much over the years. We didn't part on the best of terms but still, I would love to see her and show her how far I've come from those days in Fresno. Now that everything is out in the open…I know she would be so proud of all I've accomplished and understand why I did what I did. I wonder if she still remembers me though. She should since her brother didn't have much of a problem remembering me after all this time.*

Now back to the matter at hand. This is it. I can feel it in my bones. Jameson's wealth far exceeds any man I've been with before, including Gino. Soon it will all be within my reach. I've always made sure Lourdes enjoyed a plush lifestyle and soon I'll be in the position to provide even more than before. You just wait, precious. Mother is going to make up for everything you've gone through these past few days. You'll see.

Shelley Halima

The color crimson not only denotes love's passion, but bloodshed as well.

In the second of the Mirror series, Crimson Mirror —

Lourdes struggles to deal with the repercussions of the devastating incident in the Hamptons. She vacillates between finding forgiveness and seeking vengeance.

Lorenzo and Tyler are vying for Grace's heart. When Grace decides which man she wants to be with, the other decides if he can't have her, no one will.

Sofia and Javier have fallen madly in love but their relationship is put to the test when another woman decides she wants Javier for herself.

And after more than twenty-five years, Olivia and Pilar come face to face but the reunion may be short-lived. Over the years Olivia has made many enemies. One sets out to end her life. Will they succeed?

Coming soon *Crimson Mirror*

Made in the USA
Charleston, SC
19 January 2012